Honoré de Balzac

LA COMÉDIE HUMAINE

The Human Comedy

PRIVATE LIFE

VOLUME IX

AT COMTE OCTAVE'S, RUE PAYENNE.

———

" I bring to you the only relative left me. If I believe myself to be making a present to Your Excellency, I think also that I am giving my nephew a second father."

The *Edition Définitive* of the *Comédie Humaine* by HONORÉ DE BALZAC, now for the first time completely translated into English.

HONORINE. COLONEL CHABERT. THE INTER-DICTION. IN ONE VOLUME. TRANSLATED BY WILLIAM WALTON, AND ILLUSTRATED WITH FOUR ETCHINGS.

PHILADELPHIA : PRINTED FOR SUBSCRIBERS ONLY BY GEORGE BARRIE & SON.

HONORINE

TO MONSIEUR ACHILLE DEVÉRIA

An affectionate souvenir from the Author.

HONORINE

*

If the French are as unwilling as the English are eager to go traveling, perhaps the French and the English are both justified. Wherever we go we find something that is better than England, whilst it is excessively difficult to meet anything like the attractions of France outside of France. Other countries offer admirable landscapes, there may be found in them frequently a comfort superior to that of France, which indeed makes but the slowest progress in this respect. They display sometimes a magnificence, a grandeur, a bedazzling luxury; they are wanting neither in gracefulness nor in noble manners; but the intellectual life, the activity of ideas, the talent of conversation and that atticism so familiar in Paris, that quick understanding of that which is thought but not uttered, that genius for comprehending, which is half of the French language, is met with nowhere else. Thus the Frenchman, whose jesting is already so little comprehended, quickly withers abroad, like a transplanted tree. Emigration is a perversion of the

French nation. Very many Frenchmen, of those of whom we are here speaking, declare that they saw again with pleasure the custom-house officers of their native country,—which may be considered the most daring hyperbole of patriotism.

This little preamble has for its object the recalling to those Frenchmen who have traveled the very great pleasure which they have experienced when, as it happened, they have suddenly found all their country again, an oasis in the salon of some diplomat; a pleasure which will be comprehended with difficulty by those who have never left the asphalt of the Boulevard des Italiens, and for whom the line of the quays, on the left bank, is already no longer Paris. To find Paris again! do you know what that is, oh, Parisians? It is to find again, not the cuisine of the *Rocher de Cancale*, as Borel guards it for the gourmets who know how to appreciate it, for that is to be met with only in the Rue Montorgueil, but a service which recalls it! It is to find again the wines of France, which are quite mythological outside of France, and rare as is the woman whom we shall here discuss! It is to find again, not the wit *à la mode*, for, between Paris and the frontiers, it evaporates; but that intelligent, comprehensive, critical atmosphere in which the French live, from the poet to the workman, from the duchess to the street urchin.

In 1836, during the sojourn of the Sardinian court at Genoa, two Parisians, more or less celebrated, were enabled to believe themselves still in Paris

when they found themselves in a palace leased by
the consul-general of France and which was seated
on a hill, the last fold of the Apennines between the
gate of Saint-Thomas and that famous lighthouse
which in the keepsakes adorns all the views of
Genoa.   This palace is one of those magnificent
villas on which the Genoese nobles expended millions at the period when this aristocratic republic
was at the height of its power.   If the half-light is
beautiful anywhere, it is assuredly so at Genoa,
when it has rained as it does rain there, in torrents,
during the whole forenoon; when the purity of the
sea rivals the purity of the sky; when silence reigns
on the quay and in the groves of this villa, in its
marbles with gaping mouths from which the water
flows mysteriously; when the stars glitter, when
the waves of the Mediterranean follow each other
like the avowals of a woman from whom you draw
them one by one.   Let us admit it, this moment in
which the balmy air perfumes both the lungs and
the reveries, in which voluptuousness, visible and
mobile as the atmosphere, envelops you in your
cushioned seat while, spoon in hand, you trifle with
the ices or the sorbets, a city at your feet, beautiful
women before you,—these hours of Boccaccio are to
be found only in Italy and on the shores of the Mediterranean.   Let us suppose around the table the
Marquis di Negro, that Hospitaller brother of all
errant talents, and the Marquis Damaso Pareto, two
Frenchmen disguised as Genoese, a consul-general
having at his side a wife as beautiful as a Madonna,

and two children, silent because slumber had enveloped them, the ambassador of France and his wife,
a first secretary of the embassy who thought himself
extinguished and malicious, and finally, two Parisians who had come to take their farewells of the
consul-general's wife at a splendid dinner, you will
then have the picture which was presented by the
terrace of this villa about the middle of May, a picture dominated by one person, by a celebrated
woman on whom all looks were concentrated at
moments, and who was the heroine of this impro-
vised festival.   One of the two Frenchmen was the
famous landscape painter, Léon de Lora, the other
was a celebrated critic, Claude Vignon.   Both of
them were accompanying this woman, one of the
living illustrations of the fair sex, Mademoiselle des
Touches, known under the name of Camille Maupin
in the literary world.   Mademoiselle des Touches
had gone to Florence on business.   Through one of
those charming kindnesses of which she was so
prodigal, she had brought with her Léon de Lora to
show him Italy, and had gone as far as Rome to
show him the Campagna.   Returning by the way
of the Simplon pass, she was taking the Corniche
road to Marseilles.   Still for the benefit of the landscape painter, she had stopped at Genoa.   The consul-general had naturally wished to do the honors of
Genoa before the arrival of the Court to one who
was as strongly recommended by her fortune, her
name and her position as by her talent.   Camille
Maupin, who knew Genoa down to its smallest

chapels, had abandoned her landscapist to the cares
of the diplomat, to those of the two Genoese marquises, and was very saving of her time.   Although
the ambassador was himself a very distinguished
writer, the celebrated woman declined to yield to
his persuasions, fearing that which the English call
an *exhibition;* but she withdrew the claws of her
refusal when it became a question of a farewell day
spent at the consul's villa.   Léon de Lora said to
Camille that her presence at the villa would be the
only return he could make to the ambassador and his
wife, the two Genoese marquises and the consul
and his wife.   Mademoiselle des Touches thereupon
made the sacrifice of one of those days of complete
liberty which are not always to be found in Paris
by those on whom the world keeps its eyes.

The explanation of this reunion thus given, it is
easy to imagine that etiquette was banished from it,
as well as many women of the highest 'rank who
were curious to know if the virility of the talent of
Camille Maupin had not impaired the grace of the
pretty woman, and if, in a word, the breeches did
not show under the petticoats.   From the dinner up
to the moment when the collation was served, at
nine o'clock, if the conversation had been alternately
serious and gay, ceaselessly enlivened by the shafts
of Léon de Lora, who passed for the most malicious
man in the Paris of the day, by a good taste which
will not be thought surprising from the selection of
the guests, there had been but little discussion of
literature; but finally the wanderings of this French

tourney necessarily led up to it, were it only to touch
lightly this essentially national subject. But, before arriving at this turning of the conversation,
which gave the speech to the consul-general, it
may be useful to say a word concerning his family
and himself.

This diplomat, a man of about thirty-four years
of age, married for the last six years, was the living
portrait of Lord Byron. The celebrity of this physiognomy relieves us from the necessity of painting
that of the consul. It may, however, be observed
that there was no affectation in his dreamy air. Lord
Byron was a poet, and the diplomat was poetic; the
women know how to recognize this difference which
explains, without justifying, some of their attach-
ments. This masculine beauty, set off by a charming character, by the habits of a solitary and
laborious life, had seduced a Genoese heiress. A
Genoese heiress! this expression might cause a
smile in Genoa, where, in consequence of the exheredation of daughters, a woman is rarely rich; but
Onorina Pedrotti, the only child of a banker without
male heirs, is an exception. Notwithstanding all
the flatteries which might have been lavished by an
inspired passion, the consul-general had not seemed
to wish to wed. Nevertheless, after a residence of
two years, after some steps taken by the ambassador
during the sojourns of the Court at Genoa, the marriage was concluded. The young man withdrew
his first refusals, less because of the touching affection of Onorina Pedrotti, than in consequence of an

unknown event, one of those crises of private life
which are so promptly buried under the daily currents of interests that, later, the most natural actions
seem inexplicable.   This covering-up of causes
affects also very often the most serious events of
history.   Such was, at least, the opinion of the city
of Genoa, in which, for some women, the excessive
reticence, the melancholy of the French consul, could
be explained only by the word *passion*.   We may
remark, *en passant*, that women never complain of
being the victims of a preference, they immolate
themselves very readily in the common cause.
Onorina Pedrotti, who perhaps would have hated
the consul if she had been absolutely disdained,
loved him none the less, and perhaps more, *suo sposo,*
in knowing him to be in love.   Women admit prece-
dence in affairs of the heart.   Everything is saved so
long as it is a question of the sex.   A man is never a
diplomat with impunity; the *sposo* was as discreet
as the tomb, and so discreet that the merchants of
Genoa were disposed to see something of premedi-
tation in the attitude of the young consul, from
whom the heiress would perhaps have escaped if he
had not played this rôle of the *Malade Imaginaire* in
love.   If this were the truth, the women found it too
degrading to believe.   The daughter of Pedrotti
made of her love a consolation, she nursed these unknown sorrows in a bed of tenderness and of Italian
caresses.   *Il signor* Pedrotti had not, moreover, anything to complain of in the choice to which he had
been constrained by his beloved daughter.   Powerful

protectors in Paris watched over the fortunes of
the young diplomat.   Fulfilling the promise of the
ambassador to the father-in-law, the consul-general
was created a baron and a commander in the Legion
of Honor.   Finally, *il signor* Pedrotti was made a count
by the King of Sardinia.   The dot was a million.
As for the fortune of the *casa* Pedrotti, estimated at
two millions gained in the grain business, it fell to
the married couple six months after their union, for
the first and the last of the counts Pedrotti died in
January, 1831.   Onorina Pedrotti is one of those
beautiful Genoese, the most magnificent creatures
of Italy when they are beautiful.   For the tomb of
Julian, Michael Angelo took his models from Genoa.
Hence that amplitude, that curious disposition of the
breast in the figures of *the Day* and *the Night*, which
so many critics find to be exaggerated, but which
is peculiar to the women of Liguria.   In Genoa,
beauty no longer exists to-day except under the
mezzaro, as in Venice it is only to be met with under
the *fazzioli*.   This phenomenon may be observed
in all ruined nations.   The noble type is not only
to be found among the people, as, after the conflagration of cities, the medals are hidden in the
cinders.   But, as she is already an exception with
regard to her fortune, Onorina is another exception
as to patrician beauty.   Recall to your memory the
Night which Michael Angelo has detained forever
under *Il Pensiero,* clothe her in modern garments,
twist up that beautiful hair which is so long,
around that magnificent head, somewhat brown in

tone, put a spark of fire in those dreamy eyes,
wrap that powerful breast in a scarf, imagine the
long white dress embroidered with flowers, suppose
that the statue, risen, is seated, with arms crossed,
like those of Mademoiselle Georges, and you will
have before your eyes the consul's wife, with a
child of six years, beautiful as the desire of a
mother, and a little girl of four years on her knees,
charming as some infantile type laboriously sought
for by David the sculptor for an ornament for a tomb.
This beautiful household attracted the secret attention of Camille.   Mademoiselle des Touches thought
that the consul had a somewhat too absent air for a
perfectly happy man.

Although, during the whole of this day, the wife
and the husband presented to her the admirable spectacle of the most complete happiness, Camille asked
herself why it was that one of the most distinguished
men she had ever met, and whom she had seen in
the salons of Paris, remained consul-general at
Genoa, when he was possessed of a fortune of a
hundred and some thousand francs of income! But
she had also recognized, by a thousand of those
nothings which the women pick up with the intelligence of the Arab sage in *Zadig*, the most faithful
affection on the part of the husband.   Certainly,
these two handsome beings would love each other
without fail until the end of their days.   Camille
said to herself alternately, "What is it?"—"It is
nothing," according to the deceiving manifestations
of the consul-general's manner, who, let us say it,

possessed the absolute calm of the English, of savages, of Orientals and of consummate diplomats.

In discussing literature, the talk turned on the eternal stock in trade of the republic of letters,—the woman's fault! And it presently appeared that there were two opinions,—which, the man or the woman, was in the wrong in this fault? The three women present, the ambassador's wife, the consul-general's wife and Mademoiselle des Touches, these women naturally considered as irreproachable, were pitiless for the woman. The men undertook to prove to these three beautiful flowers of their sex that there might remain some virtue in a woman after her fall.

"How long are we going to play thus at hide-and-seek?" said Léon de Lora.

"*Cara vita*—my dear life,—go and put your children to bed, and send me by Gina, the little black portfolio which is on my piece of Boule furniture," said the consul to his wife.

She rose without making any observation, which proves that she loved her husband well, for she already knew enough French to comprehend that her husband sent her away.

"I am going to relate to you a story in which I took a part, after which we can discuss, for it seems to me to be puerile to use a scalpel on an imaginary corpse. In order to dissect, let us first take a body."

Everyone arranged himself to listen with all the more complaisance that each one had talked enough; the conversation was beginning to languish, and this moment is the opportunity which the story-teller should select.   This then is what the consul-general related :

"At the age of twenty-two, having been qualified as Doctor of Laws, my old uncle, the Abbé Loraux, then seventy-two years of age, felt the necessity of giving me a protector and of launching me on some career.   This excellent man, if indeed he were not a saint, looked upon each additional year as a new gift from God.   I do not need to tell you how readily the confessor to a royal highness can find an open-ing for a young man educated by himself, the only child of his sister.   One day, therefore, toward the end of the year 1824, this venerable old man, for the last five years curé of the Blancs-Manteaux at Paris, ascended to the chamber which I was then occupying in his residence and said to me :

"'Make your toilet, my child, I am going to pre-sent you to the person who will take you into his household as his secretary.   If I do not deceive my-self, this person will replace me, in case God should call me to Himself.   I shall have finished my mass by nine o'clock, you have three-quarters of an hour to yourself, be ready.'

"'Ah! uncle, must I then say farewell to this chamber in which I have been so happy for four years?'

"'I have no fortune to leave you,' he replied.

"'Will you not leave me the protection of your name, the remembrance of your works, and—?'

"'We will not talk of that inheritance,' he said,

smiling. 'You do not yet know the world well
enough to be aware that it pays with difficulty a
legacy of that nature, whilst, in conducting you this
morning to Monsieur le Comte—' Permit me,"
said the consul interrupting himself, "to designate
my protector to you under his baptismal name only,
and to call him the Comte Octave—'Whilst in conducting you this morning to the house of Monsieur
le Comte Octave, I believe I am giving you a protection which, if you please this virtuous statesman,
as I am sure you will, will certainly be equal to the
fortune which I would have amassed for you if the
ruin of my brother-in-law and the death of my sister
had not fallen upon me by surprise like a clap of
thunder from a clear sky.'

"'Are you the confessor of Monsieur le Comte?'

"'Eh! if I were, could I place you there? What
priest is capable of profiting by the secrets, the
knowledge of which comes to him in the tribunal of
penitence? No; you owe this protection to His
Grace the Keeper of the Seals. My dear Maurice,
you will be there as in a father's house. Monsieur le Comte will give you a fixed salary of two
thousand four hundred francs, a lodging in his hôtel,
and an allowance of twelve hundred francs for your
food; he will not admit you to his table and does
not wish to have you served separately, so that you
shall not be delivered to the service of underlings.
I have not accepted the offer which has been made
to me without having acquired the certainty that
the secretary of Comte Octave will never be merely

a first domestic.   You will be overwhelmed with
work, for the count is a great worker; but you will
come out of his house capable of filling the highest
positions.   I do not need to recommend to you discretion, the first virtue of men destined to public
functions.'

"You may judge of my curiosity!   The Comte
Octave occupied at that time one of the highest
places in the magistracy, he possessed the confidence of Madame la Dauphine, who had just named
him minister of State, he led an existence nearly
similar to that of the Comte de Sérizy, whom you
all know, I think; but a more obscure one, for he
lived in the Marais, Rue Payenne, and scarcely
ever received.   His private life escaped the public
observation by a monastic modesty and by contin-
uous labor.   Let me paint to you in a few words my
situation.   After having found in the grave head-
master of the college Saint-Louis a tutor to whom
my uncle had delegated his authority, I had finished
my studies at eighteen.   I had issued from this
college as pure as a seminarist filled with faith
issues from Saint-Sulpice.   On her deathbed my
mother had obtained from my uncle a promise that
I should not be made a priest; but I was as pious as
if I were to take holy orders.   On my *déjucher*—
coming down from the roost—from the college, to
employ an old and very picturesque word, the Abbé
Loraux took me into his rectory and caused me to
go through with my law studies.   During the four
years of studies necessary to take all the grades, I

2

worked industriously, and especially outside the arid
fields of jurisprudence.   Separated from all literature
at the college, where I lived in the house of the head-
master, I had a great thirst to extinguish. As soon as
I had read a few of the modern masterpieces, the
works of all the preceding centuries were taken up.
I developed a passion for the theatres, I attended them
every day for a long time, although my uncle only
gave me a hundred francs a month.   This parsimony,
to which his tenderness for the poor restricted this
good, old man, had for its effect to restrain the young
man's appetites within just bounds.   At the period
of my entry into Comte Octave's household, I was
not an innocent, but I considered my rare escapades
as so many crimes.   My uncle was so truly angelic,
I feared so much to distress him, that I had never
passed a night outside his doors during these four
years.   This good man waited for my return before
going to bed himself.   This maternal solicitude had
more power in restraining me than all the sermons
and all the reproaches with which the life of young
people is encrusted in puritanical families.   A
stranger to the different worlds which compose Parisian society, I knew of the women *comme il faut* and of
the bourgeoises only what I saw in my walks, or in
the boxes at the theatres, and that at the distance
from the parterre where I was.   If, at that time,
some one had said to me,—'You are going to see
Canalis or Camille Maupin,' I should have had my
head and my heart on fire.   Famous people were to
me like the gods, who did not speak, did not walk,

did not eat, like other men. How many tales of the
Thousand and One Nights are contained in one adoles-
cence!—how many *Wonderful Lamps* is it not necessary to handle before recognizing that the true
Wonderful Lamp is either chance, or work, or
genius! For some men, this dream of the awakened
intelligence is of short duration; mine still endures!
At that time I fell asleep every night grand duke
of Tuscany,—millionaire,—loved by a princess,—or
famous!

"Thus, to enter the household of the Comte Octave, to have a hundred louis a year for myself, was
to enter on an independent life. I foresaw some opportunities for entering society, for seeking there
that which my heart desired the most, a protectress
who would draw me from the dangerous way in
which young men of twenty-two years of age necessarily wander in Paris, however wise and carefully
educated they may be. I began to fear myself.
The industrious study of international law, in which
I immersed myself, did not always suffice to repress
cruel fancies. Yes, sometimes I gave myself up in
imagination to the theatrical life; I thought I had it
in me to become a great actor; I dreamed of triumphs
and of loves without end, ignorant of the deceptions
concealed behind the curtain, as everywhere else,
for every scene has its reverse side. I have sometimes issued forth, with my heart throbbing, carried
away by the desire to beat up the streets of Paris,
like a wood for game, to attach myself to some
beautiful woman whom I might encounter, to follow

her to her door, to set a watch on her, to write to
her, to confide in her entirely and to vanquish her
by strength of loving. My poor uncle, that heart
eaten up by charity, that child of seventy years,
intelligent as God, ingenuous as a man of genius,
divined doubtless the tumult of my soul, for he
never failed to say to me,—'Here, Maurice, you are
one of the poor also! here are twenty francs, amuse
yourself, you are not a priest!' when he felt the
cord by which he retained me stretched too tightly
and liable to break. If you could have seen the
will-o'-the-wisp fire which then came like gold into
his gray eyes, the smile which parted his kindly
lips and lifted them at the corners, in short, the
adorable expression of this august visage, the primitive ugliness of which was rectified by an apostolic
spirit, you could comprehend the sentiment which
compelled me, for all response, to embrace the curé
of the Blancs-Manteaux as if he were my mother.

" 'You will not find a master,' said my uncle to
me as we went to the Rue Payenne, 'you will find
a friend in the Comte Octave; but he is suspicious,
or, to speak more correctly, he is prudent. The
friendship of this statesman is only to be acquired
in the course of time; for, notwithstanding his deep
perspicacity and his habit of judging men, he was
deceived by him whom you succeed, he all but became the victim of an abuse of confidence. This is
enough to say to you concerning your conduct in his
household.'

"When we knocked at the immense great gate of

a hôtel as vast as the Hôtel Carnavelet and situated
between a court and a garden, the sound re-echoed
as through a solitude.   While my uncle asked an
old porter in livery for the count, I threw one of
those glances which see everything on the court in
which the pavement disappeared under the grass,
upon the blackened walls which enclosed little gardens superior to all the decorations of a charming
architecture, and upon roofs as high as those of the
Tuileries.   The balustrades of the upper galleries
were rusted.   Through a magnificent arcade I perceived a second court, a lateral one, in which were
the servant's quarters, the doors of which were de-
caying.   An old coachman was there washing an old
carriage.   From the careless air of this domestic it
was readily to be presumed that the sumptuous
stables in which so many horses formerly neighed
now sheltered two at the most.   The superb façade
of the court seemed to me to be gloomy, like that
of a hôtel belonging to the State or to the Crown
and which is abandoned to some public service.
The stroke of a bell sounded as we went, my uncle
and I, from the porter's lodge—there was still to be
seen above the door, 'Inquire of the Porter'—toward the perron, from which descended a valet
whose livery resembled that of the Labranches of
the Théâtre Français in the old repertoire.   A visit
was so rare that the domestic finished getting
into his great coat as he opened a glass door with
little panes, on each side of which the smoke of the
two lamps had designed stars upon the walls.   A

peristyle of a magnificence worthy of Versailles
allowed to be seen one of those staircases such as
are no longer constructed in France, and which occupy the space of a modern house. In ascending
the stone steps, cold as tombstones, and on which
eight persons might march abreast, our footsteps
resounded under enormous vaults. You could have
believed yourself in a cathedral. The balustrades
interested the eye by the miracles of that gold-
smith's work of the ironworker in which unroll
themselves the fantasies of some artist of the reign
of Henri III. Enveloped in an icy mantle which
fell upon our shoulders, we traversed the antecham-
bers, a range of salons with polished wood floors,
carpetless, furnished with those superb old-fashioned
pieces which, from such places as these, fall into
the hands of the dealers in curiosities. Finally we
arrived at a grand cabinet situated in a square
pavilion all the windows of which opened on a great
garden.

"'Monsieur le Curé des Blancs-Manteaux and his
nephew, Monsieur de l'Hostal!' announced the La-
branche to whose care we had been confided by the
theatrical valet in the first antechamber.

"The Comte Octave, who was dressed in a redingote of gray swanskin and pantaloons with feet,
like hose, rose from an immense desk, came to the
chimney-piece and made me a sign to be seated,
taking my uncle's hands and pressing them
warmly.

"'Although I am of the parish of Saint-Paul,' he

said to him, 'it would be strange if I had not heard
of the curé of the Blancs-Manteaux, and I am happy
to make his acquaintance.'

"'Your Excellency is very kind,' replied my
uncle. 'I bring to you the only relative left me.
If I believe myself to be making a present to Your
Excellency, I think also that I am giving my
nephew a second father.'

"'I can reply to you concerning that, Monsieur
l'Abbé, when we have tried each other, your nephew
and I,' said Comte Octave. 'What is your name?'
he asked me.

"'Maurice.'

"'He is a Doctor of Laws,' observed my uncle.

"'Good, good,' said the count, looking at me from
head to foot. 'Monsieur l'Abbé, I hope that, for your
nephew in the first place, and secondly for myself,
you will do me the honor to dine here every Monday.
It will be our dinner, our family gathering.'

"My uncle and the count began to talk religion
from the political point of view, works of charity,
suppression of offences, and I could then examine at
my ease the man on whom my destiny was to depend. The count was of medium stature, his garments prevented me from judging of his proportions;
but he seemed to me to be thin and dry. His countenance was harsh and sunken. The features expressed shrewdness and intelligence. The mouth,
somewhat large, indicated at once irony and goodness. The forehead, too vast perhaps, terrified as
if it had been that of a madman, all the more so

that it was in strong contrast with the lower part of the face, which terminated suddenly in a little chin brought up very close to the under lip. Two eyes of a turquoise blue, as keen and intelligent as those of the Prince de Talleyrand, whom I admired later, and, like those of the prince, equally endowed with the power of non-expression until they became actually dull, contributed to the strange character of this face, not pale, but yellow. This color seemed to indicate an irritable character and violent passions. The hair, already silvered, carefully brushed, marked the head with the alternate colors of black and white. The fastidiousness of this dressing of the hair interfered with the resemblance which I found in the count to that extraordinary monk whom Lewis has brought on the scene after the *Schedoni* of the *Confessional of the Black Penitents*, which seems to me to be a creation superior to that of the *Monk*. As became a man who had to present himself at the Palais at an early hour, the count was already shaved. Two four-branched candlesticks, furnished with shades, placed at the two extremities of his desk, and the candles of which were still burning, revealed with sufficient clearness that the magistrate had risen before daylight. His hands, which I saw when he took hold of the bellcord to ring for his valet de chambre, were very handsome, and as white as those of a woman—

"In relating to you this history," said the consul-general, interrupting himself, "I do not give you the exact social position or the titles of this personage,

though I show him to you in a situation analogous
to his own.   Position, dignity, luxury, fortune,
manner of life, all these details are true; but I do
not wish to betray my benefactor or abandon my
habits of discretion.

"Instead of feeling myself that which I really
was," resumed the consul-general after a pause,
"speaking of social position, an insect before an
eagle, I experienced I know not what undefinable
sentiment at the count's aspect, and which I can
explain to-day. The artists of genius—" and he
made a slight and graceful inclination before the
ambassador, the famous woman and the two Parisians,—"the true statesmen, the poets, a general
who has commanded armies, in short, the really
great personages, are simple; and their simplicity
puts you on the same footing with themselves.
You who are superior in intelligence, perhaps you
have remarked," he said, addressing his guests,
"how much feeling abridges the mental separations
created by society.   If we are inferior to you in intelligence, we may equal you in friendly devotion.
In the temperature—permit me this expression—of
our hearts, I felt myself as near to my protector as
I was inferior to him in rank.   In short, the soul
has its clairvoyance, it is conscious of the sorrow,
the vexation, the joy, the reproof, the hatred, in
the heart of another.   I recognized vaguely the
symptoms of a mystery, in recognizing in the count
the same revelations of the physiognomy that I had
observed in my uncle.   The exercise of the virtues,

the serenity of the conscience, the purity of the thought, had transfigured my uncle, who from ugly, had become very beautiful. I perceived a reversed metamorphosis in the count's visage; at the first glance I had taken him for fifty-five, but, after an attentive examination, I recognized a youthfulness buried under the ice of a profound grief, under the fatigue of obstinately pursued studies, under the warm tones of some passion crossed. At a word from my uncle, the count's eyes became for a moment as fresh as a periwinkle, he had an admiring smile which revealed him to me at an age which I thought to be the true one, about forty. I did not make these observations at that time, but later, in recalling the circumstances of this visit.

"The valet de chambre entered, carrying a waiter on which was his master's déjeuner.

"'I did not ring for my déjeuner,' said the count, 'leave it there however, and take monsieur upstairs to show him his apartment.'

"I followed the valet de chambre, who conducted me to a pretty suite of rooms all complete, situated below the flat roof, between the court of honor and the servant's offices, over a gallery by means of which the kitchens communicated with the grand staircase of the hôtel. When I returned to the count's cabinet, I heard, before I opened the door, my uncle pronouncing this judgment upon me:

"'He may commit a fault, for he has a great deal of heart, and we are all liable to honorable errors; but he has no vices.'

" 'Well,' said the count, giving me an affectionate glance, 'will you please yourself there, do you think? There are so many apartments in this barracks that, if you are not comfortable there, I can lodge you elsewhere.'

" 'I have only one room in my uncle's house,' I replied.

" 'Well, you can move in this evening,' said the count to me, 'for you have doubtless the furniture of all students, a hackney coach will suffice to transport it. For to-day, we will dine together, we three,' he added, looking at my uncle.

"A magnificent library adjoined the count's cabinet, he led us into it, showed me a coquettish little corner ornamented with paintings, which had formerly served as an oratory.

" 'There is your cell,' he said to me; 'you will keep yourself there when you have to work with me, for you shall not be fastened with a chain.'

"And he proceeded to detail to me the nature and the duration of my occupations while with him; as I listened to him I recognized in him a great political preceptor. I took about a month to familiarize myself with things and people, to study the duties of my new position and to accustom myself to the count's methods. A secretary necessarily observes closely the man in whose service he is. The tastes, the passions, the character, the whims of this man become the object of an involuntary study. The union of these two intelligences is at the same time more and less than a marriage. During three

months the Comte Octave and I, we spied on each
other reciprocally.   I learned with astonishment that
the count was only thirty-seven.   The purely exterior peacefulness of his life and the wisdom of his
conduct did not proceed solely from a profound sentiment of duty and from stoical reflection; in associ-
ating with this man, extraordinary for those who
knew him well, I was conscious of vast depths under
his labors, under his acts of politeness, under his
mask of benevolence, under his resigned attitude,
which resembled calmness so closely that one
might readily be deceived.   As in walking through
a forest, there are certain localities which announce
by the sound under the feet whether you are walking over great rocks or concealed hollows; in the
same manner, the concentrated egotism hidden
under the flowers of politeness and the voids caused
by unhappiness sound hollow at the perpetual contact of daily life.   It was sorrow and not discourage-
ment that dwelt in this truly great soul.   The count
had comprehended that action, that the fact, is the
supreme law of the social man.   Thus he went on
his way notwithstanding his secret wounds, and
regarded the future with a serene eye, like a martyr
full of faith.   His hidden grief, the bitter deception
which he had suffered, had not ended by bringing
him to the philosophical regions of incredulity; this
courageous statesman was religious, but without any
ostentation: he went to the early mass which was
given at Saint-Paul for the workpeople and pious
domestics.   None of his friends, no one at Court,

knew that he was so faithful in his religious observances. He practised the worship of God as certain honest people practise a vice, in profound secrecy. Thus was I to find one day the count lifted upon an Alp of unhappiness much more lofty than those on which they maintain themselves who believe themselves the most tried, who rail at the passions and the beliefs of others because they have vanquished their own, who play variations on all the tones of irony and of disdain. He had no mockery then, either for those who follow hope into all the sloughs into which she leads you, or for those who ascend a lofty peak there to isolate themselves, or for those who persist in maintaining the struggle, reddening the arena with their blood and strewing it with their illusions; he saw the world in its entirety, he surmounted the beliefs, he listened to the complaints, he mistrusted the affections and, above all, the devotions; but this great, this severe magistrate was sympathetic, he admired them, not with a passing enthusiasm, but by his silence, by an inward withdrawing, by the communion of a soul made tender. He was a species of Manfred, catholic and without crime, carrying curiosity in his faith, melting the snows in the heat of a volcano without an outlet, holding converse with a star which he alone saw! I recognized many obscure things in his outward life. He concealed himself from my observation, not like the traveler who, following a route, disappears according to the inequalities of the land in bogs or in ravines, but like a watchful skirmisher who wishes to conceal himself and who seeks for shelter. I did not understand his frequent absences, at the moments when he was the most occupied, and which he did not conceal from me, for he said to me, in confiding to me his task,—'Continue this for me.' This man, so completely enveloped in the triple obligations of the statesman, the magistrate and the orator, pleased me by that taste for flowers which reveals a noble soul, and which nearly all delicate natures have. His garden and his cabinet were full of the most curious plants, which he always bought faded. Perhaps he amused himself with this image of his own destiny!— he was withered like these flowers ready to die, and the almost decomposed perfumes of which caused him strange intoxications. The count loved his country, he devoted himself to the public interests with the fury of a heart which wishes to master another passion; but neither study nor the labors into which he plunged sufficed him; there took place within him frightful conflicts, some flashes of which reached me. In short, he allowed to be perceived heart-breaking aspirations toward happiness, and it seemed to me that he might yet be happy; but what was the obstacle? Was he in love with a woman? This was a question that I put to myself. You may judge of the extent of the circles of sorrow which my mind must have interrogated before arriving at so simple and so formidable a question. Notwithstanding his efforts then, my patron did not succeed in smothering the action

of his heart. Under his austere pose, under the
silence of the magistrate, there was struggling a
passion repressed with so much power that no one
except myself, his messmate as it were, had suspected this secret. His device seemed to be, —'I
suffer and I am silent.' The accompaniment of respect and of admiration which followed him, the
friendship of intrepid workers like himself, of the
Presidents Granville and Sérizy, had no hold on
the count; either he revealed to them nothing, or
they knew all. Impassive, carrying his head high
in public, the count betrayed the man only at rare
intervals, when, alone in his garden, in his cabinet,
he thought himself unobserved; but then he became
a child again, he gave free vent to the tears concealed under his toga, to the exaltations which, perhaps wrongly interpreted, might have injured his
reputation for perspicacity as a statesman. When
all these things had arrived at the state of certainty
for me, the Comte Octave had acquired all the attractions of a problem, and had obtained as much
affection as if he were my own father. Can you
comprehend curiosity repressed by respect?—What
misfortune had overwhelmed this learned man devoted, from the age of eighteen, like Pitt, to the
studies that lead to power, and who had no ambition; this judge who was versed in diplomatic law,
political law, civil and criminal law, and who could
draw thence arms against all disquietudes or against
all errors; this profound legislator, this serious
writer, this religious celibate whose life revealed

clearly enough that he incurred no reproach? A
criminal would not have been punished more severely
by God than was my patron: grief had destroyed
the half of his slumber, he never slept more than
four hours! What contest existed at the bottom of
these hours which passed apparently calm, studious,
without noise or murmur, and during which I have
often surprised him with the pen fallen from his
fingers, his head supported on his hand, his eyes
like two stars fixed and sometimes wet with tears?
How was it that the water of this living spring
flowed over a burning strand without being dried up
by the subterranean fires?—Was there, as under the
sea, between it and the internal fires of the globe, a
bed of granite? In short, would the volcano break
out?—Sometimes, the count looked at me with the
keen and sagacious curiosity, though rapid, with
which a man examines another when he seeks a con-
federate; then he avoided my eyes when he saw
them open, as it were, like a mouth which desires a
response and which seems to say,—'Do you speak
first.' Occasionally the Comte Octave betrayed a
wild and morose sadness. If the explosions of this
humor wounded me, he knew how to make returns
without asking my pardon in the least; but his
manners then became gracious even to the extent of
the humility of the Christian. When I had conceived a filial attachment for this man, mysterious
for me, so comprehensible for the world to whom
the word *original* suffices to explain all the enigmas
of the heart, I brought about a change in the aspect

of the household.   The neglect of his own interests
amounted with the count to stupidity in the conduct of his affairs.   With a fortune of about a hundred and sixty thousand francs of income, without
counting the emoluments of his offices, three of
which were not subject to the law against holding
two offices at once, he expended sixty thousand
francs, thirty of which, at the least, went to his
domestics.   At the end of the first year I sent away
all these scamps, and requested His Excellency to
use his interest to aid me in finding honest people.
At the end of the second year, the count, better fed,
better served, enjoyed some of the modern comforts;
he had some fine horses belonging to a coachman to
whom I gave so much a month for each horse; his
dinners, on his reception days, served by Chevet at
a price that had been carefully settled, did him honor;
his daily fare was the care of an excellent cook whom
my uncle had procured, aided by two kitchen maids;
the expense, not including the purchases, did not
amount to more than thirty thousand francs; we had
two more domestics whose cares restored to the
hôtel all its poetry, for this old place, so beautiful
in its decay, had a majesty which was dishonored
by neglect.

" 'I am no longer surprised,' he said on learning
these results, 'at the fortunes which my servants
have made.   In seven years I have had two cooks
become rich restaurant keepers!'

" 'You have lost three hundred thousand francs
in seven years,' I replied.   'And you, a magistrate,

3

who sign at the Palais, judgments against crime, you have encouraged robbery in your own house.'

"At the commencement of the year 1826, the count had doubtless concluded his observations upon me, and we were as united as two men can be when one is the subordinate of the other. He had said nothing to me of my future; but he had devoted himself, like a master and like a father, to my instruction. Frequently he caused me to reassemble all the materials of his most arduous labors, I drew up some of his reports, and he corrected them, indicating to me the differences between his interpretations of the law, his views, and mine. When, finally, I had produced a work that he could give out as his own, he manifested a joy which served me as a recompense, and he perceived that I took it as such. This little incident, so momentary, produced upon this soul, severe in appearance, an extraordinary effect. The count passed judgment upon me, to make use of judicial language, as a court of last appeal, and supreme; he took hold of me and kissed me on the forehead.

" 'Maurice,' he exclaimed, 'you are no longer my companion, I do not know yet what you will be to me; but if my life does not change, perhaps you may stand to me in place of a son!'

"The Comte Octave had presented me in the best houses of Paris, where I went in his place, with his servants and his carriage, on the too frequent occasions when, ready to set out, he changed his mind and sent for a public cabriolet, to go—where?

There was the mystery. By the welcome which I received, I divined the sentiments which the count entertained for me, and the serious nature of his recommendations. As attentive as a father, he supplied all my needs with so much the more liberality that my discretion obliged him always to think of me. About the end of the month of January, 1827, at Madame la Comtesse de Sérizy's I experienced such a constant run of ill fortune at play that I lost two thousand francs, and I did not wish to take them from the sum entrusted to me. The next day, I said to myself:

" 'Should I go and ask my uncle for them, or confide in the count?'

"I resolved on the latter course.

" 'Yesterday,' I said to him while he took his déjeuner, 'I lost constantly at play, I was nettled, I kept on, I owe two thousand francs. Will you permit me to take these two thousand francs on account from my allowance for the year?'

" 'No,' he said with a charming smile. 'When you play, in society, you should have a sum for play. Take six thousand francs, pay your debts; we shall have settled half our account to-day, for, if you usually represent me, at least your self-respect should not suffer for it.'

"I did not thank the count. Thanks would have seemed to him to be superfluous between us. This slight detail will indicate to you the nature of our relations. Nevertheless, we had not an unlimited confidence in each other, he did not reveal to me

those immense subterranean crypts which I had
recognized in his secret life, and, for my part, I did
not say to him,—'What troubles you? from what
evil are you suffering?' What did he do during his
long evenings? Frequently he returned on foot, or
in a public cabriolet, while I came home in a carriage, I, his secretary! A man so pious, was he
then the prey of vices hypocritically concealed?
Did he employ all the forces of his intelligence in
satisfying a jealousy more skilful than that of
Othello? Was he living with a wife who was unworthy of him? One morning when returning from
I do not remember what purveyor, living between
St. Paul and the Hôtel de Ville, where I had been
to pay a bill, I surprised the Comte Octave in so
animated a conversation with an old woman that he
did not perceive me. The countenance of this old
woman awoke strange suspicions within me, suspicions all the better founded that I did not see the
count making any use of his savings. Is it not a
dreadful thought? I was constituting myself the
censor of my patron. At that moment I knew that
he had more than six hundred thousand francs to
invest, and if he had employed them in purchasing
shares of stock, his confidence in me was so complete that I could not have remained in ignorance of
it. Sometimes the count walked up and down in his
garden in the morning, turning and returning like a
man to whom the walk was the hippogriff on which
a melancholy dreamer might mount. He came! he
went! he rubbed his hands as though he would take

the skin from them! And when I came suddenly
upon him, accosting him at the turning of an alley,
I saw his countenance expand. His eyes, instead
of having the dryness of the turquoise, took on that
velvet quality of the periwinkle which had struck
me so forcibly at my first visit, because of the surprising contrast between these two so different expressions, that of the happy man and that of the
unhappy man. On two or three occasions, at these
moments, he seized me by the arm, he led me away,
then he said to me,—'What were you going to ask
me?' instead of pouring his joy into my heart which
opened to him. Frequently also, the unhappy man,
especially when I could replace him in his labors and
draw up his reports, remained for entire hours
watching the goldfish which swam about in a magnificent marble basin in the midst of his garden, and
around which the most beautiful flowers formed an
amphitheatre. This statesman seemed to have succeeded in making a passion of the mechanical pleasure of crumbling bread for the fishes.

"It was in this manner that was finally discovered
the drama of this inward existence so profoundly
ravaged, so agitated, and where, in a circle forgotten
by Dante in his *Inferno*, there were begotten horrible joys—"

The consul-general made a pause.

"On a certain Monday," he resumed, "it so happened that Monsieur le Président de Granville and
Monsieur de Sérizy, then vice president of the
council of State, came to have a consultation with

the Comte Octave.   These three constituted a commission of which I was the secretary.   The count
had already caused me to be appointed an auditor to
the council of State.   All the material required for the
examination of the political question secretly sub-
mitted to these gentlemen was laid out on one of the
long tables in our library.   Messieurs de Granville and de Sérizy had sent them to the Comte
Octave for the preliminary examination of the documents relating to their task.   In order to avoid the
transportation of the papers to the house of Monsieur
de Sérizy, the president of the commission, it had
been agreed that the meeting should take place at
first in the Rue Payenne.   The cabinet of the Tuileries attached a great deal of importance to this
work, which principally devolved upon me, and to
which I was indebted, in the course of this year,
for my appointment as referendary.   Although the
Comtes de Granville and de Sérizy, whose habits
resembled those of my patron, never dined outside
their own houses, we were surprised debating still
at an hour so advanced that the valet de chambre
asked for me to say to me:

" 'Messieurs the curés of Saint-Paul and of the
Blancs-Manteaux have been waiting in the salon for
two hours.'

"It was nine o'clock!

" 'You will be obliged, messieurs, to put up with
a curé's dinner,' said the Comte Octave, laughing, to
his colleagues.   'I do not know if Granville can
overcome his repugnance to the cassock.'

" 'That depends on the curés.'

" 'Oh! one is my uncle and the other is the Abbé Gaudron,' I replied to him. 'You need not fear, the Abbé Fontanon is no longer vicar of Saint-Paul—'

" 'Well, let us dine,' replied Président de Granville. 'A hypocrite terrifies me; but I do not know any one as cheerful as a truly pious man!'

"And we went into the salon. The dinner was charming. Men who are really well-informed, politicians to whom the conduct of affairs gives a consummate experience and the habit of speaking, are admirable story-tellers when they know how to relate. There is no medium for them, they are either heavy or they are sublime. At this charming diversion, the Prince de Metternich is as expert as Charles Nodier. Polished in facets, like a diamond, the jesting of statesmen is clean cut, sparkling and full of sense.—Confident that the conventionalities would be observed among these three men of superior minds, my uncle gave free play to his own wit, a delicate wit, of a penetrating softness, and fine as is that of all those men accustomed to concealing their thoughts under their black robes. Remember, moreover, that there was nothing of common or of idle in this conversation, which I would willingly compare, as to its effect on the soul, to the music of Rossini. The Abbé Gaudron was, as Monsieur de Granville said, a Saint-Peter rather than a Saint-Paul, a peasant filled with faith, square cut in the base as in the height, a sacerdotal ox

whose ignorance in matters of the world and of literature served to animate the conversation by ingenuous astonishments and unforeseen interrogations.
Finally the talk turned on one of the wounds inherent
in the social state and with which we had just been
occupied, adultery!   My uncle called attention to
the wide divergence which the legislators of the
Code, still under the effects of the storms of the
Revolution, had established in it between the civil
law and the religious law, and from which, he
thought, came all the evil!

   " 'For the Church,' he said, 'adultery is a crime;
for your tribunals, it is only a misdemeanor.   Adultery goes in a carriage to appear before the correctional police, instead of taking its place on the
prisoners' bench in the court of assizes.   Napoléon's
council of State, full of tenderness for the culpable
wife, betrayed great incapacity.   Would it not be
advisable to bring into accord in this the civil and
the religious law, and send to the convent for the
rest of her life, as formerly, the culpable wife?'

   " 'To the convent!' replied Monsieur de Sérizy;
'it would be necessary in the first place to create
convents, and, in these times, they are converting
the monasteries into barracks.   And then, think of
it, Monsieur l'Abbé,—to give to God that which society will not have!—'

   " 'Oh!' said the Comte de Granville, 'you do
not know France.   They have been obliged to leave
to the husband the right of complaint; well, there
are not ten complaints of adultery in a year.'

" 'Monsieur l'Abbé preaches for his saint, for it was Jesus Christ who created adultery,' said Comte Octave. 'In the Orient, that cradle of humanity, woman was only a thing of pleasure and one thing was accepted,—no other virtues were asked of her but obedience and beauty. By making the soul superior to the body, the modern European family, the daughter of Jesus, has invented the indissoluble marriage, it has made of it a sacrament.'

" 'Ah! the Church has indeed recognized all the difficulties in the way,' cried Monsieur de Granville.

" 'This institution has produced a new world,' resumed the count, smiling; 'but the manners of this world will never be those of those climates in which the woman attains the nubile age at seven, and is more than old at twenty-five. The Catholic Church has forgotten the necessities of half the globe. Let us then speak of Europe only. Is woman inferior to us or superior? that is the true question with relation to ourselves. If woman is inferior to us, in elevating her as high as the Church has done, it has necessitated terrible punishments for adultery. Therefore, formerly, it was so carried out. The cloister or death, this was the whole of the ancient legislation. But, since, manners have modified the laws, as always happens. The throne has even served as a couch for adultery, and the progress of this pretty crime has marked the enfeeblement of the dogmas of the Catholic Church. To-day, where the Church no longer demands anything but a sincere repentance from the erring wife, society

contents itself with a brand instead of a torture.
The law, it is true, still condemns the culpable ones,
but it no longer intimidates them. Finally, there are
two codes of morals,—that of the world and that of
the Code. In that in which the Code is feeble, I
recognize it as well as our dear abbé, the world is
audacious and mocking. There are but few judges
who would not have wished to commit the misdemeanor against which they launch the good-natured
thunders of their *preambles*. The world, which de-
nies the law, in its fêtes, by its customs, by its
pleasures, is more severe than the Code and the
Church; the world punishes bungling after having
encouraged hypocrisy. All the provisions of the
law concerning marriage seem to me to require re-
vision, from top to bottom. Perhaps French law
would be perfect if it proclaimed the exheredation
of daughters.'

" 'We know this question, we three, all the way
to the bottom,' said the Comte de Granville, laughing. 'For myself, I have a wife with whom I cannot
live. Sérizy has a wife who will not live with him.
Yours, Octave, yours has left you. We sum up
among ourselves then, we three, all the conditions
of the conjugal conscience; therefore, we shall
doubtless compose the commission, if ever the subject of divorce is returned to.'

"Octave's fork fell on his glass, broke it, broke
the plate. The count, suddenly pale as death, threw
upon Président de Granville an overwhelming
look in which he indicated me, and which I caught.

" 'Forgive me, my friend, I did not see Maurice,' replied Président de Granville. 'Sérizy and I, we were your confederates after having served you as your witnesses; I did not think, then, of committing an indiscretion in the presence of these two venerable ecclesiastics.'

"Monsieur de Sérizy changed the conversation by relating all that he had done to please his wife, without having ever succeeded. This old man concluded by finding it impossible to regulate human sympathies and antipathies by too many rules; he maintained that the social law is never more perfect than when it approaches the natural law. Now, nature takes no account of the union of souls, her aim is accomplished by the propagation of the species. Therefore, the present Code had been very wise in leaving an enormous latitude to chance. The exheredation of daughters, so long as there are male heirs, was an excellent modification, either for preventing the degeneracy of the race, or for rendering households more happy by suppressing scandalous unions, by causing the moral qualities and beauty to be the only attractions sought.

" 'But,' he added, lifting his hand with a gesture of disgust, 'what chance is there of perfecting legislation when a country insists upon bringing together seven or eight hundred legislators!—After all,' he resumed, 'if I should be sacrificed, I have a child who will succeed me—'

" 'Putting aside all the religious question,' replied my uncle, 'I would observe to Your Excellency that

Nature owes us only life, and that society owes us
happiness. Are you a father?' my uncle asked
him.

"And I, have I children?' said the Comte Octave
in a hollow voice, the accent of which caused such
an impression that there was no more talk either of
wives or of marriage.

"When we had taken coffee, the two counts and
the two curés went away on seeing the poor Octave
fall into such a state of melancholy that he was not
able to perceive these successive disappearances.
My protector was seated on a couch at the corner of
the fire, in the attitude of a man overwhelmed.

"'You know the secret of my life,' he said to me
when he perceived that we were alone. 'After
three years of marriage, one evening on my return
home I was handed a letter in which the countess
announced to me her flight. This letter was not
wanting in nobility, for it is in the nature of women
to preserve still some virtues even in committing
this horrible fault—To-day, my wife is thought to
have embarked on a vessel that was shipwrecked,
she is considered dead. I have been living alone
for seven years!—Enough for this evening, Maurice.
We will talk further of my situation when I shall
have become accustomed to the idea of speaking to
you about it. When one suffers from a chronic
malady, is it not advisable to make the best of it?
Often the best appears to be only another aspect of
the malady.'

"I went to bed in great trouble, for the mystery,

far from being cleared up, seemed to me more and more obscure. I divined some strange drama, for I comprehended that there could be nothing commonplace between a wife whom the count had chosen and a character like his own. And then the events which had driven the countess to leave a man so noble, so considerate, so perfect, so loving, so worthy of being loved, must have been at least singular. Monsieur de Granville's phrase had been like a torch thrown into the gloomy caverns in which I had so long been wandering; and, although this flame lit them up but imperfectly, my eyes could now discover their extent. I was able to explain to myself the count's sufferings, without knowing either their depth or their bitterness. His yellow mask, his withered temples, his gigantic studies, his moments of reverie, the least details of the life of this married celibate, took on a luminous relief during this hour of mental examination which is like the twilight of sleep and to which any man with a heart would have yielded himself as I did. Oh! how I loved my poor patron! he seemed to me sublime. I read a melancholy poem, I perceived a perpetual action in that heart which I had accused of inertia. A supreme sorrow, does it not always attain to immobility? This magistrate who wielded so much power, had he avenged himself? did he glut himself on a long agony? Is there not such a thing in Paris as a wrath that boils for ten years? What had Octave done since this great misfortune, for this separation of a married couple is the great

misfortune in our epoch in which the private life
has become, what it was not formerly, a social
question? We passed several days in mutual observation, for the great sufferings have their
modesty; but finally, one evening, the count said
to me in a grave voice:

"'Remain!'

"This is, very nearly, his recital:

"'My father had a ward, rich, beautiful, and sixteen years of age at the period of my return from
college to this old hôtel. Brought up by my mother,
Honorine was then awakening to life. Full of
graces and of youthfulness, she dreamed of happiness as she would have dreamed of an ornament,
and perhaps happiness was for her the ornament of
the soul? Her piety was not unaccompanied by
slight joys, for everything, even religion, was a
poetry for this ingenuous heart. She looked forward to her future as to a perpetual festival. Innocent and pure, no frenzy had ever troubled her
slumber. Shame and vexation had never marked
her cheek or made tearful her eyes. She did not
even investigate the secret of her involuntary emotions on a fine day of spring. In short, she felt
herself weak, destined to obedience, and awaited
marriage without desiring it. Her laughing imagination was ignorant of the corruption, perhaps necessary, that literature inoculates by the portrayal of
the passions; she knew nothing of the world, and
was acquainted with none of the dangers of society.
The dear child had suffered so little that she had

not even displayed her courage.   Her candor, indeed,
would have made her walk without fear in the midst
of serpents, like that ideal figure which a painter
has created, of Innocence.   Never was there a forehead more serene and, at the same time, more smiling than hers.   Never was there permitted to a
mouth to strip more completely of their true meaning interrogations stated with so much ignorance.
We lived together like two brothers.   At the expiration of a year I said to her, in the garden of this
hôtel, before the fountain while throwing bread to
the fishes:

" ' "Are you willing that we should be married?
With me you can do whatever you wish, while
another man would make you unhappy."

" ' "Mamma," she said to my mother, who came
toward us, "it is arranged between Octave and me
that we shall be married—"

" ' "At seventeen!—" replied my mother.   "No,
you shall wait eighteen months; and, if in that
eighteen months you please each other, well, you
are of equal birth and fortune, you shall make at
the same time a marriage *de convenance* and of mutual
inclination."

" 'When I was twenty-six and Honorine was nine-
teen, we were married.   Our respect for my father
and mother, old people of the ancient Court, prevented us from arranging this hôtel in modern style,
from changing the furniture, and we remained here,
as formerly, like children.   Nevertheless, I went out
into the world, I initiated my wife into the life of

society, and I considered it as one of my duties to instruct her. I recognized later that the marriages contracted under conditions similar to ours present a danger against which may be broken many affections, many prudences, many existences. The husband becomes a pedagogue, a professor if you prefer; and love perishes under the ferule which, sooner or later, wounds; for a wife young and beautiful, discreet and joyous, will admit of no superiorities above those with which she is endowed by nature. Perhaps I committed errors? perhaps I assumed, in the difficult beginnings of a household, a magistral tone? Perhaps, on the contrary, I committed the fault of confiding absolutely in that candid nature, and I did not keep a surveillance over the countess, whose rebellion would have seemed to me impossible? Alas! it is not known yet, either in politics or in the household, whether empires and happiness perish through too much confidence or through too much severity. Perhaps, also, the husband did not realize for Honorine the dreams of the young girl? Do we know, during the days of happiness, in what precepts we have failed?'

—"I only remember in the bulk the reproaches which the count addressed to himself, with the directness of an anatomist searching for the causes of a malady which had escaped his confrères; but his clement indulgence seemed to me at the time truly worthy of that of Jesus Christ when he saved the woman taken in adultery.—

"'Eighteen months after my father's death, he

preceding my mother by a few months to the tomb,'
he resumed after a pause, 'came the terrible night
when I was surprised by Honorine's letter of farewell. By what poetry had my wife been seduced?
Was it the senses? was it the magnetism of unhappiness or of genius? which of these forces was it
that had surprised her or carried her away? I have
wished to know nothing. The stroke was so cruel
that I remained, as it were, stupefied for a month.
Later, reflection advised me to remain in my ignorance, and the misfortunes of Honorine have instructed me too much in these things. Up to the
present, Maurice, everything is very commonplace;
but everything is changed by this word,—I love
Honorine, I have not ceased to adore her! From the
day of my abandonment I have lived on my souvenirs, I resume, one by one, the pleasures for
which doubtless Honorine had no taste.

"'Oh!' he said, seeing the astonishment in my
eyes, 'do not make of me a hero, do not think me
stupid enough, as a colonel of the Empire would
have said, not to have sought for distractions. Alas!
my child, I was either too young or too much in
love;—I have not been able to find another woman
in the entire world. After frightful conflicts with
myself I sought to benumb myself; I went, money
in hand, as far as the threshold of infidelity; but
there rose up before me, like a white statue, the
memory of Honorine. In recalling the infinite delicacy of that smooth skin through which could be seen
the blood circulating and the nerves palpitating; in

4

seeing again that ingenuous head, as naïve the evening before my misfortune as on the day on which
I said to her,—"Are you willing that we should be
married?" in remembering a perfume as heavenly as
that of virtue; in seeing again the light of her
glance, the prettiness of her gestures, I fled like a
man who had gone to violate a tomb and who had
seen issue from it the transfigured soul of the dead.
At the council, at the Palais, at night, I dream so
constantly of Honorine, that it requires of me an
excessive strength of soul to recall myself to what I
am doing, to what I am saying.   This is the secret
of my labors.   Well, I feel no more anger toward
her than a father would have in seeing his dear child
in a danger into which it had fallen through imprudence.   I have comprehended that I had made of
my wife a poem which I enjoyed with so much intoxication that I believed my intoxication shared. Ah!
Maurice, a love without discretion is, on the part of
a husband, a fault which may prepare the way for
all the crimes of a wife! I had probably left without
employment the powers of this child, cherished like
a child; I had perhaps wearied her with my love
before the hour of love had arrived for her.   Too
young to foresee the devotion of the mother in the
constancy of the wife, she had taken this first trial
of marriage for life itself, and the pouting child had
rebelled against life unknown to me, not daring to
complain to me, through modesty perhaps! In so
cruel a situation she found herself defenceless against
a man who had violently agitated her.   And I, this

so sagacious magistrate, as I was called, I whose
heart is good but whose mind was occupied, I had
divined too late these laws of the unacknowledged
feminine code, I had read them in the light of the
conflagration which consumed the roof over my
head.   Then I constituted in my heart a tribunal,
according to the law; for the law makes of the husband a judge;—I acquitted my wife and I condemned myself.   But love then took on within me
the form of passion, of that mean and arbitrary passion which takes possession of certain old men.
To-day, I love Honorine absent as one loves, at
threescore, a woman who must be had at any price,
and I feel within me the strength of a young man.
I have the audacity of the old and the restraint of
the adolescent.   My friend, society has nothing
but mockery for this frightful conjugal situation.
Where it would be pitiful for a lover, it sees in the
husband I know not what impotence; it laughs at
those who do not know how to keep a wife whom
they have acquired under the canopy of the Church
and before the scarf of the mayor.   And I have been
obliged to keep silent!   Sérizy is happy.   He owes
to her indulgence the pleasure of seeing his wife, he
protects her, he defends her; and, as he adores her, he
knows the excessive pleasures of the benefactor who
is not worried about anything, not even about ridicule, for he baptizes with it his paternal pleasures.

" ' "I remain married only because of my wife!"
said Sérizy to me one day as we came out of the
council.

" 'But I!—I have nothing, not even ridicule to affront, I who sustain myself only by a love with nothing to feed on! I who have not a word to say to a woman of the social world! I who am repelled by prostitution! I, faithful through incantation! Had it not been for my religious faith, I should have killed myself. I have challenged the abyss of work, I have plunged into it, I have issued from it alive, burning, ardent, having lost the power of sleep!—'

"—I cannot recall to myself the words of this man so eloquent, and to whom passion gave an eloquence so superior to that of the tribune that, like himself, my cheeks were furrowed by tears as I listened to him! You may judge of my impressions when, after a pause during which we dried our eyes, he finished his recital by this revelation:—

" 'This is the drama in my soul, but it is not the outward drama which is being played at this moment in Paris! The inward drama interests no one. I am aware of it, and you will recognize it one day, you who weep at this moment with me;— no one piles up on his heart or on his epidermis, another's sorrow. The measure of all sorrows is within us. You, yourself, you comprehend my suf‧ ferings only by a very vague analogy. Are you able to see me calming the most violent rage of despair by the contemplation of a miniature in which my eyes find again her forehead to kiss it, the smile of her lips, the outline of her visage, where I can inhale the purity of her skin, and which per- mits me almost to feel, to handle, the black clusters of her curling hair? Have you ever surprised me when I leaped for hope, when I writhed under the thousand shafts of despair, when I walked through the mud of Paris in order to overcome my impatience by fatigue? I have periods of enervation comparable to those of consumptives, of hilarity like a madman, of the apprehension of an assassin when he encounters a brigadier of gendarmes. In short, my life is a continual paroxysm of terrors, of joys, of despairs. As to the drama, this is it:—You believe me occupied with the council of State, with the Chamber, with the Palais, with political affairs! —Eh! Mon Dieu, seven hours of the night suffice for all, so much has the life I lead over-excited my faculties. Honorine is my great occupation. To reconquer my wife, that is my sole study; to watch her in the cage in which she is without her being aware of my power; to satisfy her needs, to supervise the little pleasure which she permits herself, to be ceaselessly near her, like a sylph, without allowing myself to be either seen or suspected, for then all my future would be lost, this is my life, my real life! For the last seven years I have never slept without going to see the light of her night-lamp, or her shadow on the window curtain. She left my house without wishing to take away with her anything but the garments she was wearing on that day. The child carried her nobility of sentiments to the point of stupidity! Moreover, eighteen months after her flight she was abandoned by her lover, who was terrified by the bitter and cold, the

sinister and infectious aspect of poverty, the coward!
This man had doubtless counted upon the happy and
gilded existence in Switzerland and in Italy, which
the great ladies permit themselves after leaving
their husbands. Honorine had in her own right
sixty thousand francs of income. This wretch left
the dear creature enceinte and without a sou! In
1820, in the month of November, I succeeded in
getting the best obstetrician in Paris to assume the
rôle of a little surgeon of the faubourg. I persuaded
the curé of the quarter in which the countess lived
to relieve her needs as if he were accomplishing a
work of charity. To conceal my wife's name, to
assure her her incognito, to find her a housekeeper
who was devoted to me and who would be an intelligent confidante—bah! this was an undertaking
worthy of Figaro. You understand that to discover
my wife's asylum, it was sufficient for me to wish
it. After three months of hopelessness rather than
of despair, the thought of consecrating myself to
Honorine's happiness, in taking God for a witness
of my conduct, was one of those poems which fall
only on a lover's heart whatever happens! All absolute love wishes something to feed upon. Ah!
should I not protect this child, culpable through my
imprudence only, against new disasters; accomplish, in short, my rôle of guardian angel? After
seven months of nursing, the infant son died, happily for her and for me. My wife lay for nine
months between life and death, abandoned at the
moment when she had the greatest need of a man's

arm, but this arm,' he said, extending his own with a movement of angelic energy, 'was stretched over her head. Honorine was cared for as if she had been in her own hôtel. When, restored to health, she asked how, by whom, she had been succored, she was answered,—"The Sisters of Charity of the quarter,—The Maternity Society,—the curé of the parish who was interested in her." This woman, in whom pride goes to the extent of becoming a vice, has displayed in unhappiness a strength of resistance which, on certain evenings, I designate as the obstinacy of a mule. Honorine wished to earn her own living! my wife work!—For the last five years I have kept her in a charming pavilion in the Rue Saint-Maur, where she makes flowers and millinery. She believes she sells the products of her elegant handiwork to a merchant, who pays her for them at such a rate that she makes twenty francs a day, and for six years she has not had a single suspicion. She pays for all her daily needs nearly the third of what they are worth, so that with six thousand francs a year she lives as though she had fifteen thousand francs. She has a taste for flowers, and gives a hundred écus to a gardener who costs me, myself, twelve hundred francs in wages, and who sends me statements of two thousand francs every three months. I have promised to this man a kitchen garden and the house with it adjoining the lodge of the concierge of the Rue Saint-Maur. This property belongs to me under the name of a register's clerk of the court. A single indiscretion

would make the gardener lose everything. Honorine has her pavilion, a garden, a superb hothouse,
for five hundred francs of rent a year. She lives
there, under the name of her housekeeper Madame Gobain, this old woman of a discretion proof
against anything, whom I found, and by whom she
has made herself loved. But this zeal is, like that
of the gardener, sustained by the promise of a
recompense on the day of success. The concierge
and his wife cost me horribly dear, for the same
reasons. In short, for the last three years Honorine has been happy, she thinks she owes to her
labor the luxury of her flowers, her toilet and her
comforts.

"'Oh!—I know what you wish to say,' cried the
count, seeing an interrogation in my eyes and on my
lips. 'Yes, yes, I made an attempt. My wife lived
previously in the Faubourg Saint-Antoine. One
day when, on the word of the Gobain, I believed in
the chances of a reconciliation, I sent, by the post,
a letter in which I endeavored to persuade my wife,
a letter written, recommenced twenty times! I will
not describe to you my anguish. I went from the
Rue Payenne to the Rue de Reuilly, like a condemned man who proceeds from the Palais to the
Hôtel de Ville; but he is in a cart, and I, I walked!
—It was night, there was a fog. I went to meet Madame Gobain who was to come to tell me what my
wife had done. Honorine, on recognizing my hand-
writing, had thrown the letter in the fire without
reading it.

" ' "Madame Gobain," she said, "I shall not be in to any one to-morrow!—"

" 'Was this a dagger-stroke, this speech, for a man who finds unlimited joys in the deception by means of which he procures the finest velvet of Lyons at twelve francs a yard, a pheasant, a fish, fruits at a tenth of their value, for a woman ignorant enough to believe that she is paying sufficiently, with two hundred and fifty francs, Madame Gobain, the cook of a bishop?—You have surprised me at times rubbing my hands and a prey to a kind of happiness. Well, this has been when I have just succeeded in carrying out a trick worthy of the theatre;—I had deceived my wife by sending her by a female dealer in toilet articles an Indian shawl, offered to her as coming from an actress who had scarcely worn it, but in which I, the grave magistrate whom you know, I had slept for one night! In short, to-day, my life is summed up in the two words in which can be expressed the most violent of torments:—I love and I wait! I have in Madame Gobain a faithful spy upon the adored heart. I go every night to talk with this old woman, to learn from her everything that Honorine has done during the day, the lightest words which she has spoken, for a single exclamation might deliver to me the secrets of this soul which has made itself deaf and mute. Honorine is pious; she attends the services, she prays; but she has never gone to confession and does not take the communion;—she knows what a priest would say to her. She does not wish to hear

the advice, the order, to return to me. This horror
of myself terrifies me and confounds me, for I never
did the least injury to Honorine; I have always been
good to her. If we admit that I was sometimes
quick in instructing her, that my man's irony
wounded her legitimate pride of a young girl,—is
that a reason for persevering in a resolution which
the most implacable hatred alone could inspire?
Honorine has never revealed her identity to Madame Gobain, she preserves an absolute silence
concerning her marriage, so that this honest and
worthy woman cannot say a word in my favor, for
she is the only one in the household who has my
secret. The others know nothing; they live under
the terror which the name of the prefect of police inspires and in veneration of the power of a minister.
It is then impossible for me to penetrate into this
heart; the citadel is mine, but I cannot enter. I
have not a single means of action. Any violence
would ruin me for ever. How to combat reasons of
which you are ignorant? To write a letter, to have
it copied by a public writer, and place it under the
eyes of Honorine?—I have thought of it. But would
that not be to risk a third breaking-up? The last
one cost me a hundred and fifty thousand francs.
This purchase was at first made in the name of
the secretary whom you replaced. The wretch,
who did not know how lightly I slept, was surprised
by me opening with a false key the chest in which
I had placed the counter-deed; I coughed, he became frightened; the next day I forced him to sell

the house to my actual borrowed name, and I put him out the door. Ah! if I did not feel within me all the noble faculties of man satisfied, happy, expanded; if the qualities of my rôle did not pertain to those of the divine paternity, if I did not enjoy through every pore, there would be moments in which I would believe myself the victim of some monomania. There are nights in which I hear the tinkling of Folly's bells, I am afraid of these violent transitions from a feeble hope, which sometimes blazes up and shoots out, to a complete despair which falls as far as a man can fall. I meditated seriously, a few days ago, on the atrocious dénouement of Lovelace with Clarissa, saying to myself:

" " "If Honorine had a child by me, would it not be necessary for her to return to the conjugal roof?"

" 'Finally, I have such faith in a happy future that, ten months ago, I acquired and paid for one of the handsomest hôtels in the Faubourg Saint-Honoré. If I reconquer Honorine, I do not wish her to see this hôtel again, or the chamber from which she fled. I wish to put my idol in a new temple where she may believe in a life entirely new. I am having made of this hôtel a marvel of taste and of elegance. I have heard of a poet who, almost mad with love for a cantatrice, had, at the beginning of his passion, purchased the most beautiful bed in Paris, without knowing the ending which the actress reserved for his passion. Well, there is the coldest of magistrates, a man who is thought to be the gravest counselor of the Crown, all the fibres of

whose heart were stirred by this anecdote. The
orator of the Chamber comprehended this poet who
fed his ideal on a material possibility. Three days
before the arrival of Marie-Louise, Napoléon rolled
himself in her nuptial bed at Compiègne—All
gigantic passions have the same features. I love
like a poet and an emperor!—'

"When I heard these last words I believed in the
reality of Comte Octave's fears: he rose, walked
about, gesticulated, but he stopped as though frightened by the violence of words.

" 'I am very ridiculous,' he resumed, after a very
long pause, seeking for a look of compassion.

" 'No, monsieur, you are very unhappy—'

" 'Oh! yes,' he said, resuming the flow of his
confidences, 'more than you think! From the violence of my words you might, and indeed you probably do, believe it to be a case of the most intense
physical passion, since for the last nine years it has
annulled all my faculties; but this is nothing in
comparison with the adoration which is inspired in
me by the soul, the intelligence, the manners, the
heart, all that which in the woman is not the
woman; in short, those ravishing divinities in the
train of Love with whom life is passed, and who are
the daily poetry of a fugitive pleasure. I can see,
through a retrospective phenomenon, those graces of
the heart and of the spirit of Honorine to which I
gave but little attention in the days of my happiness, like all happy people! I have, from day to
day, recognized the extent of my loss in recognizing

the divine qualities with which was endowed this
capricious and unruly child, who has become so
strong and so proud under the heavy hand of poverty, under the blow of the most cowardly abandonment.   And this celestial flower is withering
solitary and hidden! Ah! the law of which we
were speaking,' he resumed with a bitter irony,
'the law, it is a picket of gendarmes, it is my wife
seized and brought here by force!—Would that not
be to conquer a dead body? Religion has had no
hold upon her, she wished for some poetry in her
life, she prays without listening to the command-
ments of the Church.   For myself, I have exhausted
everything in the way of clemency, kindness, love.
—I have come to the end.   There remains only one
method of succeeding;—the shrewdness and the
patience with which the bird-catchers finally trap
the most suspicious, the most active, the most fan-
tastic and the rarest birds.   Thus, Maurice, when
the very excusable indiscretion of Monsieur de
Granville revealed to you the secret of my life, I
finally came to see in this incident one of those
commands of fate, one of those notifications which
the gamblers ardently desire and to which they
listen in the midst of their most furious games—
Have you enough affection for me to be romantically
devoted to me?—'

   " 'I anticipate you, Monsieur le Comte,' I replied,
interrupting him, 'I divine your intentions.   Your
first secretary wished to pick the lock of your strong-
box; I know the heart of the second, he is capable

of loving your wife.   And can you devote him to
misfortune by sending him to the fire?   To put
his hand in a brasier without burning it, is that
possible?'

   " 'You are a child,' replied the count, 'I will send
you gloved!   It is not my secretary who will come
to take up his lodging in the Rue Saint-Maur, in the
little house of the kitchen gardener which I have
caused to be vacated, it will be my young cousin,
the Baron de l'Hostal, referendary—'

   "After a moment of surprise I heard the stroke of
a bell and a carriage rolled up to the perron.   Presently the valet de chambre announced Madame de
Courteville and her daughter.   Comte Octave had
very many relatives on his mother's side.   Madame
de Courteville, his cousin, was the widow of a judge
of the tribunal of the Seine, who had left her with
a daughter and without any fortune whatever.   How
could a woman of twenty-nine compare with a
young girl of twenty, as beautiful as the imagination could desire for an ideal mistress?

   " 'Baron, referendary, keeper of the seals, while
waiting for something better, and this old hôtel for
a dot, will you have reasons enough for not loving
the countess?' he said in my ear as he took me by
the hand and presented me to Madame de Courteville and her daughter.

   "I was dazzled, not by so many advantages which
I had never dared to dream of, but by Amélie de
Courteville, all whose beauties were set off by one
of those brilliant toilets which the mothers give

their daughters when it is a question of marrying them.

"We will not speak of myself," said the consul, making a pause;—

"Twenty days later," he resumed, "I went to live in the house of the kitchen gardener, which had been cleaned, arranged and furnished with that celerity which is explained by three words,— Paris! the French workman! money! I was as much in love as the count could desire for his own security. Would the prudence of a young man of twenty-five suffice for the stratagems which I had undertaken and in which was involved the happiness of a friend? To resolve this question, I admit to you that I counted a good deal on my uncle, for I was authorized by the count to take him into my confidence in case I should deem his intervention necessary. I took a gardener, I made myself a most zealous florist, I occupied myself furiously, like a man who could be distracted by nothing, in digging up the kitchen garden and preparing the soil for the cultivation of flowers. After the manner of the maniacs of Holland or of England, I gave myself out for a monoflorist. I cultivated dahlias especially, bringing together all the known varieties. You will understand that my line of conduct, even in its slightest deviations, was traced by the count, all whose intellectual qualities were then attentive to the last events of the tragic comedy which was about to be played in the Rue Saint-Maur. As soon as the countess had retired, almost every evening, between eleven o'clock and midnight, a council was held between Octave, Madame Gobain and myself. I heard the old woman rendering an account to Octave of the least movements of his wife during the day; he informed himself of everything, the meals, the occupations, the conduct, the ménu for the next day, the flowers which she proposed to imitate. I comprehended that this was a love to the point of despair, since it was composed of that triple love which proceeds from the head, the heart and the senses. Octave lived only during this hour. During the two months that the work lasted, I did not turn my eyes on the pavilion in which my neighbors lived. I had not even asked if I had a neighbor, although the garden of the countess was separated from mine only by a paling fence, along which she had caused to be planted cypress, already four feet high. One fine morning, Madame Gobain announced to her mistress, as a great misfortune, the intention of some original character who had become her neighbor, of building, toward the end of the year, a wall between the two gardens. I will not speak to you of the curiosity by which I was devoured. To see the countess!—this desire paled even my budding love for Amélie de Courteville. My project of building the wall was a frightful menace. No more air for Honorine, whose garden would become a species of alley enclosed between my wall and her pavilion. This pavilion, formerly a pleasure house, resembled a château of cards, it was only about thirty feet in depth with a front of

about a hundred. The façade, painted in the German fashion, imitated a trellis of flowers to the
height of the first story, and presented a charming
specimen of that Pompadour style which is so well
named *rococo*. It was reached through a long avenue
of linden trees. The garden of the pavilion and my
kitchen garden resembled the blade of a hatchet,
the handle of which was represented by the avenue.
My wall would cut off three-quarters of the hatchet.
The countess was heartbroken over it, and said,
in the midst of her despair :

"'My poor Gobain, what sort of a man is this
florist?'

"'Upon my word,' she replied, 'I do not know
that it is possible to do anything with him, he seems
to hold all women in horror. He is the nephew of a
curé in Paris. I have only seen the uncle once, a
fine old man of seventy-five, very ugly but very
gentle and kind. It may well be that this curé en-
courages his nephew, as is said in the quarter, in
his passion for flowers so that he may not do worse—'

"'But what?'

"'Well, your neighbor is a harebrained fellow!—'
said the Gobain, pointing to her own head.

"The quiet fools are the only men of whom women
have no mistrust in matters of sentiment. You
will perceive in the end how clearly the count had
seen in choosing this rôle for me.

"'But what is the matter with him?' asked the
countess.

"'He has over-studied,' replied the Gobain, 'he

5

has become wild. Finally, he has his reasons for not loving women any more—there, since you wish to know all that is said.'

" 'Well,' replied Honorine, 'crazy people frighten me less than sensible ones, I will speak to him myself! Say to him that I ask him to come and see me. If I do not succeed with him, I will see the curé.'

"The morning after this conversation, as I was walking in my laid-out garden paths, I caught a glimpse of the curtains of a window on the first floor of the pavilion drawn aside and of the face of a woman looking out curiously. The Gobain accosted me. I glanced brusquely at the pavilion and made a brutal gesture, as though I said,—'Well, it is but little I care for your mistress!'

" 'Madame,' said the Gobain, returning to render an account of her embassy, 'the crazy fellow asked me to leave him alone, saying that every man was master in his own house, especially when he has no wife.'

" 'He is doubly right,' replied the countess.

" 'Yes, but he ended by saying to me,—'I will go!' when I told him that he would make very unhappy a person who lived a retired life, and who found great diversion in the culture of flowers.'

"The next morning I was aware by a sign from the Gobain that my visit was expected. After the countess's déjeuner, as she was walking in her pavilion, I broke through the palings and went to her. I had arrayed myself like a countryman;—old pantaloons with feet, of gray swanskin, heavy sabots,

an old hunting vest, a cap on my head, a cheap
handkerchief around my neck, my hands soiled
with earth and a gardener's trowel in my hand.

" 'Madame, this is the monsieur who is your
neighbor!' cried the Gobain.

"The countess was not frightened. I finally saw
that woman whom her own conduct and the count's
confidences had rendered such an object of curiosity.
We were then in the first days of the month of May.
The pure air, the blue sky, the greenness of the first
leaves, the scent of the spring, made a frame for this
creation of sorrow. When I saw Honorine, I comprehended the passion of Octave and the truthfulness of that observation, a celestial flower! Her
whiteness struck me at first by its peculiarity, for
there are as many whites as there are blues and reds.
In looking at the countess, the eye served to touch
that smooth skin in which the blood flowed through
bluish threads. At the slightest emotion, this blood
spread itself out under the tissues like a vapor in
rosy sheets. As we met, the rays of the sun, passing through the thin foliage of the acacias, surrounded Honorine with that yellow and liquid
nimbus which Raphael and Titian, alone among
painters, have represented surrounding the Virgin.
Her brown eyes expressed at once tenderness and
gaiety; their light was reflected on her countenance
through the long, lowered lashes. With the movement of these silky lashes Honorine threw a charm
upon you, so much was there of feeling, of majesty,
of terror, of scorn, in her manner of raising or

lowering this veil of her soul. She could freeze you
or animate you by a glance. Her hair of a pale
brown, was gathered up negligently upon her head
and outlined a forehead like a poet's, large, powerful, dreamy. The mouth was entirely voluptuous.
Finally, as a great privilege, rare in France but
common in Italy, all the lines, the contours of this
head, had a character of nobility which would be
able to arrest the ravages of time. Although slender, Honorine was not thin, and her outlines seemed
to me to be those which would awaken love again
when it thought itself extinguished. She was
well entitled to the appellation of *mignonne*, for she
belonged to that species of little, supple women
who allow themselves to be taken, flattered, abandoned and taken up again like cats. Her little feet,
which I heard on the gravel, made upon it a slight
noise which was in keeping with them and which
harmonized with the rustling of her dress; there
resulted a species of feminine music which engraved itself on the heart and which would have
distinguished her walk among a thousand other
women. Her carriage recalled all her quarterings
of nobility with so much haughtiness that in the
streets the most audacious of the proletariat would
have stood aside for her. Mirthful and tender,
proud and imposing, she could not be comprehended
otherwise than as endowed with these qualities
which seem to exclude each other, and which nevertheless left her a child. But the child might become
as strong as an angel; and, like the angel, once

wounded in her true nature, she would be implacable. The coldness on this visage was doubtless
no less than death for those on whom her eyes had
smiled, for whom her lips had opened, for those
whose souls had welcomed the melody of this voice
which gave to words the poetry of song by peculiar
accentuations. When I scented the violet perfume
which she exhaled, I understood how the memory of
this woman had arrested the count on the threshold
of debauchery, and how impossible it would be to
ever forget her who was truly a flower to the touch,
a flower to look at, a flower by scent, and a celestial flower for the soul.—Honorine inspired devotion,
a devotion chivalric and without recompense. You
said to yourself on seeing her, 'Think, and I will
divine your thoughts; speak, I will obey. If my
life, sacrificed in torment, can procure you a day
of happiness, take my life; I will smile like the
martyrs on their funeral piles, for I will carry that
day to God like a pledge which a father would
fulfil on recognizing a pleasure given to his child.'
Many women arrange for themselves a physiognomy
and succeed in producing effects similar to those
which you would have experienced on seeing the
countess; but, with her, everything proceeded from
a delicious naturalness, and this inimitable naturalness went straight to the heart. If I speak to you
thus, it is because the question is here only of her
soul, of her thoughts, of the delicacy of her heart,
and because you would have reproached me for not
having sketched them for you. I was on the point

of forgetting my rôle of a man reputed crazy, brutal and with very little chivalry.

"'They have told me that you love flowers, madame?'

"'I am a workwoman in flowers, monsieur,' she replied. 'After having raised the flowers, I copy them, like a mother who is enough of an artist to give herself the pleasure of painting her children.— Is not that enough to say to you that I am poor, and unable to pay for the concession which I wish to obtain from you?'

"'And how is it,' I replied with the gravity of a magistrate, 'that a person who seems to be as distinguished as you are occupies herself with such a vocation? Have you then, like myself, reasons for keeping your hands busy so that your head may not do any work?'

"'Let us remain on the party wall,' she replied, smiling.

"'But we are at the foundations,' I said. 'Is it not necessary that I should know, from our two sorrows, or, if you prefer, from our two crotchets, which of us should yield to the other?—Ah! what a pretty cluster of narcissus! they are as fresh as this morning!'

"I declare to you that she had created for herself, as it were, a museum of flowers and shrubs, in which the sun alone penetrated, the arrangement of which had been dictated by an artistic genius, and which the most unsensitive of landlords would have respected. The masses of flowers, arranged with all

the science of a florist or disposed in clusters, produced a pleasant effect on the soul.   This quiet and
solitary garden exhaled consoling balsam and inspired only gentle thoughts, graceful images, voluptuous ones even.   In it might be recognized that
ineffable signature which our true character im-
prints upon everything, when nothing constrains
us to obey the various hypocrisies, otherwise necessary, which society requires.   I looked alternately
at the heap of narcissus and at the countess, seeming
to be more attracted by them than by her, to carry
out my rôle.

"'You love flowers, then, very much?' she said
to me.

"'They are,' I said, 'the only beings which do
not abuse our care and our tenderness.'

"Then I launched into so violent a tirade, drawing a parallel between botanical things and the
world, that we found ourselves a thousand leagues
from the party wall, and that the countess must
have taken me for a suffering soul, wounded and
worthy of pity.   Nevertheless, at the end of a half-
hour my neighbor brought me back naturally to the
question; for the women, when they are not in love,
have all the coolness of an old attorney.

"'If I allow you to keep the paling fence,' I said
to her, 'you will learn all the secrets of the cultivating which I wish to conceal, for I am seeking for
the blue dahlia, the blue rose, I am crazy on blue
flowers.   Is not blue the favorite color of fine souls?
We are neither of us in our own house; we might

as well put in a little open-work gate which would
unite our two gardens.—You love flowers, you would
see mine, I should see yours. If you receive no
one, I am visited only by my uncle, the curé des
Blancs-Manteaux.'

" 'No,' she said, 'I do not wish to give anyone
the right to enter my garden, my home, at any hour.
Come in, you will be always received like a neighbor with whom I wish to live on friendly relations;
but I love my solitude too much to burden it with
any dependence whatever.'

" 'As you like!' I said.

"And I leaped over the paling with a bound.

" 'Of what use would a gate be?' I cried when I
was on my own ground, turning toward the countess
and mocking her with a gesture, with a crazy
grimace.

"I remained two weeks without seeming to think
of my neighbor. On a beautiful evening, about the
end of the month of May, it happened that we were
each on our own side of the paling, walking with
slow steps. When we came to the end, it seemed
to be necessary to exchange some words of politeness; she found me so completely crushed, plunged
into so dolorous a reverie, that she spoke to me of
hope, throwing to me some phrases which were like
those songs with which nurses put their children to
sleep. Then I crossed the hedge and found myself
for the second time near her. The countess made
me come into her house, wishing to lighten my sorrow. I thus penetrated finally into that sanctuary

in which everything was in harmony with the woman whom I have endeavored to depict to you. There reigned throughout an exquisite simplicity. This pavilion, in its interior, was indeed the pretty little box invented by the art of the eighteenth century for the cheerful debauchery of a grand seigneur. The walls of the dining-room, situated on the ground floor, were covered with paintings in fresco representing flowers on trellis work, of an admirable and marvelous execution. The wall of the staircase presented charming decorations in cameo. The little salon, which was opposite to the dining-room, was greatly damaged, but the countess had hung on the walls curious old tapestries that had formed parts of ancient screens. A bath-room was adjoining. Upstairs, there was only one chamber with its dressing-room and a library metamorphosed into a workroom. The kitchen was concealed in the basement over which the pavilion rose, for it was necessary to mount to it by a perron of several steps. The balustrades of the gallery and its garlands of Pompadour flowers disguised the roof, of which nothing could be seen but the pinnacles in lead. In this retreat, you were a hundred leagues from Paris. Were it not for the bitter smile which sometimes played over the beautiful red lips of this pale woman, you would have believed in the happiness of this violet buried in its forest of flowers. In the course of a few days, we arrived at a state of confidence which sprang from our being neighbors and from the certainty which the countess

had of my complete indifference to women. One
look might have compromised everything, and never
did a single thought of her appear in my eyes!
Honorine wished to see in me something like an old
friend. Her manners with me proceeded from a
sort of compassion. Her looks, her voice, her conversation, everything revealed the fact that she was
a thousand leagues from those coquetries which the
most severe woman would perhaps have permitted
herself under similar circumstances. It was not
long before she gave me the right of entrance into
the charming workroom in which she made her
flowers, a retreat crowded with books and curiosities, adorned like a boudoir, and the richness of
which redeemed the commonness of the working
utensils. The countess had, in the long run, poet-
ized, as it were—which is the antipodes of poetry
—a manufacture. Of all the vocations which
women can pursue, that of making artificial flowers
is, perhaps, the one of which the details permit
them to display the most gracefulness. To color
them, a woman must lean over a table and give all
her faculties, with a certain amount of intenseness,
to this semi-painting. Tapestry weaving, followed
as assiduously as it must be by a workwoman who
wishes to earn her living by it, is apt to produce pul-
monary consumption, or curvature of the spine.
The engraving of plates of music is one of the
labors the most tyrannical by its minuteness, by the
care and the intelligence which it requires. Sew-
ing, embroidery, do not give the workwoman thirty

sous a day. But the manufacture of flowers and
that of feminine fashions necessitate a multitude
of movements, of gestures, of ideas even, which
leave a pretty woman still in her own sphere; she
is still herself, she may talk, laugh, sing, or think.
Certainly there was an artistic sentiment in the
manner in which the countess disposed on a long
table of yellow pine the myriad of colored petals
which served to compose the flowers upon which she
had decided. Her cups of color were of white porcelain, and always clean, ranged in such a manner as
to permit the eye to find immediately the desired
shade in the whole gamut of tints. The noble artist
thus economized her time. A pretty piece of furniture in ebony inlaid with ivory, with a hundred
Venetian drawers, contained the matrices of steel
with which she struck the leaves or certain petals.
A magnificent Japanese bowl contained the paste,
which she never allowed to become sour, and to
which she had adapted a cover with a hinge so light,
so movable, that she lifted it with the tip of her
finger. The iron and the brass wire were kept in a
little drawer of her work-table, before her. The
living flower, with which she proposed to compete,
rose before her eyes in a Venetian glass, swelling
out like a calix upon its stem. She had a passion
for the most difficult masterpieces, she undertook
the most impossible tasks, bunches of grapes, the
most delicate corolla, heath, nectarines of the most
capricious shades. Her hands, as active as her
thoughts, went from her table to her flower as

lightly as those of an artist on the keys of a piano.
Her fingers seemed to be *fairies*, to make use of an
expression of Perrault, so well did they conceal,
under the gracefulness of the movement, the different forces of twisting, of application of weight required by each work, while adapting with instinc-
tive clearness each movement to the result desired.
I did not weary of the pleasure of admiring her
while she composed a flower as soon as all its parts
had been assembled before her, and perfecting,
covering a stem with down, and attaching the
leaves to it. She displayed the genius of a painter
in her audacious enterprises, she imitated faded
flowers, yellow leaves; she struggled with the field
flowers, with all that were the most natural, the
most complicated in their simplicity.

  " 'This art,' she said to me, 'is still in its infancy. If Parisian women had a little of that
genius which the slavery of the harem requires in
the women of the Orient, they would give a complete language to the flowers which they wear on
their heads. I have made, for my own artistic satisfaction, faded flowers with the leaves of the color
of Florentine bronze, as they are found before or
after the winter.—This wreath, on the head of a
young woman whose life has been a disappointment,
or who is devoured by a secret grief, would it
lack poetical meaning? How many things could a
woman not express by her coiffure? Are there not
flowers for the drunken bacchantes, flowers for the
gloomy and rigid pious souls, thoughtful flowers for

wearied women? Botany may express, it seems to me, all the sensations and the thoughts of the soul, even the most delicate ones!'

"She made use of me to stamp the leaves, to cut out, to prepare the wire for the stems. My pretended wish for distraction soon rendered me skilful. We talked all the time we were working. When I had nothing to do, I read the news to her, for I could not lose sight of my rôle, and I feigned the man wearied with life, worn out by griefs, morose, sceptical, bitter. My appearance procured me adorable little jests upon the purely physical resemblance —excepting the lame foot—to Lord Byron. It was accepted as beyond question, that her own unhappinesses, concerning which she wished to preserve the most profound silence, outweighed mine, although already the causes for my misanthropy would have satisfied Young or Job. I will not speak to you of the sentiments of shame which tortured me in thus assuming for my heart, as do the beggars in the streets for their limbs, false scars in order thus to excite the pity of this admirable woman. I soon came to understand all the extent of my devotion in comprehending all the baseness of spies. The testimonials of sympathy which I then received would have consoled the greatest of misfortunes. This charming creature, severed from the world, alone for so many years, had, outside of love, treasures of affection to bestow, she offered them to me with childlike effusion, with a pity which certainly would have filled with bitterness the roué who might

have loved her; for, alas! she was all charity, all
compassion. Her renunciation of love, her terror of
what is called happiness for women, broke out with
as much force as ingenuousness. These happy days
proved to me that the friendship of women is much
superior to their love. I permitted the confidences
of my griefs to be drawn from me with as many
affectations as the young ladies assume when seating
themselves at the piano, so conscious are they of
the weariness which they are about to inflict. As
you may imagine, the necessity of overcoming my
repugnance to speak had ended by forcing the countess to draw closer the bonds of our intimacy; but
she found again in me so completely her own an-
tipathy to love, that she seemed to me to be happy
because of the chance which had sent to her in her
solitary island a species of man Friday. Perhaps
the solitude had commenced to weigh upon her.
Nevertheless, she was without the slightest coquetry, she had no longer anything of the woman,
she was no longer conscious of any heart, she said
to me, but in the ideal world in which she sought
refuge. Involuntarily I drew the comparison between these two existences, that of the count, all
action, all agitation, all emotion; that of the countess, quite passive, all inactivity, all motionless.
The woman and the man admirably obeyed each
his own nature. My misanthropy authorized me
to launch against men and women certain cynical in-
vectives, which I permitted myself, hoping thereby
to bring Honorine to some avowals; but she did not

allow herself to be drawn into any trap, and I began
to comprehend that *obstinacy of a mule,* more common
among women than is thought.

" 'The Orientals are right,' I said to her one
evening, 'in shutting you up and in considering you
as only the instruments of their pleasures.   Europe
has been well punished for having admitted you as
part of the world, and for accepting you on a footing
of equality.   In my opinion the woman is the most
dishonest and the most contemptible being that can
be encountered.   And it is to that cause, moreover,
that she owes her charms;—there is very little
pleasure in hunting a domestic animal!   When a
woman has inspired a man with a passion, she is
forever sacred to him; she is, in his eyes, clothed
with an imprescriptible privilege.   With man, the
gratitude for past pleasures is eternal.   If he find
again his mistress old, or unworthy of him, this
woman still has certain rights over his heart; but,
for you women, a man whom you have loved is no
longer anything; more than that, he is guilty of an
unpardonable wrong, that of living!—You dare not
avow it; but you all have in your heart that thought
which the popular calumnies called tradition ascribe
to the Lady of the Tour de Nesle.—What a pity it
is that you cannot nourish yourself on love as you
can on fruits! and that, of a repast partaken, there
nothing could remain to you but the feeling of
pleasure!—'

" 'God,' she said, 'has doubtless reserved this
perfect pleasure for Paradise.—But,' she went on,

'if your argument seems to you very intelligent, it has for me the misfortune of being false. What are those women who give themselves up to several loves?' she asked me, looking at me as the Virgin of Ingres looked at Louis XIII. offering her his kingdom.

"'You are a genuine comédienne,' I replied, 'for you have just given me one of those looks which would make the fortune of an actress. But, beautiful as you are, you have loved; therefore, you forget.'

"'I,' she replied, eluding my question, 'I am not a woman, I am a nun, of the age of seventy-two years.'

"'How then can you affirm so authoritatively that you feel with more sensitiveness than I? Unhappiness for women has only one form, they consider as misfortunes only deceivings of the heart.'

"She looked at me with a gentle air, and did as do all women, when, caught between the two horns of a dilemma, or clutched in the grasp of truth, they persist none the less in their will; she said to me:

"'I am a nun, and you speak to me of a world in which I can no longer set foot.'

"'Not even in thought?' I said to her.

"'Is the world so worthy of being envied?' she replied. 'Oh! when my thoughts wander, they go much higher.—The angel of perfection, the beautiful Gabriel, often sings in my heart,' she said. 'I should be rich, I would work none the less, so that I might not mount too often on the variegated wings of the angel and fly away into the kingdom of fancy.

There are certain contemplations which are our un-doing, we women! I owe much of my tranquillity to my flowers, though they do not always succeed in occupying me. On certain days, I feel my soul invaded by an objectless expectation; I cannot ban-ish a thought which takes possession of me, which seems to make my fingers heavy. I believe that a great event is preparing, that my life is about to change; I listen in empty space, I look into the shadows, I am without interest in my work, and I find again, after a thousand fatigues, life—daily life. Is it a forewarning from Heaven? That is what I ask myself—'

"After three months of the struggle between two diplomatists, one concealed under the skin of a melancholy juvenile and the other a woman ren-dered invincible by loathing, I told the count that it appeared to be impossible to make this tortoise come out of her house. It would be necessary to break her shell. The evening before, in a last discussion, perfectly friendly, the countess had ex-claimed:

" 'Lucretia wrote with her dagger and her blood the first word of the charter of all women: *Liberty !*'

"The count gave me from this time carte blanche.

" 'I have sold for a hundred francs the flowers and bonnets which I have made this week!' said Honorine to me, joyously, one Saturday evening when I went to see her in the little salon on the ground floor, the gildings of which had been renewed by the pretended owner.

6

"It was ten o'clock. A July twilight and a magnificent moon contributed their clouded light. There were whiffs of mingled perfumes that caressed the soul, the countess clinked in her hand the five pieces of gold received from a false dealer in millinery, another ally of Octave, whom a judge, Monsieur Popinot, had found for him.

"'To earn one's livelihood while amusing one's self,' she said, 'to be free, when men, armed with their laws, have wished to make slaves of us! Oh! every Saturday I have emotions of pride. In fact, I love Monsieur Gaudissart's gold pieces as much as Lord Byron, your twin, loved those of Murray.'

"'It is scarcely a woman's rôle,' I replied.

"'Bah! am I a woman? I am a youth endowed with a tender soul, that is all; a youth whom no woman can torment—'

"'Your life is a negation of your entire being,' I replied. 'What, you for whom God has expended his most curious treasures of love and of beauty, do you not desire sometimes—?'

"'What?' she asked, sufficiently mistrustful at a phrase which, for the first time, contradicted my assumed character.

"'A pretty child with curling hair, coming, going among these flowers, like a flower of life and of love, crying to you: "Mamma!"—'

"I waited for a reply. A silence somewhat too prolonged made me perceive the terrible effect of my words, which the darkness had concealed from me.— Reclining on her divan, the countess had not fainted,

but was chilled by a nervous attack, the first shiver-
ings of which although gentle, like everything
which emanated from her, resembled, as she after-
wards said, the first effects of the most subtle of
poisons. I called Madame Gobain, who came and
carried her mistress away, placed her upon her bed,
unlaced her, undressed her, restored her, not to life
but to the consciousness of a horrible pain. I
walked up and down the alley which ran in front of
the house, weeping, doubting of success. I would
have resigned my rôle of bird-catcher, so impru-
dently accepted. Madame Gobain, who came down
and found me with my face covered with tears, went
back promptly to say to the countess:

"'Madame, what has happened? Monsieur Maurice is weeping bitterly, like a child.'

"Stimulated by the dangerous interpretation
which might be put upon our mutual agitation, she
found a superhuman strength, put on a wrapper,
descended and came to me.

"'You are not the cause of this attack,' she said
to me; 'I am subject to spasms, a species of cramp
of the heart—'

"'And you wish to conceal from me your griefs?'
—I said to her, drying my tears, and in that voice
which does not dissemble. 'Have you not just told
me that you have been a mother, that you have had
the sorrow of losing your child?'

"'Marie!' she cried suddenly, ringing the bell.

"The Gobain made her appearance.

"'Some lights, and the tea,' she said, with the

coolness of a lady armed with pride by that atrocious British education which is known to you well.

"When the Gobain had lit the candles and closed the shades, the countess presented to me a countenance which revealed nothing; her indomitable pride, her gravity of a savage, had already resumed their sway; she said to me:

"'Do you know why I love Lord Byron so much? —He suffered as the animals suffer. Of what use is a complaint when it is not an elegy like that of Manfred, a bitter jesting like that of Don Juan, a reverie like that of Childe Harold? No one will know anything of me!—My heart is a poem that I carry to God!'

"'If I wished—' I said.

"'If?' she repeated.

"'I am not interested in anything,' I replied, 'I cannot be curious; but, if I wished, I would know to-morrow all your secrets.'

"'I defy you to do so!' she said with an ill-concealed anxiety.

"'Are you in earnest?'

"'Certainly,' she said, shaking her head, 'I should know if this crime be possible.'

"'In the first place, madame,' I replied, indicating to her her hands, 'those pretty fingers, which reveal clearly enough that you are not a young workwoman, were they made for labor? Then, you call yourself Madame Gobain, you who, before me, the other day, when you received a letter said to Marie,—'Here, it is for you,' Marie is the true Madame Gobain. Therefore, you hide your own name under that of your housekeeper. Oh! madame, from me you need fear nothing. You have in me the most devoted friend that you will ever have—*Friend,* you understand? I give to this word its holy and touching meaning, so profaned in France, where we baptize with it our enemies. This friend, who will defend you against everything, wishes you to be as happy as a woman like you should be. Who knows if the pain I caused you involuntarily was not a voluntary action?'

" 'Yes,' she replied with a menacing audacity, 'I wish it, you may become curious, and tell me all that you can learn about me, but—' she said, raising her finger, 'you will tell me also through what sources you have derived this information. The preservation of the feeble happiness which I enjoy here depends upon your steps.'

" 'That is to say, that you would fly—'

" 'As quickly as possible, and to the New World—'

" 'Where you would be,' I interrupted her, 'at the mercy of the brutality of the passions which you would inspire. Is it not the quality of genius and of beauty to shine, to attract all regards, to excite covetousness and wickedness? Paris is the desert without the Bedouins; Paris is the only spot in the world in which one can conceal himself when obliged to live by his own labor. Of what do you complain? Who am I? one domestic the more, I am Monsieur Gobain, that is all. If you have some duel on hand, you will require a second.'

"'Nevertheless, discover who I am. I have already said:—*I wish it!* now, I entreat you,' she repeated with a grace, which you always have at your command," said the consul, looking at the ladies.

"'Very well, to-morrow, at this hour, I will tell you what I have discovered,' I replied. 'But do not conceive a hatred against me. Will you do as the other women do?'

"'What is it the other women do?'

"'They command us to make immense sacrifices, and, when they are accomplished, they reproach us with them a little later, as though they were injuries.'

"'They are right, if what they have demanded of you have seemed to you to be sacrifices—' she replied, maliciously.

"'Replace the word sacrifices by the word efforts, and—'

"'That would be,' she said, 'an impertinence.'

"'Forgive me,' I said to her, 'I forgot that women and the Pope are infallible.'

"'*Mon Dieu!*' she said after a long pause, 'two words only can trouble this peace so dearly purchased, and which I enjoy as if it were a fraud—'

"She rose, paying no more attention to me.

"'Where to go?' she said. 'What to become— Will it be necessary to leave this soft retreat, prepared with so much care that I might finish my days in it?'

"'Finish your days in it?' I said to her with a visible terror. 'Has it then never occurred to you that there will come a time when you can no longer work, or when the price of flowers and of millinery will have fallen through competition?—'

"'I have already a thousand écus of savings!' she said.

"'*Mon Dieu!* how many privations this sum must represent?—' I cried.

"'Till to-morrow,' she said to me, 'leave me. This evening I am not myself, I wish to be alone. Should I not gather my forces in case of misfortune? for, if you should know something, the others who have informed you, and then—Adieu,' she said, in a quick tone and with an imperative gesture.

"'To-morrow, the combat,' I replied smiling, so as not to lose the careless character which I had given to this scene.

"But, in going away by the long avenue, I repeated to myself:

"'To-morrow, the combat.'

"And the count, whom I went to find, as every evening, on the boulevard, cried likewise:

"'To-morrow, the combat.'

"Octave's anxiety equaled that of Honorine. We remained, he and I, until two o'clock in the morning, walking up and down along the moats of the Bastille, like two generals who, the evening before a battle, weigh all the chances, examine the

ground, and recognize that in the midst of the combat the victory may be decided by an accident to
be taken advantage of. These two beings, violently
separated, were both watching, the one in the hope,
the other in the dread, of a reunion. The dramas
of life are not in the events, they are in the feelings
they take place in the heart, or, if you prefer, in that
immense world which we must call the spiritual
world. Octave and Honorine acted, lived exclusively in this world of the great intelligences.

"I was prompt. At ten o'clock in the evening,
for the first time, I was admitted into a charming
chamber, white and blue, into the nest of this
wounded dove. The countess looked at me, wished
me to speak, and was terrified by my respectful air.

"'Madame la Comtesse—' I said to her, smiling
gravely.

"The poor woman, who had risen, fell back in
her armchair and remained there in an attitude of
distress which I could have wished some great
painter to seize.

"'You are,' I said continuing, 'the wife of the
most noble of men and one of the greatest consideration, of a man who is accepted as great, but who
is much more so toward you than he is in the eyes
of the world. You and he, you are two lofty characters. Where do you think you are, here?' I
asked her.

"'In my house,' she replied, opening eyes which
were dilated by astonishment.

"'In the house of Comte Octave!' I replied.

'We have been tricked. Monsieur Lenormand, the
clerk of the court, is not the true proprietor, it is
the assumed name of your husband. The admirable peacefulness which you enjoy here is the work
of the count, the money that you earn comes from
the count, and his protection extends to the very
slightest details of your existence. Your husband
has saved you in the eyes of the world, he has
given plausible motives for your absence, he
ostensibly hopes that you were not lost in the ship-
wreck of the *Cécile,* the vessel upon which you
embarked to go to Havana, in order to secure the
inheritance of an old relative who might possibly
have forgotten you; you traveled in the company of
two women of his family and of an old steward!
The count claims that he has sent agents to those
distant localities, and that he has received letters
which give him a great deal of hope.—He takes, to
conceal you from all eyes, as many precautions as
you, yourself.—In short, he obeys you—'

"'Enough,' she replied. 'I wish to know only
one thing more. From whom do you obtain these
details?'

"'Eh! *Mon Dieu!* madame, my uncle secured
the place of secretary in the office of the commissary
of police of this quarter for a young man without
fortune. This young man has told me everything.
If you should leave this pavilion secretly this evening, your husband will know where you go, and his
protection will follow you everywhere. How could
a woman of intelligence be able to believe that the

shopkeepers could pay as much for flowers and bonnets as they sell them for? If you had asked of
them a thousand écus for a bouquet, they would
have given it to you! Never was the tenderness of
a mother more ingenious than that of your husband.
I have learned from the concierge of your house that
the count often comes, when everything is quiet,
behind the hedge, to watch the light of your night
lamp! Your great cashmere shawl is worth six
thousand francs.—The merchant from whom you
buy your toilet articles sells you as *second-hand*
goods that come from the very best manufactories—
In short, you here realize perfectly, Venus in the
toils of Vulcan; but you are caught in them alone,
and by the invention of a sublime generosity, sublime for the last seven years, and at every moment.'

"The countess trembled as trembles a captive
swallow, and which, in the hand in which it is held,
stretches its neck, looks around it with a terrified
eye. She was agitated by a nervous convulsion,
and examined me with a mistrustful look. Her dry
eyes emitted a light that was almost warm; but she
was still a woman!—there came a moment in which
her tears broke forth, and she wept, not because
she was touched, she wept at her helplessness, she
wept with despair. She had thought herself independent and free, marriage weighed upon her like
the prison upon the captive.

" 'I will go,' she said, through her tears, 'he
forces me to it, I will go there where, certainly, no
one will follow me!'

" 'Ah!' I said, 'you will kill yourself—Come,
madame, you must have very powerful reasons for
not wishing to return to Comte Octave's house.'

" 'Oh! certainly!'

" 'Well, tell them to me, tell them to my uncle;
you will have in us two devoted counselors. If my
uncle is a priest in a confessional, he never is in
a salon. We will listen to you, we will endeavor to
find a solution to the problems which you will propose to us: and, if you are the dupe or the victim
of some misunderstanding, perhaps we may be able
to clear it up. Your soul seems to me pure; but, if
you have committed a fault, you have well expiated
it.—Finally, remember that you have in me the
most sincere friend. If you wish to save yourself
from the tyranny of the count, I will furnish you
with the means, he will never find you.'

" 'Oh! there is the convent,' she said.

" 'Yes, but the count, become Minister of State,
would cause you to be refused by all the convents
in the world. Although he is very powerful, I
would save you from him,—but—when you have
demonstrated to me that you cannot, that you should
not, return to him. Oh! do not think that you
would fly from his power to fall into mine,' I went
on, as I received from her a horrible glance of mistrust and one full of an exaggerated nobility. 'You
will have peace, solitude, and independence; in
short, you will be as free and as respected as if you
were an ugly and wicked old maid. I shall not be
able, myself, to see you without your consent.'

" 'And how? by what means?'

" 'That, madame, is my secret.   I do not deceive
you in the least, of that you may be certain.
Demonstrate to me that this life is the only one
which you can lead, that it is preferable to that of
the Comtesse Octave, rich, honored, in one of the
finest hôtels in Paris, adored by her husband, a
happy mother—and I will decide your cause in your
favor.'

" 'But,' she said, 'will there ever be a man who
will comprehend me?—'

" 'No,' I replied.   'Therefore I have called in religion to judge us, the curé of the Blancs-Manteaux
is a saint, seventy-five years of age.   My uncle is
not the grand inquisitor, he is Saint-John; but he
will make himself Fénelon for you, the Fénelon who
said to the Duc de Bourgogne:—"Eat veal on Friday;
but be a Christian, monseigneur!"'

" 'No, monsieur, the convent is my last resource
and my sole asylum.   There is no one but God who
can comprehend me.   No man, were he Saint-
Augustine, the most tender of the Fathers of the
Church, could enter into the scruples of my conscience, which for me are the insurmountable circles of Dante's *inferno*.   Another than my husband,
another, however unworthy of this offering he may
have been, has had all my love!   He has not had
it, for he did not take it; I gave it to him as a
mother gives to her child a marvelous toy, which
the child breaks.   For me, there were not two loves.
Love for certain souls makes no attempts; either it

is, or it is not. When it shows itself, when it rises, it is all complete. Well, this life of eighteen months was for me a life of eighteen years, I brought to it all the faculties of my being, they were not impoverished by their effusion, they were exhausted in that deceitful intimacy where I alone was frank. For me, the cup of happiness is neither emptied nor empty, nothing can fill it again, for it is broken. I am out of the combat, I have no longer any weapons —After having thus given myself up completely, what am I? the remnant of a feast. They gave me only one name, Honorine, as I have but one heart. My husband has had the young girl, an unworthy lover has had the woman, there is nothing left! Allow myself to be loved? that is the great word which you are going to say to me. Oh! I am still something, and I revolt at the idea of being a prostitute! Yes, I have seen clearly in the light of the conflagration; and, yes,—I could conceive of yielding to the love of another; but to Octave?—oh! never.'

"'Oh! you love him,' I said to her.

"'I esteem him, I respect him, I venerate him, he has never done me the least harm; he is good, he is tender; but I can no longer love him—However,' she said, 'let us speak no more of that. Discussion makes everything little. I will convey to you in writing, my ideas on this subject; for, at this moment, they suffocate me, I have a fever, my feet are in the ashes of my Paraclete. Everything that I see, those things which I believed I had won by my labor, recall to me now everything that I wish to forget. Ah! I shall have to fly from here, as I went away from my house.'

" 'To go where?' I said. 'Can a woman exist without a protector? At thirty, in all the glory of beauty, rich with forces which you do not suspect, full of tenderness to bestow, will you go to live in the desert where I can hide you?—Remain in peace. The count, who in five years has not shown himself here, will never enter here without your consent. You have for a guarantee of your tranquillity, his sublime life for the last nine years. You can then deliberate in all security on your future, with my uncle and me. My uncle is as powerful as a Minister of State. Calm yourself then, do not exaggerate your misfortune. A priest whose head has grown white in the exercise of his sacred functions, is not a child, you will be comprehended by one to whom all passions have been confided for nearly fifty years, and who weighs in his hands the burdened hearts of kings and princes. If he is severe under the stole, my uncle will be, before your flowers, as gentle as they, and indulgent as his Divine Master.'

"I left the countess at midnight, I left her in appearance calm, but sad, and cherishing secret dispositions which no perspicacity could divine. I found the count a few steps away, in the Rue Saint-Maur, for he had quitted the designated locality on the boulevard, drawn toward me by an invincible force.

" 'What a night the poor child is going to pass!' he cried, when I had recounted to him the scene which had just taken place. 'If I should go there,' he said, 'if, suddenly, she should see me?'

" 'At this moment, she is a woman to throw herself out of the window,' I replied. 'The countess is of those Lucretias who will not survive a violation, even from a man to whom they have given themselves.'

" 'You are young,' he answered me. 'You do not know that the will, in a soul agitated by such cruel debates, is like the waves of a lake over which a tempest is passing, the wind changes at every moment, and the current sets now toward one shore and now toward another. During this night, there are as many chances that, on seeing me, Honorine will throw herself into my arms as that she will throw herself out of the window.'

" 'And you would accept this alternative?' I asked him.

" 'Come,' he replied, 'I have, at my house, to enable me to wait till to-morrow evening, a dose of opium which Desplein has prepared for me so that I may sleep without danger!'

"The next day, at noon, the Gobain brought me a letter, saying that the countess, worn out with fatigue, had gone to rest at six o'clock and that, thanks to a draught of almond-milk, prepared by the druggist, she was sleeping. Here is that letter, I have kept a copy of it,—for, mademoiselle," said the consul, addressing Camille Maupin, "you

are acquainted with the resources of art, the tricks
of style, and the efforts of very many writers who do
not lack skilfulness in their compositions; but you
will recognize that literature would not know how
to find such writings as this in its affected entrails;
there is nothing so terrible as the true. See what
this woman wrote, or, rather, this sorrow:

" 'MONSIEUR MAURICE:

" 'I know all that your uncle could say to me, he
is not better informed than my conscience. Conscience is in man the interpreter for God, I know
that if I do not reconcile myself with Octave, I shall
be damned: such is the decree of the religious law.
The civil law commands me to obedience, whatever
happens. If my husband does not repulse me, everything is said, the world will consider me as pure, as
virtuous, whatever I may have done. Yes, marriage
has this of the sublime in it, that society ratifies
the husband's pardon; but it has forgotten that it
is necessary that the pardon should be accepted.
On legal, on religious, on worldly grounds, I should
return to Octave. If we confine ourselves to the
human question, is there not something cruel in
refusing him happiness, in depriving him of children, in effacing his name from the golden book of
the peerage? My sorrows, my repugnances, my
sentiments, all my egotism—for I know myself to be
egotistical—should be immolated for the benefit of
the family. I should be a mother, the caresses of
my children would dry a great many tears! I should

be very happy, I should certainly be honored, I
should pass by, proud and opulent, in a brilliant
equipage! I should have domestics, a hôtel, a household, I should be the queen of as many festivals as
there are weeks in the year. The world would give
me welcome. In short, I should not remount into
the patrician heaven, I should not even have
descended from it. Thus God, the law, society,
everything is in accord. Against what do you
rebel? is said to me from the height of Heaven,
from the pulpit, from the tribunal and from the
throne, the august intervention of which would be
invoked, if necessary, by the count. Your uncle
would even speak to me, if it were required, of a
certain celestial grace which would inundate my
heart when I should be conscious of the pleasure of
having done my duty. God, the law, the world,
Octave, wish that I should live, is it not so? Well,
if there be no other difficulty, my reply will cut
through all; I will not live! I shall become very
white, very innocent, for I shall be in my shroud,
adorned with the irreproachable paleness of death.
There is not here the least *obstinacy of a mule*.
This obstinacy of a mule, of which you have accused
me, laughingly, is, in a woman, the effect of a certainty, a vision of the future. If my husband, through
love, has the sublime generosity to forget everything,
I will not forget, I will not! Does forgetfulness depend upon us? When a widow marries, love makes
her a young girl, she marries a man beloved; but I
cannot love the count. Everything is in that, you

7

see. Every time that my eyes met his I should see
in them forever my fault, even when the eyes of my
husband were full of love. The greatness of his
generosity would attest before me the greatness of
my crime. My eyes, always mistrustful, would be
forever reading an invisible sentence. I should have
in my heart confused souvenirs which would combat each other. Never would marriage awaken in
my being the cruel delights, the mortal delirium of
passion; I should kill my husband by my coldness,
by comparisons which would suggest themselves,
though concealed in the depths of my consciousness.
Oh! on that day when, in a line in the forehead, in
a saddened look, in an imperceptible gesture, I
should perceive some involuntary reproach, even
though repressed, nothing would retain me;—I
should be lying with my head crushed on a pavement which I should find more kindly than my husband. This horrible and gentle death would perhaps
be entirely due to my over-sensitiveness. I should
die, perhaps, the victim of some momentary impatience which an event had caused Octave, or deceived by an unjust suspicion. Alas! I might,
perhaps, mistake a proof of love for a proof of contempt. What a double torture! Octave would be
forever doubting me, I should be forever doubting
him. I should oppose to him, quite involuntarily, a
rival unworthy of him, a man whom I despise, but
who has made me know voluptuousnesses engraved
in characters of fire, of which I am ashamed, and
which I am irresistibly compelled to remember. Is

this enough to reveal to you my heart? No one, monsieur, can prove to me that love recommences, for I cannot, and I do not wish to accept the love of anyone. A young girl is like a flower which you have just plucked; but the culpable wife is a flower which has been trodden upon. You are a florist, you should know if it be possible to straighten up again this stem, to revive these faded colors, to bring back the sap in these tubes so delicate and on the perfect uprightness of which depends all vegetative power.—If some botanist should give himself up to this operation, would this man of genius be able to smooth out the wrinkles of the rumpled texture? He would remake a flower, he would be God! God alone can make me new. I drink the bitter cup of expiation; but, in drinking it, I have terribly spelled out this sentence:—*To expiate is not to efface.* In my pavilion, alone, I eat a loaf watered with my tears; but no one sees me eating it, no one sees me weep. To enter again Octave's house, would be to renounce my tears, my tears would offend him. Oh! monsieur, how many virtues would it not be necessary to tread under foot in order, not to give one's self, but to yield one's self, to a husband whom one has deceived?—who can count them? God only, for He only is the confidant and He it is who prompts in our hearts these terrible sensitivenesses, which might make even His angels turn pale. Ah! I will even go further. A wife has courage before a husband who knows nothing; she displays then in her hypocrisies

an untamed strength, she deceives in order to give
a double happiness. But a mutual certainty, is
it not debasing? For myself, I should exchange
humiliations for ecstasies. Would not Octave end
by finding depravity in my consentings? Marriage is founded on esteem, on sacrifices made on
one side and the other; but neither Octave nor I
can foretell the future of our reunion: he will dishonor me by some old man's love for a courtesan;
and I, I should have the perpetual shame of being a
thing instead of being a lady. I should not be virtue, I should be pleasure in my household. These
are the bitter fruits of a fault. I have made myself
a conjugal bed in which I can only turn myself on
live coals, a bed in which there is no slumber.
Here, I have hours of peacefulness, hours in which
I forget; but, in my own hôtel, everything would
recall to me the stain which dishonors my wife's
robe. When I suffer here, I bless my sufferings,
I say to God: *Thanks!* But in his house, I should
be full of fright, tasting joys which are not my
due. All this, monsieur, is not reasoning, it is
the conviction of a soul greatly experienced, for
it has been furrowed for seven years by pain.
Finally, should I make to you this frightful avowal?
I feel my breasts forever bitten by an infant conceived in intoxication and joy, in the belief in
happiness, by an infant which I nourished during
seven months, of which I shall be pregnant all my
life. If new infants should draw from me their nourishment, they would drink tears which, mingled with

my milk, would turn them sour. I am apparently light-hearted, I seem to you childish—Oh! yes I have the memory of the child, that memory that renews itself on the edge of the tomb. Thus, as you see, there is not one situation in the beautiful life to which the world and the love of a husband wish to bring me back, which is not false, which does not conceal snares for me, which does not open before me precipices over which I should roll, torn by pitiless crags. It is now five years that I have been wandering in the barren wastes of my future without finding there a suitable place for my repentance, because my soul has been taken possession of by a true repentance. To all this, religion has its replies, and I know them by heart. These sufferings, these difficulties, are my punishment, it says, and God will give me the strength to support them. This, monsieur, is a reason for certain pious souls, endowed with an energy in which I am wanting. Between the hell in which God will not prevent me from blessing him, and the hell which waits for me in the house of Comte Octave, my choice is made.

"'One last word. If I were a young girl, and were it not for my actual experience, I would still choose my husband; but this is precisely the reason for my refusal,—I do not wish to blush before this man. What! I should be always on my knees, he would be always standing before me! And, if we changed our positions, I should find him despicable. I do not wish to be better treated by him because of my fault. The angel who would dare to commit certain

brutalities that are permitted on both sides when
they are mutually irreproachable, that angel does
not exist on earth; he is in Heaven! Octave is full
of delicacy, I know it; but there do not exist in that
soul—however grand they may make it, it is still a
man's soul—any guarantees for the new existence
which I should lead in his house. Come then to tell
me where I can find that solitude, that peace, that
silence, the friends of irreparable misfortunes, which
you have promised me?'

"After having taken of this letter the copy which
you see, so as to keep this memorial complete, I went
to the Rue Payenne. Anxiety had overcome the
power of the opium. Octave was walking up and
down like a madman in his garden.

"'Reply to that,' I said to him, giving him his
wife's letter. 'Endeavor to reassure modesty that
is instructed. It is somewhat more difficult than to
circumvent modesty that is ignorant of itself, which
curiosity delivers up to you.'

"'She is mine!'—cried the count, whose countenance expressed his happiness in proportion as he
progressed in his reading.

"He made me a sign with his hand to leave him
alone, feeling himself watched in his joy. I comprehended that excessive happiness, like excessive
sorrow, obeys the same laws; I went to receive
Madame de Courteville and Amélie, who were to
dine with the count that day. However beautiful
Mademoiselle de Courteville may have been, I was

conscious, on seeing her again, that love has three faces, and that the women who inspire in us a complete love are very rare. While comparing involuntarily Amélie with Honorine, I found more charm in the wife in fault than in the pure young maid. For Honorine, fidelity was not duty, but the fatality of the heart; whilst Amélie was about to take the most solemn promises with a serene air, without knowing either their range or their obligations. The exhausted wife, reputed dead, the penitent sinner to be lifted, seemed to me sublime, she excited the natural generosities of man, she demanded of the heart all its treasures, of the strength, all its resources; she filled life, she brought into it a contest in the happiness; while Amélie, chaste and confiding, would enclose herself in the sphere of a peaceful maternity, where the commonplace should be poetical, where my spirit would find neither combat nor victory.

"Between the plains of La Champagne and the snowy and tempestuous but sublime Alps, where is the young man who would choose the chalky and peaceful level? No, such comparisons are fatal and evil on the threshold of the mayor's office. Alas! it is necessary to have had experience with life to know that marriage excludes passion, that the family should in no wise be founded upon the storms of love. After having dreamed of an impossible love with its innumerable ideal delights, after having tasted the cruel deliciousness of the ideal, I had before my eyes a modest reality. What would you have; give

me your pity! At the age of twenty-five, I had
doubts of myself; but I took a virile resolution.   I
went in search of the count again, under the pretext
of informing him of the arrival of his cousins and I
found him become young again in the reflection of
his hopes.

" 'What is it, Maurice?' he asked me, struck with
the alteration in my looks.

" 'Monsieur le Comte—'

" 'You no longer call me Octave! you to whom I
shall owe life, happiness—'

" 'My dear Octave, if you succeed in bringing
the countess back to her obligations, I have carefully observed her—' he looked at me as Othello
must have looked at Iago, when Iago had succeeded
in communicating the first suspicion to the Moor—
'she should never see me again, she should be ignorant that you have had Maurice for a secretary;
never pronounce my name, let no one recall me,
otherwise, everything will be lost.—You have caused
me to be named referendary; well, obtain for me
some diplomatic post abroad, a consulate, and think
no more about marrying me to Amélie—Oh! have
no fears,' I went on, as I saw him start, 'I will carry
out my part to the end—'

" 'Poor fellow!'—he said to me, taking me by the
hand, pressing it, and suppressing the tears which
moistened his eyes.

" 'You gave me gloves,' I replied, laughing, 'I did
not put them on, that is all.'

"We then came to an agreement as to what I

should do that evening at the pavilion, to which I
returned at the end of the day. It was then the
month of August, the day had been warm, stormy,
but the storm had remained in the air, the sky was
like brass, the perfumes of the flowers were heavy,
I seemed to be in a sweating-chamber, and surprised myself wishing that the countess had gone
to the Indies; but she was wearing a redingote of
white muslin trimmed with knots of blue ribbons,
without a headdress, her crisp curls falling down
the sides of her cheeks, and seated on a wooden
bench made in the shape of a settee, under a sort
of little grove, her feet on a little wooden stool,
and showing a few inches below her dress. She did
not rise, she indicated to me with her hand a place
near her, saying to me:

"'Is not life without any outlook for me?'

"'The life that you have made for yourself,' I
said to her, 'but not that which I wish to make
for you; for, if you wish it, you may be very
happy—'

"'And how?' she asked.

"All her body asked the question.

"'Your letter is in the hands of the count.'

"Honorine rose like a startled fawn, sprang away
three steps, walked about, taking turns in her garden, remained standing for a few moments, and
finally went to take a seat alone in her salon, where
I rejoined her when I had left her a little time in
which to accustom herself to the pain of this dagger-
stroke.

" 'You! a friend!—Say rather a traitor, some spy for my husband, perhaps?'

" Instinct, in women, is the equal of the perspicacity of the greatest men.

" 'An answer was required for your letter, was there not? and there was only one man in the world who could write it—You will then read the reply, dear countess, and, if you do not find any outlook for your life after this reading, the spy will prove to you that he is a friend, for I will put you in a convent whence the count's power will never wrest you; but, before going there, let us hear the other side. There is a law, divine and human, which hatred itself feigns to obey, and which commands not to condemn without hearing the defence. You have, up to the present, condemned, like the children, while stopping your ears. A devotion of seven years has its rights. You will then read the reply which your husband will make. I have sent to him by my uncle the copy of your letter, and my uncle has asked him what his reply would be if his wife should write him a letter conceived in similar terms. Thus you are in no way compromised. The good man will himself bring the count's letter. Before this holy man and before me, through respect for yourself, you should read it, or you would be only a rebellious and angry child. You will make this sacrifice to the world, to the law, to God.'

"As she did not see in compliance any affront to her woman's will, she consented. All this labor of four or five months had been built up for this

moment. But do not the pyramids terminate by a
point upon which a bird can balance itself?—The
count rested all his hopes on this supreme hour,
and he had finally reached it. I do not know anything, in all the memories of my life, more formidable than the entrance of my uncle into this Pompadour salon at ten o'clock in the evening. That
head, whose silver hair was set off by garments all
of black, and that countenance of a divine calm,
produced a magic effect upon the Comtesse Honorine; she felt the freshness of a balm upon her
wounds, she was enlightened by a reflection of
that virtue, brilliant but unconscious.

"'Monsieur le Curé des Blancs-Manteaux!' said
the Gobain.

"'Do you come, my dear uncle, with a message
of peace and of happiness?' I asked him.

"'Happiness and peace will always be found in
observing the commands of the Church,' he replied,
presenting the countess with the following letter:

"'MY DEAR HONORINE,

"'If you had done me the kindness not to doubt
me, if you had read the letter which I wrote you
five years ago, you would have spared yourself five
years of useless toil and of privations which have
afflicted me. I then proposed to you a compact, the
stipulations of which would have destroyed all your
fears and rendered possible our domestic life. I
have many reproaches to address to myself, and I
have become conscious of all my faults in seven

years of grief. I misunderstood marriage. I was
not able to suspect the danger when it threatened
you. An angel was in my house, the Lord had said
to me: Guard her well! the Lord has punished the
rashness of my confidence. You cannot give yourself a single blow without striking me. Have compassion on me, my dear Honorine! I have so well
comprehended your sensitiveness that I have not
been willing to bring you back to the old hôtel of
the Rue Payenne, in which I can live without you,
but which I should not want to see again with you.
I am adorning with pleasure another house in the
Faubourg Saint-Honoré, into which I conduct, in
anticipation, not a wife whom I owe to her ignorance of life, duly acquired by law, but a sister who
will permit me to deposit on her forehead the kiss
which a father gives to a daughter daily blessed.
Will you deprive me of the right which I believed
myself to have conquered from your despair, that of
watching most closely over your needs, over your
pleasures, over your life even? Women have a
heart of their own, always full of excuses, that of
their mother; you have never known any other
mother than mine, who would have brought you
back to me; but how is it that you have not divined
that I have for you the heart both of my mother and
of your own! Oh! Dear, my affection is neither
petty nor caviling, it is of those which do not allow
to contradiction even time enough to wrinkle the
countenance of an adored child. For whom do you
take the companion of your infancy, Honorine, in

believing him capable of accepting kisses given in
trembling, of sharing joy and mistrust? Do not fear
that you may have to endure the lamentations of a
mendicant passion. I have not wished for you until
after having assured myself of the power of leaving
to you your complete liberty. Your solitary pride has
exaggerated the difficulties; you could share the life
of a brother or of a father, without suffering and
without joy, if you wished; but you would find
around you neither mocking nor indifference, nor
misconstruing of intentions. The warmth of the
atmosphere in which you live shall be always
equable and mild, without storms, without possible
disturbances. If, later, after having acquired the
certainty of being in your home as you are in your
pavilion, you should be willing to introduce in it
other elements of happiness, pleasures, diversions,
you will enlarge the circle at your will. The tenderness of a mother has neither disdain nor pity;
what is it? love without desire;—well, in me, admiration will conceal all the sentiments in which
you might see offences. We may thus be able to
hold ourselves nobly, side by side. In you, the
kindness of a sister, the caressing spirit of a friend,
will be sufficient to satisfy the ambition of him who
wishes to be your companion, and you may measure
his tenderness by the efforts which he makes to
conceal it from you. We shall have, neither of us,
any uneasiness concerning our past, for we can
recognize in each other sufficient intelligence to
look ahead of us only. Therefore, you will be in

your own house, in your hôtel, everything that you
are in the Rue Saint-Maur,—inviolable, solitary,
occupied as you please, governed by your own laws;
but you will have, moreover, a lawful protection
which will then be under obligations to display for
you the most chivalric love, and that consideration
which adds so much lustre to women, and a fortune
which will permit you to undertake so many good
works. Honorine, when you wish a useless abso-
lution, you will come and ask for it; it will not be
imposed upon you, either by the Church or by the
Code; it will depend entirely upon your pride, upon
your own volition.   My wife might have to fear all
that which terrifies you, but not the friend or the
sister toward whom I shall hold myself constrainéd
to display all the manners and all the considerations
of politeness.   To see you happy will suffice for my
contentment, I have proved it during seven years.
Ah! the guarantees of my word, Honorine, are in
all the flowers which you have made, preciously
kept, watered by my tears, and which are, like the
quipos of the Peruvians, a history of our sorrows.
If this secret compact does not content you, my
child, I have requested the holy man who carries
this letter, not to say a word in my favor.   I do not
wish to be indebted for your return either to the
terrors impressed upon you by the Church, or to
the commands of the Law. I wish to receive only
from yourself the simple and modest happiness
which I ask.   If you persist in imposing upon me
the sombre life, deprived of any fraternal smile,

which I have led for nine years, if you remain in
your desert, solitary and unmoved, my will will
give way before yours.   Be sure of this,—you will
not be molested any more than you have been until
to-day.   I will give his dismissal to that lunatic
who has interfered in your affairs, and who perhaps
has vexed you—'

"'Monsieur,' said Honorine, interrupting her
letter, which she put in her corsage, and looking at
my uncle, 'I thank you, I will take advantage of the
permission which Monsieur le Comte has given me
to remain here—'

"'Ah!' I exclaimed.

"This exclamation procured me from my uncle
an unquiet look, and from the countess a malicious
glance which enlightened me as to her motives.
Honorine had wished to know if I were an actor, a
bird-catcher, and I had the sorrowful satisfaction
of deceiving her by my exclamation, which was
one of those cries of the heart which women know
so well.

"'Ah! Maurice,' she said to me, 'you know how
to love, you do!'

"The light which shone in my eyes was another
response which would have dissipated the countess's distrust, if she had had any still.   Thus the
count was served by me up to the last moment.
Honorine then resumed her letter from her husband,
to finish it.   My uncle made me a sign, I rose.

"'We will leave madame,' he said to me.

"'Are you going already, Maurice?' she inquired of me without looking at me.

"She rose, followed us out, still reading, and on the threshold of the pavilion she took my hand, pressed it very affectionately, and said to me:

"'We shall see each other again—'

"'No,' I replied, grasping her hand till she cried out. 'You love your husband! To-morrow, I go away.'

"And I fled precipitately, leaving my uncle, to whom she said:

"'What is the matter with your nephew?'

"The poor abbé completed my task by making the gesture of indicating his head and his heart as if to say: 'He is crazy, you must excuse him, madame!' with much more truthfulness than he thought. Six days later, I set off with my appointment as vice-consul in Spain, in a large commercial city, where I could in a short time qualify myself for the consular career, to which I limited my ambition. After my installation, I received this letter from the count:

"'MY DEAR MAURICE,

"'If I were happy, I would in no wise write to you; but I have commenced another life of pain,—I have become young again through desire, with all the impatiences of a man who has passed forty, with the wisdom of the diplomat who knows how to moderate his passion. When you went away, I was not yet admitted to the pavilion in the Rue Saint-

HONORINE AND MAURICE.

_____

"*On the threshold of the pavilion she took my hand, pressed it very affectionately, and said to me:*

"'*We shall see each other again—*'

"'*No,' I replied, grasping her hand till she cried out. 'You love your husband! To-morrow I go away.'*"

Maur; but a letter had promised me the permission
to go there, the gentle and melancholy letter of a
woman who dreads the emotions of an interview.
After having waited more than a month, I risked
presenting myself, asking through the Gobain if I
should be received. I seated myself on a chair in
the avenue, near the lodge, my head in my hands,
and I remained there nearly an hour.

" ' "Madame wishes to dress," said the Gobain to
me in order to conceal under a feminine coquetry
which should be creditable to me, Honorine's irreso-
lutions.

" 'During a long quarter of an hour we had been,
each of us, affected by an involuntary nervous
trembling, as strong as that which seizes the orators
on the stand, and we addressed to each other frightened phrases, like people surprised who make a pre-
tence of conversation.

" ' "See Honorine," I said to her, my eyes full
of tears, "the ice is broken, and I am so trembling with happiness that you must forgive the
incoherence of my language. It will be so for a
long time."

" ' "It is not a crime to be in love with your
wife," she replied with a forced smile.

" ' "Do me the favor not to work any more as you
have done. I know from Madame Gobain that you
have been living for the last twenty days on your
savings, you have sixty thousand francs income of
your own, and, if you will not give me your heart,
at least do not leave me your fortune."

8

"'"I have known your kindness for a long time—" she said.

"'"If it pleases you to remain here," I replied, "and to preserve your independence; if the most ardent love does not find favor in your eyes, do not work any more—"

"'I presented her with three certificates each of twelve thousand francs interest, she took them, opened them indifferently, and, after having read them, Maurice, she gave me a look for sole reply. Ah! she comprehended perfectly that it was not money which I gave her, but liberty.

"'"I am vanquished," she said to me, extending to me a hand which I kissed, "come to see me as often as you wish."

"'Thus she had only received me by doing violence to herself. The next day I found her armed with a counterfeit gaiety, and it has required two months of accustoming before seeing her in her true character. But this was then like a delicious May, a springtime of love which gave me ineffable joys; she had no more fears, she studied me. Alas! when I proposed to her to go over to England with me in order to join me ostensibly, in her house, to resume her rank, to live in her new hôtel, she was seized with terror.

"'"Why not live always this way?" she said.

"'I resigned myself without a word.

"'"Is this an experiment?" I asked myself as I left her.

"'In going from my own house to the Rue Saint-

Maur, I became animated, thoughts of love swelled my heart, and I said to myself, like the young men:

"'"This evening she will yield—"'

"'All this strength, factitious or real, was dissipated by a smile, by a command in her eyes, proud and calm, which passion never changed. That terrible saying which you repeated: *Lucretia wrote with her blood and her dagger the first word of the charter of women,*—LIBERTY, came back to me, chilled me. I was profoundly convinced of the necessity of the consent of Honorine, and of the impossibility of wresting it from her. Did she have any suspicion of those storms which agitated me as well during the return as during the going? I finally depicted to her my situation in a letter, renouncing speaking to her about it. Honorine did not reply to me, she remained so mournful that I acted as if I had not written. I was greatly pained at having afflicted her, she read in my heart and forgave me. You shall know how. Three days ago, for the first time, she received me in her white and blue chamber. The room was full of flowers, adorned, illuminated. Honorine had assumed a toilet which made her ravishing. Her hair enclosed with its light rolls that face which you know; on her head she wore some tufts of Cape heather; she wore a dress of white muslin, a white girdle with long floating ends. You knew what she is in this simplicity; but, on this day, she was a bride, she was the Honorine of the early days. My joy was immediately frozen, for her countenance had a character of terrible gravity, there was fire under that ice.

" ' "Octave," she said to me, "when you wish it, I will be your wife; but, know it well, this submission has its dangers, I can resign myself—"

" 'I made a gesture.

" ' "Yes," she said, "I understand you, resignation offends you, and you wish that which I cannot give, love! Religion, compassion, have caused me to renounce my vow of solitude, you are here!"

" 'She made a pause.

" ' "In the first place," she went on, "you did not ask more; now, you want your wife. Well, I give up to you Honorine, such as she is, and without deceiving you as to what she will be. What shall I become? A mother! I wish it. Oh! believe it, I wish it sincerely. Endeavor to transform me, I consent to it; but if I die, my friend, do not curse my memory, and do not accuse of obstinacy that which I should call the worship of the ideal, if it were not more natural to call the indefinable sentiment which will kill me, the worship of the divine! The future does not concern me, it is you who are charged with it, take counsel!—"

" 'She then seated herself in that serene attitude which you have admired, and looked at me growing pale under the pain which she had caused me. My blood was chilled. When she saw the effect of her words, she took my hands, placed them in her own and said to me:

" ' "Octave, I love you, but in another manner than that in which you wish to be loved; I love your soul—But, know it, I love you enough to die in your service, like an Eastern slave, and without regret. This will be my expiation."

" 'She did more, she placed herself on her knees on a cushion before me, and, in an accession of divine charity, she said to me:

" ' "After all, perhaps I shall not die?—"

" 'Here are the words with which I wrestle. What can I do?—My heart is too full, I have sought that of a friend to throw into it this cry: What can I do?'

"I made no reply. Two months later, the newspaper announced the arrival, by an English packet-boat, of the Comtesse Octave, restored to her family, after a voyage, the events of which were invented with a sufficient plausibility to be contested by no one. On my arrival at Genoa, I received a letter announcing the happy accouchement of the countess, who presented her husband with a son. I held the letter in my hands for two hours, on that terrace seated on that bench. Two months later, tormented by Octave, by Messieurs de Granville and Sérizy, my protectors, overwhelmed by the loss of my uncle, I consented to marry.

"Six months after the Revolution of July, I

received the following letter, which concludes the history of this household:

" 'MONSIEUR MAURICE,

" 'I am dying, although a mother, and perhaps because I am a mother. I have played well my part as wife; I have deceived my husband, I have had joys as real as the tears shed on the stage by actresses. I die for society, for the family, for marriage, as the first Christians died for God. I do not know of what I am dying, I seek for it in good faith, for I am not obstinate; but I desire to explain to you my malady, to you who brought the heavenly surgeon, your uncle, to whose words I yielded myself; he has been my confessor, I took care of him in his last illness, and he showed Heaven to me in commanding me to continue to do my duty. And I have done my duty. I do not blame those who forget, I admire them as strong natures, necessary ones; but I have the infirmity of remembering! That love of the heart which we identify with the man loved, I have not been able to feel twice. Up to the last moment, as you know, I cried in your heart, in the confessional, to my husband: *Have pity on me!*—Everything was without pity. Well, I am dying. I die in displaying an unheard-of courage. Never was courtesan more gay than I. My poor Octave is happy, I allow his love to feed itself on the mirages of my heart. In this terrible game, I expend all my forces, the actress is applauded, fêted, covered with flowers; but the invisible rival comes to seek every day his prey, a portion of my life. Torn apart, I smile! I smile on two children, but the eldest, the dead one,— triumphs! I have already said it to you,—the dead child will call me, and I go to him. Intimacy without love is a situation in which my soul dishonors itself every hour. I can neither weep nor abandon myself to my reveries but when alone. The requirements of the world, those of my household, the care of my child, that of the happiness of Octave, do not leave me an instant in which to renew my strength, to acquire new forces as I did in my solitude. The perpetual *qui-vive* always surprises my heart with a start. I have not in the least been able to fix in my soul that vigilance of the quick ear, of the lying word, of the lynx eye. It is not a beloved mouth which drinks my tears and which blesses my eyelids, it is a handkerchief which stanches them; it is water which refreshes my inflamed eyes, and not beloved lips. I am a comédienne with my soul; and this is perhaps why I die! I suppress my grief with so much care that nothing of it appears on the outside; it has indeed to devour something, it attacks my life. I said to the doctors who discovered my secret:

" ' "Make me die of some plausible malady; otherwise, I shall drag my husband with me."

" 'It is then agreed, between Messieurs Desplein, Bianchon and myself that I am dying of the softening of some bone, I do not know which, that science has perfectly described. Octave believes himself

adored! Do you understand me perfectly? Thus
I am afraid that he will follow me. I write to you
to entreat you to be, in that case, the guardian of
the young count. You will find enclosed a codicil in
which I express this wish: you will only make use
of it when it becomes necessary, for perhaps I am
foolishly mistaken. My concealed devotion will
perhaps leave Octave inconsolable, but living!
Poor Octave! I wish for him a wife better than I
am, for he indeed deserves to be loved. Since my so
clever spy is married, let him remember that which
the fair florist of the Rue Saint-Maur here bequeaths
him as a testament,—See that your wife is very soon
a mother! Throw her into the most commonplace
materialities of the household; prevent her from
cultivating in her heart the mysterious flower of the
ideal, that celestial perfection in which I have believed, that enchanted flower with burning colors,
and the perfume of which inspires disgust for real-
ities. I am a Saint-Theresa who can nourish herself only with ecstasies, in the depth of a convent
with the Divine Jesus, with an irreproachable angel,
winged, so as to come and go at pleasure. You
have seen me happy in the midst of my well-beloved
flowers. I have not told you all; I saw love flourishing under your feigned madness, I concealed from
you my thoughts, my poesies; I did not give you
entrance into my beautiful kingdom. Finally you
will love my child for the love of me, if he should
be left some day without his poor father. Guard my
secrets as the tomb will guard me. Do not weep

for me: I have been dead a long time, if Saint-Bernard was right in saying that there is no more life where there is no more love."

"And," said the consul, folding his letters and locking his portfolio with a key, "the countess is dead."

"Is the count still living?" asked the ambassador, "for, since the Revolution of July, he has disappeared from political life."

"Do you remember, Monsieur de Lora," said the consul-general, "of having seen me conducting back to the steamer—?"

"A man with white hair, an old man?" asked the painter.

"An old man of forty-five, going in quest of health, of diversions, to southern Italy. This old man, he was my poor friend, my protector, who passed through Genoa to say adieu to me, to confide to me his testament—He appoints me the guardian of his son. I was not under the necessity of telling him of Honorine's wish."

"Is he aware of his character of assassin?" said Mademoiselle des Touches to the Baron de l'Hostal.

"He suspects the truth," replied the consul, "and it is that which is killing him. I remained on the steamer which is carrying him to Naples until we were in the roadstead; there was a barque to bring me back. We remained for some time exchanging our farewells, which, I fear, will be eternal. God knows how we love the confidant of our love, when she who has inspired it is no more! 'That man has a charm,' said Octave to me, 'he wears an aureole.' When we came out on the prow, the count looked at the Mediterranean; as it happened, the weather was fine, and, doubtless, moved by this spectacle, he left me these last words: 'In the interest of human nature, would it not be necessary to investigate that irresistible power which makes us sacrifice to the most fleeting of all pleasures, and against our reason, a divine creature?—I have heard cries in my conscience. Honorine was not the only one who cried. And yet I wished!—I am devoured by remorse! I died, in the Rue Payenne, of the pleasures which I had not; I shall die in Italy of the pleasures which I have tasted!—Whence comes this discord between two natures equally noble, I dare to say?' "

A profound silence prevailed on the terrace for some moments.

"Was she virtuous?" asked the consul of the two ladies.

Mademoiselle des Touches rose, took the consul by the arm, led him off for a few steps, and said to him:

"Are not men also culpable to come to us, to make of a young girl a wife, while keeping at the bottom of their hearts angelic images, comparing us to unknown rivals, to perfections often drawn from more than one memory, and then finding us always inferior?"

"Mademoiselle, you would be right if marriage

were founded on passion, and this was the error of the two beings who soon will both be no more. Marriage, with a heart's love between the two spouses, that would be paradise."

Mademoiselle des Touches left the consul and was rejoined by Claude Vignon, who said to her in her ear:

"He is somewhat vain and silly, Monsieur de l'Hostal."

"No," she replied, slipping in Claude's ear this sentence, "he has not yet discovered that Honorine would have loved him. Oh!" she said, seeing the consul's wife coming, "his wife has heard him, the unfortunate man!—"

Eleven o'clock was sounded by the clocks, all the guests returned on foot, along the sea beach.

"All that is not life," said Mademoiselle des Touches. "That woman is one of the rarest exceptions, and perhaps the most monstrous of intelligences, a pearl! Life is composed of various accidents, of sorrow and pleasures alternated. The Paradise of Dante, that sublime expression of the ideal, that constant blue, is found only in the soul, and to demand it of the things of life is a voluptuousness against which nature protests every hour. For such souls, the six feet of a cell and a prie-Dieu suffice."

"You are right," said Léon de Lora. "But, however much of a good-for-nothing I may be, I cannot restrain my admiration for a woman capable, as was that one, of living by the side of an atelier, under the roof of a painter, without ever descending, or seeing the world, or getting muddy in the streets."

"That has been seen for a few months at a time," said Claude Vignon with a profound irony.

"The Comtesse Honorine is not the only one of her kind," replied the ambassador to Mademoiselle des Touches. "A man, we will even say a man of politics, a bitter writer, was the object of a love of this kind, and the pistol-shot that killed him touched only him: she whom he loved was as if cloistered."

"There are still to be found, then, great souls in this century!" said Camille Maupin, remaining thoughtful, leaning against the quay for several minutes.

Paris, January, 1843.

COLONEL CHABERT

TO MADAME LA COMTESSE IDA DE BOCARMÉ,
NÉE DU CHASTELER

COLONEL CHABERT

*

"Hello! there is our old box-coat again!"

This exclamation suddenly escaped a clerk who was one of that species known in the lawyers' offices as *saute-ruisseaux*—gutter-jumpers—and who at this moment was biting with a very good appetite into a piece of bread; out of it he took a small portion of the soft part to make a pellet, and threw this as a joke through the small open pane of the window on which he was leaning. The pellet, very well aimed, rebounded almost to the height of the window frame after having struck the hat of an unknown man who was crossing the court of a house situated in Rue Vivienne, in which dwelt Maître Derville, attorney.

"See here, Simonnin, no playing tricks upon people, or I will put you out of the office. However poor a client may be, he is still a man, what the devil!" said the head clerk, interrupting himself in the addition of a memorandum of costs.

The *saute-ruisseau* is generally, as was Simonnin, a youth of thirteen or fourteen years of age who in all offices is under the special orders of the

9   (129)

principal clerk, whose commissions and whose bil-
lets-doux occupy much of his time even when engaged in carrying summonses to the bailiffs and
petitions to the Palais. He belongs to the *gamins*
of Paris by his manners, and to chicanery by his
destiny. This youth is nearly always without
pity, under no restraint, not to be disciplined, a
lampooner, a banterer, greedy and lazy. Nevertheless, nearly all these little clerks have an old
mother, living on a fifth floor, with whom they
divide the thirty or forty francs which are allotted
to them per month.

"If he is a man, why do you call him *old box-
coat?*" said Simonnin with the air of a scholar who
catches his master napping.

And he went on eating his bread and cheese,
leaning his shoulder against the upright of the window; for he took his rest standing, like the van
horses, one of his legs raised and supported against
the other, on the toe of his shoe.

"What trick could we play on that *bloke?*" said,
in a low voice, the third clerk, whose name was
Godeschal, stopping in the midst of an argument
which he was originating in the midst of an application engrossed by the fourth clerk and of which the
copies were being made by two neophytes lately
come from the provinces.

Then he continued his improvisation:

"*—But, in his noble and benevolent wisdom, His
Majesty Louis the Eighteenth*—spell that all out, *hé*,
Desroches the wise who does the engrossing!—*at*

the moment when he resumed the reins of his kingdom, comprehended—what is it that he comprehends, that great joker ?—*the high mission to which he had been called by divine Providence !*—a point of admiration and six periods; they are religious enough at the Palais to allow us that,—*and his first thought was, as is proved by the date of the ordinance hereunder designated, to repair the misfortunes caused by the frightful and mournful disasters of our Revolutionary period, in restoring to his faithful and numerous servants*—'numerous' is a flattery that should please the tribunal—*all their property that has not been sold, whether it be found in the public domain, whether it be found in the ordinary or extraordinary domains of the Crown, whether, finally, it be found in the endowments of public establishments, for we are and we claim ourselves able to maintain, that such is the spirit and the sense of the celebrated and so loyal ordinance rendered in*—Wait," said Godeschal to the three clerks, "this blackguard of a phrase has filled the end of my page.—Well," he resumed, wetting with his tongue the back of his quire so as to be able to turn the thick page of his stamped paper, "well, if you wish to play a trick upon him, we must say to him that the master can only see his clients between two and three o'clock in the morning; we shall see if he will come, the old scamp !"

And Godeschal went on with the phrase commenced:

"*Rendered in*—Are you ready ?" he asked.

"Yes," cried the three copyists.

Everything went forward together, the application, the conversation and the conspiracy.

"*Rendered in*—I say, papa Boucard, what is the date of the ordinance? we must put the dots on the i's, *saquerlotte!* That makes the pages."

"*Saquerlotte!*" repeated one of the copyists before Boucard the head clerk could reply.

"What! have you written *saquerlotte?*" cried Godeschal, looking at the newcomer with an air at once severe and derisory.

"Why yes," said Desroches, the fourth clerk, leaning over his neighbor's copy, "he has written, —*We must put the dots on the i's,* and *sakerlotte* with a k."

All the clerks broke into a great shout of laughter.

"How, Monsieur Huré, you take *saquerlotte* for a legal term, and you say that you came from Martagne!" cried Simonnin.

"Strike that out!" said the head clerk. "If the judge who examines the papers should see things like that, he would say that everything was made fun of. You would make it disagreeable for our employer. Come now, do not commit any more stupidities like that, Monsieur Huré! A Norman should not write out an application carelessly. It is the *Carry Arms!* of bazoche."

"*Rendered in—in?*—" asked Godeschal. "Tell me when it was, Boucard?"

"June, 1814," replied the head clerk without leaving his work.

A knock at the door of the office interrupted the

phrases of the prolix application. Five clerks with good sets of teeth, with lively and mocking eyes, with crisp heads of hair, lifted their noses toward the door after having all cried in chorus:

"Come in!"

Boucard remained with his head buried in a pile of papers, called *broutille*—rubbish—in the slang of the Palais, and continued to draw up the memorandum of costs on which he was engaged.

The office was a large room ornamented with that classic stove which garnishes all these dens of chicanery. The pipes traversed the apartment diagonally and entered a walled-up chimney, on the marble shelf of which might be seen divers pieces of bread, triangles of Brie cheese, cutlets of fresh pork, glasses, bottles, and the cup of chocolate of the head clerk. The odor of these comestibles combined so well with the disagreeable smell of the stove heated to an immeasurable degree, with the particular perfume of the office and of the old papers, that the smell of a fox would not have been perceptible there. The floor was already covered with filth and snow brought in by the clerks. Near the window was placed the cylindrical secretary of the principal clerk, against which was backed up the little table destined for the second in rank. The second at this moment was *doing* the Palais. It might be eight or nine o'clock in the morning. The office had for sole ornament those great yellow posters which announced the seizure of real estate, sales, public auctions to transfer from majors to minors, adjudications definite or preparative, the glory of offices ! Behind the head clerk was an enormous case of pigeon-holes which rose from the bottom of the wall to the top, and each compartment of which was crammed with bundles of papers from which hung an infinite number of tickets and ends of red tape which give their peculiar appearance to legal documents. The lower ranks of this case were full of portfolios yellowed by usage, bordered by blue paper, and on which might be read the names of the important clients whose juicy affairs were at this moment being duly cooked. The dirty panes of the window allowed but little light to pass. Moreover, in the month of February there are very few offices in Paris where, before ten o'clock, you can write without the aid of a lamp, for they are all treated with a carelessness which may readily be conceived;—everyone goes to them, nobody stays in them, there is no personal interest attached to that which is so commonplace; neither the attorney, nor the litigants, nor the clerks, are concerned with the elegance of a locality which is for some a class, for the others a passage-way, for the master a laboratory. The dirty furniture is transferred from attorney to attorney with a scrupulousness so religious that certain offices still possess boxes for remainders, measures for parchment *slips*, bags which had belonged to the procureurs of the *Chlet*, an abbreviation of the word CHATELET, a jurisdiction in the ancient order of things which is represented by the present inferior court for civil causes. This gloomy office, thick with dust, had then, like all the others, something in it repulsive for the litigants, which made it one of the most hideous of the Parisian monstrosities. Certainly, if the damp sacristies in which prayers are weighed and paid for like groceries, if the shops of the dealers in old clothes in which hang the rags that flout all the illusions of life in showing us to what all our festivals come, if these two cloacæ of all poetry did not exist, an attorney's office would be of all social places of barter the most horrible. But it is so also of the gambling house, of the police court, of the lottery bureau and of the house of ill-fame. Wherefore? Perhaps in these localities the drama which takes place in the human soul renders it indifferent to all the accessories, — which might explain also the simplicity of the great thinkers and of the greatly ambitious.

"Where is my penknife?"

"I am eating my breakfast."

"Will you be careful, there is a pâté on the application!"

" 'Ssh, messieurs."

These various exclamations were all uttered at once at the moment that the old client closed the door behind him with that sort of humility which perverts all the movements of the unfortunate man. The unknown endeavored to smile, but the muscles of his countenance relaxed when he had vainly sought for some symptoms of amenity on the inexorably indifferent faces of the six clerks. Accustomed doubtless to judging men, he addressed himself very politely to the *saute-ruisseau,* hoping that this fag at least would reply civilly.

"Monsieur, can your master be seen?"

The malicious *saute-ruisseau* did not reply to the poor man other than by giving with the fingers of his left hand repeated little taps on his ear, as if to say, "I am deaf."

"What do you want, monsieur?" asked Godeschal, at the same time swallowing a piece of bread large enough to have charged a four-pounder, flourishing his knife and crossing his legs in such a manner as to bring that one of his feet which happened to be in the air up to the level of his eye.

"I come here, monsieur, for the fifth time," replied the patient one. "I wish to speak to Monsieur Derville."

"Is it on business?"

"Yes, but I can only explain it to Monsieur—"

"The master is asleep; if you wish to consult him on some difficult question, he only goes to work seriously at midnight. But, if you would state your case to us, we could, as well as he, give you—"

The unknown remained impassive. He began to look modestly around him, like a dog which, having slipped into a strange kitchen, fears a beating. It is one of the advantages of their condition that the clerks have no fear of thieves; they had no suspicions, therefore, of the man in the box-coat and permitted him to make his observations of the locality, in which he vainly sought a seat on which to rest himself, for he was visibly fatigued. The attorneys systematically leave very few chairs in their offices. The ordinary client, weary of waiting while standing, goes away grumbling, but he does not take up time which, to adopt the expression of an old procureur, is not counted in taxing costs.

"Monsieur," he replied, "I have already had the honor to inform you that I can only explain my business to Monsieur Derville, I will await his awakening."

Boucard had finished his computation. He smelt the odor of his chocolate, rose from his cane-seated armchair, came to the chimney, surveyed the old man, looked at the box-coat and made an indescribable grimace. He probably was of the opinion that, in whatever manner this client might be twisted, it would be impossible to wring out of him a centime; he therefore intervened with a brief speech with the intention of disembarrassing the office of an unprofitable case.

"They are telling you the truth, monsieur. The master only works at night. If your business is important, I would advise you to return at one o'clock in the morning."

The client looked at the head clerk with a stupid air, and remained for a moment motionless. Accustomed to all the changing expressions and to the singular caprices produced by indecision or by meditation which characterize the litigious, the clerks continued to eat, making as much noise with their jaws as would so many horses at the manger, and disquieting themselves no further about the old man.

"Monsieur, I will come this evening," said the latter finally, seeming to wish, with the tenacity peculiar to the unfortunate, to detect all humanity at fault.

The only epigram which is permitted to misery is to compel Justice and Benevolence to unjust denials. When the unfortunate have convicted Society of falsehood, they throw themselves more eagerly into the bosom of God.

"What a famous swaggerer!" said Simonnin, without waiting till the old man had closed the door.

"He looks as if he had been dug up," replied the clerk.

"It is some colonel claiming back-pay," said the head clerk.

"No, it is a former concierge," said Godeschal.

"Who will bet that he is noble?" cried Boucard.

"I will bet that he has been a porter," replied Godeschal. "The porters alone are endowed by nature with second-hand box-coats, greasy and ragged at the bottom as is that of this old fellow. You did not see, then, his boots down at the heels which let in the water, and his cravat which serves him for a shirt. He has been sleeping under the bridges."

"He may be noble and have pulled the concierge's door cord," cried Desroches. "Such things have been!"

"No," replied Boucard in the midst of the

laughter, "I maintain that he was a brewer in 1789, and a colonel under the Republic."

"Ah! I will bet a theatre for the crowd that he never was a soldier," said Godeschal.

"It is a bargain," replied Boucard.

"Monsieur! Monsieur!" cried the little clerk, opening the window.

"What are you doing, Simonnin?" asked Boucard.

"I am calling him to ask him if he is a colonel or a porter; he ought to know, he ought."

All the clerks commenced to laugh. As for the old man, he was already remounting the stairs.

"What are we going to say to him?" cried Godeschal.

"Let me manage it!" replied Boucard.

The poor man re-entered timidly, lowering his eyes, perhaps so as not to reveal his hunger by looking too eagerly at the comestibles.

"Monsieur," said Boucard to him, "will you have the goodness to give us your name so that the master may know if—?"

"Chabert."

"Is it the colonel who was killed at Eylau?" asked Huré, who, having said nothing up to this time, was eager to add his mockery to that of the others.

"The same, monsieur," replied the goodman with an antique simplicity.

And he withdrew.

"*Chouit!*"

"Sacked!"

"Bankrupted!"

"Oh!"

"Ah!"

"Bâoum!"

"Ah! the old humbug!"

"*Trinn la la trinn trinn !*"

"Busted!"

"Monsieur Desroches, you will go to the theatre without paying," said Huré to the fourth clerk, giving him a slap on the shoulder that might have killed a rhinoceros.

It was a torrent of cries, of laughter, of exclamations, in the rendering of which all the onomatopœias of the language might be used.

"To what theatre shall we go?"

"To the Opéra," cried the principal.

"In the first place," replied Godeschal, "no theatre was mentioned. I can, if I want to, take you to Madame Saqui's."

"Madame Saqui's is not a theatre."

"What is a theatre?" replied Godeschal. "Let us establish first the point of departure. What did I bet, messieurs? A theatre. What is a theatre? Something that you go to see—"

"But, according to that system, you would pay us all by taking us to see the water run under the Pont Neuf?" cried Simonnin, interrupting.

"That you go to see by paying for it," said Godeschal, continuing.

"But you see by paying for them a great many

things which are not theatres. The definition is not exact," said Desroches.

"But listen to me, then!"

"You are talking nonsense, my dear fellow," said Boucard.

"Is Curtius's a theatre?" said Godeschal.

"No," replied the head clerk, "it is a gallery of wax figures."

"I will bet a hundred francs against a sou," replied Godeschal, "that the gallery of Curtius constitutes the whole of those things upon which has devolved the name of theatre. It includes something to see at different prices, according to the different places in which you put yourself."

"And *berlik berlok*," said Simonnin.

"You take care that you do not get your ears cuffed!" said Godeschal.

The clerks shrugged their shoulders.

"Moreover, it is not proven that that old monkey was not making fun of us," said he, closing his argument, smothered by the laughter of the other clerks. "The facts are, that Colonel Chabert is very dead, his wife has married again, to the Comte Ferraud, councillor of State. Madame Ferraud is one of the clients of this office!"

"The case is adjourned till to-morrow," said Boucard. "Get to work, messieurs! *Sac à papier!* nothing is done here. Finish your application there, it must be declared before the hearing in the fourth chamber. The case is tried to-day. Come, get to work!"

"If he had been Colonel Chabert, would he not have applied the toe of his boot to the posterior of that joker of a Simonnin when he pretended to be deaf?" said Desroches, considering this observation as more conclusive than that of Godeschal.

"Since nothing is decided," replied Boucard," we will agree to go to the second boxes at the Français to see Talma in Nero. Simonnin can go to the parterre."

Whereupon the head clerk seated himself at his desk, and everyone followed his example.

"Rendered in June, Eighteen Hundred and Fourteen —written out," said Godeschal. "Have you got that?"

"Yes," replied the two clerks and the engrosser, whose pens commenced to creak across the stamped paper, making in the office as much noise as a hundred cockchafers shut up by scholars in paper horns.

"And we hope that the Messieurs constituting the tribunal—" said the improvisatore.—"Halt! I must reread my sentence, I do not understand it myself."

"Forty-six—That happens very often!—and three, forty-nine," said Boucard.

"We hope," resumed Godeschal, after having read over his text, *"that the Messieurs constituting the tribunal will not be less great than the august author of the ordinance, and that they will bring to justice the miserable pretensions of the administration of the grand chancellorship of the Legion of Honor by giving*

*jurisprudence within the limits which we establish
here—*"

"Monsieur Godeschal, would you like a glass of
water?" said the little clerk.

"That scamp of a Simonnin!" said Boucard.
"Here, get out your horses with double soles to
them, take this package, and waltz over to the In-
valides."

"*Which we establish here,*" resumed Godeschal.
"Add, *in the interests of Madame*—write it all out—
la Vicomtesse de Grandlieu—"

"What!" cried the head clerk, "you have set
yourself to drawing up the applications in the affair
of the Vicomtesse de Grandlieu against the Legion
of Honor, an office case, a suit on contract? Ah!
you are a fine booby! Will you just put aside your
copies and your minutes, keep those for the case of
Navarreins against the Hospitals. It is late, I am
going to do a piece of a petition, with the *whereases*,
and I am going myself to the Palais—"

This scene represents one of those thousand
pleasures which, later, give rise to the "Ah! Those
were good times!" when thinking of our past youth.

Toward one o'clock in the morning the pretended
Colonel Chabert came to knock at the door of Maître
Derville, an attorney practising before the inferior
court for civil causes of the department of the Seine.
The porter said to him that Monsieur Derville had
not yet returned. The old man stated his appointment, and ascended to the apartment of this celebrated lawyer, who, notwithstanding his youth,

passed for one of the shrewdest men in the Palais.
After having rung, the mistrustful client was not a
little astonished to see the head clerk occupied in
arranging on the table in the dining-room of his
employer numerous bundles of documents of cases
which would come up the next day, all in order.
The clerk, not less astonished, bowed to the colonel
and requested him to take a chair; which he did.

"Upon my word, monsieur, I thought that you
were joking yesterday when you gave me such a
very early hour for a consultation," said the old man,
with the false cheerfulness of a ruined man who
forces himself to smile.

"The clerks jested and spoke the truth both at
once," replied the chief clerk, continuing his work.
"Monsieur Derville has taken this hour for examining his causes, summing up his procedure, deciding
on the conduct, arranging the defences. His pro-
digious intelligence is more at liberty at this time,
the only one in which he can obtain the silence and
the tranquillity necessary to the conceiving of the
best ideas.   You are, since he has been an attorney,
the third instance of a consultation given at this
nocturnal hour.   After he comes in, he will discuss
each case, read everything, pass perhaps four or
five hours at his task; then he will ring for me and
explain to me his intentions.   In the morning, from
ten o'clock to two, he hears his clients, then the
rest of the day is employed with his appointments.
In the evening, he goes out into society to meet
his friends.   It is then only at night that he can

arrange his actions, search the arsenals of the Code and draw up his plans of battle. He does not like to lose a single case, he has a love for his profession. He does not take, as do his confrères, every kind of a case. That is his life, which is singularly active. Also, he makes a great deal of money."

While hearing this explanation the old man remained silent, and his grotesque countenance took on an expression so devoid of all intelligence that the clerk, after having looked at him, paid no further attention to him. A few moments later Derville returned, in evening dress; his principal clerk opened the door for him, and continued the classification of his documents. The young attorney remained for a moment stupefied on seeing in the obscurity the singular client who was waiting for him. The Colonel Chabert was as perfectly motionless as one of the wax figures in that gallery of Curtius to which Godeschal had proposed to take his comrades. This immobility would not perhaps have been a subject of surprise, if it had not completed the supernatural spectacle presented by his general appearance. The old soldier was lean and thin. His forehead, purposely concealed under the hair of his smooth wig, gave him something of a mysterious air. His eyes appeared to be covered with a transparent film,—you would have said of a soiled mother-of-pearl, the bluish reflections of which changed color in the light of the candles. The visage, pale, livid, and sharp as a knife—if I may be permitted this common expression—seemed

10

deathly. The neck was surrounded by a shabby cravat of black silk. Below the brownish line described by this rag the body was so completely concealed in the shadow that an imaginative man might have taken this old head for some silhouette due to chance, or for a portrait by Rembrandt without a frame. The brim of the hat which covered the old man's forehead threw a black furrow upon the upper part of his countenance. This effect, grotesque though natural, brought out all the more by the sharpness of the contrasts, the whitish wrinkles, the cold sinuosities, the colorless quality of this cadaverous physiognomy. And finally, the absence of all movement in the body, of all warmth in the look, were in accord with a certain expression of sorrowful dementia, with the degrading symptoms which characterize idiocy, that they made of this figure something so fatal that no human speech could express it. But an observer, and especially an attorney, would have found furthermore in this shipwrecked man the signs of a profound grief, the indications of a misery which had degraded this visage, as the drops of water falling from the sky upon a beautiful marble will in the end disfigure it. A physician, an author, a magistrate, would have divined at once a complete drama from the aspect of this sublime horror, the least characteristic of which was to resemble those grotesques which the painters amuse themselves by sketching at the bottoms of their lithographic stones while talking with their friends.

When he saw the attorney, the unknown shivered with a convulsive movement like those which the poets involuntarily make when an unexpected noise arouses them from a fruitful reverie, in the midst of silence and the night. The old man uncovered promptly, and rose to salute the young man; the leathern band which lined the interior of his hat was doubtless very greasy, his wig stuck to it without his perceiving it, and left naked his bare skull horribly mutilated by a transverse scar which started at the occiput and ended at the right eye, forming throughout its length a great raised seam. The sudden removal of this dirty wig, which the poor man wore to hide his wound, did not suggest in the slightest degree anything laughable to the two men of the law, so frightful to see was this cleft cranium. The first thought suggested by the aspect of this wound was,—"Through that the intelligence has escaped!"

"If he is not Colonel Chabert, he must be a bold campaign trooper," thought Boucard.

"Monsieur," said Derville to him, "to whom have I the honor of speaking?"

"The Colonel Chabert."

"To whom?"

"He who was killed at Eylau," replied the old man.

On hearing this singular expression the clerk and the attorney threw upon each other a mutual glance which signified,—"It is a lunatic!"

"Monsieur," resumed the colonel, "I would prefer to confide to you only the secret of my situation."

One thing worthy of remark is the natural intrepidity of attorneys. Whether it be the habit of receiving a great number of people, whether it be the profound consciousness of the protection which the law affords them, whether it be confidence in their functions, they enter everywhere, without fearing anything, like the priests and the doctors. Derville made a sign to Boucard, who disappeared.

"Monsieur," said the attorney, "during the day, I am not saving of my time; but in the middle of the night, my moments are valuable. Therefore, be brief and concise. Come to the point without digressions. I will ask you myself the explanations which may seem to me necessary. Speak."

After having seated his singular client, the young man sat down himself before the table; but, whilst giving his attention to the discourse of the late colonel, he turned over his documents.

"Monsieur," said the defunct, "perhaps you know that I commanded a regiment of cavalry at Eylau. I contributed greatly to the success of the celebrated charge made by Murat, which decided the victory. Unfortunately for me, my death is an historical fact recorded in the *Victoires et Conquêtes*, where it is related in detail. We broke in two the three Russian lines which, immediately reclosing, obliged us to traverse them again in an opposite direction. At the moment when we were returning toward the Emperor, after having dispersed the Russians, I encountered a body of the enemy's cavalry. I threw myself upon those obstinate fellows. Two Russian officers, two veritable giants, attacked me at once. One of them dealt me over the head a sabre cut which went through everything, even to a cap of black silk which I was wearing, and laid my skull open deep. I fell from my horse. Murat came to my help, he passed over my body, he and all his people, fifteen hundred men, was not that enough! My death was announced to the Emperor, who, very considerately—he loved me a little, *le patron!*— wished to know if there might not be some chance of saving the man to whom he was indebted for that vigorous attack. He sent two surgeons to look for me and bring me back to the ambulances, saying to them, perhaps too carelessly, for he was occupied,— 'Go to see, then, if by chance my poor Chabert is still living.' Those confounded sawbones, who had seen me trodden under the feet of the horses of two regiments, doubtless did not give themselves the trouble of feeling my pulse, and said that I was indeed dead. The certificate of my death was then probably drawn up according to the regulations established by the military jurisprudence.''

On hearing his client express himself with a perfect clearness and relate facts so possible, though unusual, the young attorney rejected his documents, rested his left elbow on the table, his head on his hand, and looked at the colonel steadily.

"Do you know, monsieur," said he to him, interrupting him, "that I am the attorney of the Comtesse Ferraud, the widow of Colonel Chabert?"

"My wife! Yes, monsieur. Therefore, after a

hundred fruitless attempts with the lawyers, who
all thought I was crazy, I determined to come to
find you. I will speak to you of my misfortunes
later. Let me first establish the facts for you, explain to you rather how they may have come to pass
than how they actually happened. Certain circumstances, which can only be known to the Eternal
Father, oblige me to present several of them as
hypotheses. Thus, monsieur, the wounds which
I received, probably induced tetanus, or threw me
into a state analogous to the malady named, I believe, catalepsy. Otherwise, how can it be conceived that I was, according to the usages of war,
stripped of my clothes, and thrown into the soldier's
grave by those charged with the duty of burying the
dead? Here, permit me to introduce a detail which
I could not have known until after the event which
may very well be called my death. I met, in 1814,
in Stuttgart, a former quartermaster of my regiment.
This dear fellow, the only one who has been willing
to recognize me, and of whom I will speak to you
presently, explained to me the phenomena of my
preservation by telling me that my horse had received a bullet in his flank at the same moment that
I myself was wounded. The animal and the rider
then went down together like a house of cards. In
falling, whether to the right or to the left, I was
doubtless covered by the body of my horse, which
prevented me from being crushed by the hoofs or
struck by the bullets. When I came to myself,
monsieur, I was in a position and in an atmosphere

of which I could give you no idea, were I to discourse to you concerning it until to-morrow. The
little air that I breathed was nephitic. I endeavored to move and found no space. On opening my
eyes, I saw nothing. The scarcity of air was the
most threatening circumstance, and the one which
most enlightened me as to my position. I comprehended that there, where I was, the air was not
renewed and that I was going to die. This thought
took away from me the consciousness of the inexpressible pain by which I had been awakened. My
ears rang violently. I heard, or I thought I heard—
I wish to assert nothing—moans uttered by the heap
of corpses in the midst of which I was lying.
Although the memory of those moments is very
shadowy, although my remembrances are confused,
notwithstanding the impressions of suffering still
more profound which I was to experience and which
have confounded my ideas, there are nights in which
I think I still hear those smothered sighs! But
there was something more horrible than the cries, a
silence which I have never found elsewhere, the
real silence of the tomb. Finally, lifting my hands,
feeling the dead, I discovered a space between my
head and the human manure above. I could then
measure the space which had been left to me by a
chance, the cause of which was unknown to me. It
seemed that, thanks to the carelessness, or to the
precipitation, with which we had been thrown in
pell-mell, two corpses had been crossed above me in
such a manner as to describe an angle similar to

that of two cards placed one against the other by a child who is laying the foundations of a castle. In searching about promptly, for there was no time to lose, I encountered, very fortunately, an arm which was not attached to anything, the arm of a Hercules, a good bone to which I owed my salvation. Without that unhoped-for succor, I should have perished! But, with a rage which you should be able to conceive, I set myself to work to traverse the corpses which separated me from the layer of earth doubtless thrown upon us,—I say 'us,' as if we had been living! I worked well, monsieur, for here I am! But I do not know to-day how I was able to succeed in piercing the covering of flesh which put a barrier between myself and life. You will say to me that I had three arms! This lever, which I made use of with skill, procured me constantly a little air which was between the corpses which I displaced, and I regulated my breathing. Finally I saw the daylight, but through the snow, monsieur. At that moment I perceived that my head was laid open. Fortunately, my blood, that of my comrades or the mangled skin of my horse perhaps, how do I know! had, in coagulating, furnished me, as it were, with a natural plaster. Notwithstanding this crust, I fainted when my head came in contact with the snow. However, the little heat that was left in me, having melted the snow around me, I found myself, when I recovered consciousness, in the centre of a little opening through which I called as long as I could. But by this time the sun had risen, I had

then but little chance of being heard. Was there
already any one in the fields? I lifted myself up
by making with my feet a spring, the base of which
rested on the dead who had solid loins. You feel
that it was not the moment to say to them, 'Honor
to unfortunate courage!' In short, monsieur, after
having had the grief, if that word can render my
rage, at seeing for a long time, oh! yes, for a long
time, those cursed Germans run away on hearing a
voice there where they saw no man, I was finally
extricated by a woman who was sufficiently courageous, or sufficiently curious, to approach my head,
which seemed to have grown up through the ground
like a mushroom. This woman went to get her
husband, and the two carried me to their poor
cabin. It appears that I had a relapse of catalepsy,—allow me this expression with which to
describe to you a state of which I have no idea, but
which I judged, from what my hosts said, must have
been an effect of that malady. I remained for six
months between life and death, not speaking, or
raving when I did speak. Finally my hosts got me
admitted to the hospital at Heilsberg. You understand, monsieur, that I came out of the belly of
the grave as naked as out of that of my mother;
so that when, six months later, one fine morning,
I remembered that I had been the Colonel Chabert, and when, recovering my reason, I wished
to obtain from my nurse somewhat more respect
than she would have given to a poor devil, all
my comrades of the ward began to laugh. Happily

for me, the surgeon had, through his professional
pride, answered for my recovery, and was naturally
interested in his patient. When I had related to
him in their sequence, facts of my former existence,
this worthy man, whose name was Sparchmann,
had drawn up, in the judicial forms required by the
law of the country, a statement of the miraculous
manner in which I had issued from the burial ditch,
the day and the hour on which I had been found by
my benefactress and her husband; the nature, the
exact position of my wounds, joining to these different certificates a description of my person. Well,
monsieur, I have neither these important documents,
nor the declaration which I made before a notary of
Heilsberg with a view of establishing my identity!
Since the day when I was driven from that city by
the events of the war, I have constantly wandered
about like a vagabond, begging my bread, treated
as a madman when I related my adventures, and
without having either found or gained a sou with
which to procure the papers which could prove my
statements, and restore me to social life. Often my
pains detain me for six months at a time in the little
towns where they are prodigal of their cares to the
sick Frenchman, but where they laugh in the face
of this man as soon as he pretends to be Colonel
Chabert. For a long time, this laughter, these
doubts, threw me into a fury which injured me and
which even caused me to be locked up as a madman
in Stuttgart. In truth, you may judge, after my recital, whether there have been sufficient reasons for

imprisoning a man! After two years of detention to which I was obliged to submit, after having heard a thousand times my guardians saying, 'There is a poor man who thinks himself to be Colonel Chabert!' to people who replied, 'The poor fellow!' I became convinced of the impossibility of my own adventure, I became sorrowful, resigned, tranquil, and renounced calling myself Colonel Chabert, so that I might get out of prison and return to France. Oh! monsieur, to see Paris again, that was a delirium which I did not—''

With this unfinished sentence Colonel Chabert fell into a profound reverie, which Derville respected.

"Monsieur, one fine day," resumed the client, "one day in spring, they gave me my liberty and ten thalers, under the pretext that I talked very sensibly on all sorts of subjects, and that I no longer called myself Colonel Chabert. Upon my word, about that time and still to-day, at moments, my name is disagreeable to me. I could wish not to be myself. The consciousness of my rights kills me. If my malady had taken from me all memory of my past existence, I should have been happy! I would have entered the service under some name or other, and, who knows? I should perhaps have become a field marshal in Austria or Russia."

"Monsieur," said the attorney, "you confuse all my ideas. I think myself dreaming while listening to you. For mercy's sake, let us stop a moment."

"You are," said the colonel with a melancholy

air, "the only person who has listened to me so patiently. Not one functionary of the law has been willing to advance me ten napoleons in order to procure from Germany the necessary papers for commencing my suit—"

"What suit?" said the attorney, who had forgotten the unfortunate situation of his client while listening to the recital of his past miseries.

"But, monsieur, is not the Comtesse Ferraud my wife? She possesses thirty thousand francs of income which belong to me, and is not willing to give me two liards. When I say these things to the attorneys, to sensible men; when I propose, I, a beggar, to bring an action against a count and a countess; when I rise up, I, deceased, against a certificate of death, a marriage certificate and certificates of birth, they show me out, according to their character, either with that air coldly polite which you know how to put on in order to get rid of an unfortunate, or brutally, like men who think they have encountered an adventurer or a fool. I have been buried under the dead; but, now, I am buried under the living, under certificates, under facts, under society in its entirety, which wishes to put me again under ground."

"Monsieur, will you please go on now," said the attorney.

"*Will you please,*" cried the unfortunate old man, grasping the younger one's hand, "that is the first word of politeness that I have heard since—"

The colonel wept. Gratitude stifled his voice.

That penetrating and indescribable eloquence which is in the look, in the gesture, in the very silence, had ended by convincing Derville and touched him deeply.

"Listen, monsieur," he said to his client, "I have won this evening three hundred francs at play; I can well employ the half of this sum in securing the happiness of a man. I will commence the inquiries and the proceedings necessary to procure the documents of which you speak, and, until they arrive, I will remit to you a hundred sous a day. If you are Colonel Chabert, you will know how to pardon the modesty of the loan in a young man who has his fortune to make. Proceed."

The pretended colonel remained for a moment motionless and stupefied; his extreme misfortune had doubtless destroyed his beliefs. If he pursued his lost military renown, his fortune, himself, perhaps it was in obedience to that inexplicable sentiment, the seed of which is in the hearts of all men, and to which we owe the researches of the alchemists, the passion for glory, the discoveries of astronomy, of physics, everything which urges man to aggrandize himself by multiplying himself by deeds or ideas. The *ego* in his thought was no more than a secondary object, in the same manner that the vanity of triumph or the pleasure of gaining becomes dearer to the bettor than are the stakes of the wager. The words of the young attorney were then like a miracle for this man repulsed during ten years by his wife, by justice, by the entire creation of society.   To find in an attorney's house those ten pieces of gold which had been refused him during so long a time, by so many persons and in so many manners!   The colonel resembled that lady who, having had a fever for fifteen years, thought that she had only changed the malady for another the day on which she was cured.   There are felicities in which no one believes; they arrive, it is the thunder, they consume.   Therefore the gratitude of the poor man was too lively to permit him to express it.   He would have seemed cold to superficial observers, but Derville divined a complete probity in this stupor.   A cheat would have found his voice.

"Where was I?" said the colonel with the naïveté of a child or a soldier, for there is often a good deal of the child in the real soldier, and nearly always of the soldier in the child, especially in France.

"At Stuttgart.   You had just come out of prison," replied the attorney.

"Do you know my wife?" asked the colonel.

"Yes," replied Derville with an inclination of the head.

"How is she?"

"Charming, still."

The old man made a sign with his hand, and seemed to master some secret pain with that grave and solemn resignation which characterizes men tried in the blood and the fire of battle-fields.

"Monsieur," he said with a sort of gaiety,—for he breathed again, this poor colonel, he issued a

second time from the grave, a shroud of snow less
easily melted than that which had formerly encased
his head in ice had dissolved, and he inhaled the air
as though he had just left a dungeon;—"Monsieur,"
he said, "if I had been a pretty youth, not one of my
misfortunes would have happened to me. The
women believe men when they stuff their phrases
with the word 'love.' Then, they trot about, they
come and go, they will do anything, they intrigue,
they assert facts, they work like the devil for any
one who pleases them. How could I have interested
any woman? I had a face like a *Requiem*, I was
clothed like a *sans-culotte*, I resembled rather an
Esquimau than a Frenchman, I who had formerly
passed for the prettiest of the dandies in 1799! I,
Chabert, Comte de l'Empire! Well, on the very
day on which they threw me out on the sidewalk
like a dog, I met the quartermaster of whom I have
already spoken to you. The name of this comrade
was Boutin. The poor devil and I, we made the
prettiest pair of jades that I have ever seen; I saw
him on the promenade; if I recognized him it was
impossible for him to guess who I was. We went
together to a cabaret. There, when I declared myself, Boutin's mouth opened in a shout of laughter
like a mortar that bursts. This mirth, monsieur,
caused me one of my keenest mortifications! It
revealed to me without any embellishment all the
change that had taken place in me! I was then unrecognizable, even by the eye of one of the humblest
and most grateful of my friends! I had formerly

saved Boutin's life, but it was a service that I owed
him.   I will not tell how it was that he had put me
under this obligation.   The incident took place in
Italy, at Ravenna.   The house in which Boutin
saved me from being poignarded was not a very
decent one.   At that period, I was not a colonel, I
was a simple trooper, like Boutin.   Fortunately, this
history included some details that could be known
only to ourselves, and when I recalled them to him,
his incredulity diminished.   Then I related to him
the accidents of my grotesque existence.   Although
my eyes, my voice, were, he told me, singularly
altered, though I no longer had either hair, or teeth,
or eyebrows, though I was as white as an albino, he
ended by finding his colonel again in the beggar,
after a thousand interrogations to which I responded
victoriously.   He related to me his adventures, they
were not less extraordinary than mine;—he had returned from the borders of China, which he had endeavored to reach after having escaped from Siberia.
He informed me of the disasters of the campaign in
Russia, and of the first abdication of Napoléon.
This news was one of the things which afflicted me
the most!   We were two curious wrecks, after having thus rolled around the globe as roll about in the
ocean the pebbles carried by the tempests from one
shore to the other.   Between us, we had seen Egypt,
Syria, Spain, Russia, Holland, Germany, Italy and
Dalmatia, England, China, Tartary, Siberia; we
only lacked having been to India and America!
Finally, more nimble than I was, Boutin took upon

himself to go to Paris as quickly as possible in order to inform my wife of the state in which I was. I wrote to Madame Chabert a letter full of details. It was the fourth, monsieur! If I had had any relatives, perhaps none of all this would have happened to me; but, it is necessary to admit it, I was a hospital foundling, a soldier who for patrimony had his courage, for family, all the world, for country, France, for his only protector, the good God. I am mistaken! I had a father, the Emperor. Ah! if he had been about, the dear man, and if he had seen *his Chabert,* as he called me, in the condition in which I was, why, he would have flown into a rage. What would you have! our sun is set, we are all cold now. After all, the political events might have justified my wife's silence! Boutin set off. He was very happy, he was! He had two white bears, very well trained, which provided him with a living. I could not accompany him; my pains would not permit me to make long stages. I wept, monsieur, when we separated, after having walked as long as my condition would permit me in the company of his bears and himself. At Carlsruhe, I had an attack of neuralgia in the head, and remained six weeks on the straw of an inn. I would never finish, monsieur, if it were necessary to relate to you all the misfortunes of my life as a beggar. The mental sufferings, before which the physical pains paled, excited, however, less sympathy, because they could not be seen. I remember having wept before a hotel in Strasbourg where I had once given a display, and where I could obtain nothing, not even a morsel of bread. Having arranged with Boutin the itinerary which I would follow, I went to every post-office to ask if there were a letter and money for me. I came as far as Paris without having received anything. How many despairs did I not have to undergo! 'Boutin must be dead,' I said to myself. In fact, the poor devil had perished at Waterloo. I learned of his death later, and accidentally. His mission to my wife was doubtless fruitless. Finally, I entered Paris, at the same time as the Cossacks. For me, it was sorrow on sorrow. When I saw the Russians in France, I no longer remembered that I had neither shoes on my feet, nor money in my pocket. Yes, monsieur, my garments were in rags. The night before my arrival I was obliged to bivouac in the wood of Claye. The chill of the night caused an accession of I know not what malady, which suddenly seized me as I was traversing the Faubourg Saint-Martin. I fell almost fainting at the door of an iron merchant. When I came to myself, I was in a bed in the Hôtel-Dieu. There I remained during a month, sufficiently comfortable. I was presently dismissed; I was without money, but in good condition and on the good pavement of Paris. With what joy and what promptitude I hastened to the Rue du Mont-Blanc, where my wife should be living in a hôtel of mine. Bah! the Rue du Mont-Blanc had become the Rue de la Chaussée-d'Antin. I saw nothing of my hôtel, it had been sold, demolished. Some speculators had built several houses in my gardens. Not knowing that my wife had married Monsieur Ferraud, I could obtain no information. Finally, I went to see an old advocate who had formerly had charge of my affairs. The worthy man was dead, after having bequeathed his practice to a young man. The latter informed me, to my great astonishment, of the opening of my will, the settlement of my estate, the marriage of my wife and the birth of her two children. When I told him that I was Colonel Chabert, he laughed out so frankly that I left him without making the slightest observation to him. My detention in Stuttgart made me think of Charenton, and I resolved to act with prudence. Then, monsieur, knowing where my wife lived, I took my way toward her hôtel, my heart full of hope. Well," said the colonel with a movement of concentrated rage, "I was not admitted until I had announced myself under a borrowed name, and the day on which I took my own, I was shown out of her door. To see the countess returning from a ball or the theatre, in the morning, I have remained for entire nights flattened against the post of her porte-cochère. My look plunged into this carriage which passed before my eyes with the rapidity of lightning, and in which I hardly caught a glimpse of this woman who is mine and who is no longer mine! Oh! from that day I have lived for vengeance," cried the old man in a muffled voice, and rising suddenly before Derville. "She knows that I am living; she has received from me, since my return, two letters written by myself. She no longer loves me! As for myself, I do not know whether I love her or detest her! I desire her and I curse her alternately. She owes to me her fortune, her happiness; well, she has not even sent me the slightest assistance! At moments, I no longer know what will happen!"

With these words the old soldier fell into his chair again, and again became motionless. Derville remained silent, occupied in the contemplation of his client.

"The case is grave," he said finally, mechanically. "Even in admitting the authenticity of the papers which should be found at Heilsberg, I am not convinced that we could triumph at once. The suit will be brought successively before three tribunals. It will be necessary to reflect with due calmness on such a cause, it is altogether exceptional."

"Oh!" replied the colonel coldly, lifting his head with a proud movement, "if I succumb, I shall know how to die, but in company."

The old man had suddenly disappeared. The eyes of the man of energy blazed up, illuminated by the fires of desire and of vengeance.

"It will perhaps be necessary to come to an understanding," said the attorney.

"Come to an understanding!" repeated Colonel Chabert. "Am I dead, or am I living?"

"Monsieur," replied the attorney, "you will follow, I hope, my advice. Your cause shall be my cause. You will presently perceive the interest which I take in your situation, almost without prec-edent in judicial records. Meanwhile, I will give you a word to my notary who will remit to you, on your receipt, fifty francs every ten days. It will not be convenient that you should come here for assistance. If you are Colonel Chabert, you should not be at the mercy of anyone. I will give to these advances the form of a loan. You have property to recover, you are rich."

This last delicate attention wrung tears from the old man. Derville rose suddenly, for it was not perhaps customary for an attorney to show emotion; he passed into his cabinet, from which he returned with an unsealed letter which he handed to the Comte Chabert. When the poor man took it be-tween his fingers, he felt two gold pieces through the paper.

"Will you designate to me the certificates, give me the name of the city, of the kingdom?" said the attorney.

The colonel dictated the desired information, verifying the spelling of the names of the locali-ties; then he took his hat in one hand, looked at Derville, offered him the other hand, a callous hand, and said to him in a simple voice:

"Upon my word, monsieur, after the Emperor, you are the man to whom I shall owe the most! You are *a brave*."

The attorney struck his hand in that of the colo-nel, conducted him as far as the stairway and lighted him down.

"Boucard," said Derville to his head clerk, "I have just heard a story which will cost me perhaps twenty-five louis. If I am robbed, I shall not regret my money, I shall have seen the most skilful actor of our epoch."

When the colonel found himself in the street and before a lantern, he took out of the letter the two pieces of twenty francs which the attorney had given him, and looked at them for a moment in the light. He saw gold again, for the first time in nine years.

"I am going to smoke some cigars!" he said to himself.

About three months after this consultation in the night between Colonel Chabert and Derville, the notary charged with the disbursement of the half-pay which the attorney allotted to his singular client came to confer with him upon an important affair, and commenced by claiming from him six hundred francs remitted to the old soldier.

"You amuse yourself, then, by maintaining the old army?" laughingly said this notary, a young man named Crottat, who had bought out the office in which he had been head clerk, and the principal of which had taken flight, after a frightful bankruptcy.

"I thank you, my dear maître," replied Derville, "for reminding me of that affair. My philanthropy will not go beyond twenty-five louis, I fear already to have been the dupe of my patriotism."

As Derville finished his sentence, he saw upon his desk the packages which his head clerk had

placed there.   His eyes were attracted by the aspect of the stamps, oblong, square, triangular, red,
blue, affixed to a letter by the Prussian, Austrian,
Bavarian and French post-offices.

"Ah!" said he laughing, "here is the dénouement
of the comedy, we will see if I have been trapped."

He took the letter and opened it, but could read
nothing, it was written in German.

"Boucard, go yourself and have this letter translated, and return promptly," said Derville, half
opening the door of his cabinet and extending the
letter to his head clerk.

The Berlin notary whom the attorney had addressed announced to him that the certificates which
he had asked for would reach him a few days after
this letter of notification.   The papers, he said,
were perfectly regular, and clothed with all the
legal formalities necessary to make them valid in
law.   Moreover, he notified him that nearly all
the witnesses of the facts recorded in the documents were living in Prussich-Eylau; and that
the woman to whom Monsieur le Comte Chabert
owed his life, still dwelt in one of the faubourgs of
Heilsberg.

"This is becoming serious," cried Derville when
Boucard had given him the substance of this letter.
"But I say, my good fellow," he went on, addressing the notary, "I am going to need some information which should be in your office.   Was it not in
the office of that old scamp of a Roguin—"

"We say the unfortunate, the unhappy Roguin,"

interrupted the Maître Alexandre Crottat, laughingly.

"Was is not in the office of that unfortunate who succeeded in carrying away eight hundred thousand francs from his clients, and reducing several families to despair, that the settling of the inheritance Chabert took place? It seems to me that I have seen that in our Ferraud papers."

"Yes," replied Crottat, "I was then third clerk; I have made the copies of this settling and carefully studied it.   Rose Chapotel, wife and widow of Hyacinthe, called Chabert, Comte de l'Empire, grand officer of the Legion of Honor; they were married without contract, the property was therefore held in common.   As well as I can remember, the actual property amounted to about six hundred thousand francs.   Before his marriage, the Comte Chabert had made a will in favor of the hospitals of Paris by which he devoted to them a quarter of the fortune of which he should be in possession at the moment of his death, the State inherited another fourth.   There was auction, sale and division, because the attorneys put things through.   At the time of the liquidation, the monster who then governed France restored by a decree, to the colonel's widow, the portion due to the exchequer."

"Thus the personal fortune of the Comte Chabert amounts then only to some three hundred thousand francs?"

"Consequently, my good fellow!" replied Crottat. "You are sometimes perfectly exact, you attorneys, although you are accused of falsifying in your pleadings, as much for, as against."

The Comte Chabert, whose address might be read at the bottom of the first receipt which he had given to the notary, lived in the Faubourg Saint-Marceau, Rue du Petit-Banquier, in the house of an old quartermaster of the Imperial Guard, who had turned milk-dealer and was named Vergniaud. When he arrived there, Derville was obliged to go on foot in search of his client; for his coachman refused to commit himself to a street unpaved, the ruts of which were a little too deep for the wheels of a cabriolet. By looking about him on all sides the attorney ended by discovering, in that part of the street which was in the neighborhood of the boulevard, between two walls built with bones and clay, two dilapidated pilasters in rough stone which had been damaged by the passage of vehicles, notwithstanding pieces of wood placed to protect them. These pilasters supported a beam covered by a coping in tiles, on which these words were marked in red,—VERGNIAUD, NOURICEURE. To the right of this name might be seen some eggs; to the left, a cow, all painted in white. The gate was open, and doubtless remained so throughout the day. At the back of a sufficiently spacious court, opposite the gate, was a house, if, however, this name can be applied to one of those wretched buildings erected in the faubourgs of Paris, and which are comparable to nothing, not even to the poorest dwellings in the country, of which they have all the poverty

without having any of the poetry. In fact, in the
midst of the fields, the cabins have still a grace
which is given them by the purity of the air, the
verdure, the aspect of the fields, a hill, a winding
road, vines, a living hedge, the moss of the roofs,
and the agricultural utensils; but in Paris, poverty
is only increased by its horror. Although recently
constructed, this building seemed to be ready to fall
in ruins. Not one of its materials was applied to
its appropriate use, they all came from the demoli-
tions which daily take place in Paris. Derville
read on a shutter made with the boards of a sign,—
Magasin de nouveautés. The windows had no resemblance among themselves, and were absurdly
placed. The ground floor, which appeared to be the
habitable portion, was raised up on one side, whilst
on the other, the chambers were buried by a de-
clivity. Between the gate and the house extended
a morass strewn with manure and irrigated by pools
of rain water and those proceeding from the establishment. The wall against which this miserable
lodging leaned, and which appeared to be more solid
than the others, was garnished with boxes with
slats within which real rabbits produced their numerous families. To the right of the porte-cochère
was situated the cow-house, surmounted by a forage
loft, and which communicated with the house
by a dairy. To the left was a poultry-yard,
a stable, and a pig-sty which had been finished,
like the house, with broken planks of white wood,
nailed one upon the other and badly covered with

rushes. As in nearly all the localities in which are
prepared the materials for that great repast which
Paris devours every day, the court in which Derville now set foot showed signs of that hurry required by the necessity of arriving at a certain hour.
Those great cans of dented tin in which the milk is
transported, and the pots which contain the cream,
were thrown about pell-mell before the dairy, with
their stoppers of linen. The tattered cloths which
served to dry them were floating in the sunlight,
suspended from cords attached to pickets. That
pacific horse whose species is only found in dairies,
had made a few steps before his cart and waited
before the stable, the door of which was closed. A
goat was browsing on the branches of the thin and
dusty vine which adorned the yellow and cracked
wall of the house. A cat was crouching among the
cream pots and licking them. The chickens,
frightened at Derville's approach, fled with much
outcry, and the watch dog barked.

"The man who decided the victory at the battle
of Eylau lives there!" said Derville to himself, em-
bracing with one glance the whole of this ignoble
spectacle.

The house had been left under the protection of
three boys. One of them, perched upon the top of
a cart loaded with green hay, was pitching stones
into the chimney of a neighboring house, hoping
that they would fall into the pot over the fire. The
second was endeavoring to induce a pig to venture
upon the floor of the cart which rested upon the

earth, whilst the third, hanging at the other end, was waiting till the pig should have done so to lift him in the air by making a see-saw of the cart. When Derville asked them if Monsieur Chabert lived there, none of them replied, and all three looked at him with a lively stupidity, if it be permissible to combine these two words. Derville repeated his question without success. Vexed at the jeering air of these three scamps, he addressed them with those sharp words spoken good-naturedly which young people think themselves privileged to offer to children, and the boys broke their silence with a brutal laugh. Derville grew angry. The colonel, who had heard, came out from a little low chamber situated near the dairy and appeared on the threshold of his door with a military phlegm quite inexpressible. He had in his mouth one of those pipes notably *culottées*—darkened, a technical expression of the smokers,—one of those humble pipes of white clay called *brûle-gueule*—mouth-burners. He lifted the peak of a horribly greasy cap, saw Derville and crossed the manure heap to come more promptly to his benefactor, crying in a friendly voice to the boys:

"Silence in the ranks!"

The children immediately fell into a respectful silence, which revealed the authority which the old soldier exercised over them.

"Why have you not written to me?" said he to Derville. "Go along by the cow-house! See, there, the way is paved," he cried, noticing the attorney's hesitancy, he not wishing to wet his feet in the manure.

By leaping from place to place, Derville reached the threshold of the door out of which the colonel had come. Chabert seemed to be affected disagreeably at being obliged to receive him in the chamber which he occupied. In fact, Derville saw there but one chair. The colonel's bed consisted of some bundles of straw over which his hostess had spread two or three pieces of those old hangings, picked up I know not where, with which the milk-sellers cover the seats of their carts. The floor was simply of trodden earth. The walls, full of saltpetre, greenish and cracked, diffused so much humidity in the air that the wall against which the colonel slept was hung with a mat of rushes. The famous box-coat hung on a nail. Two pairs of poor boots lay in a corner. No vestige of linen. On the worm-eaten table, the *Bulletins de la Grande Armée*, reprinted by Plancher, lay open, and appeared to have furnished the colonel's reading matter; his face was calm and serene in the midst of this poverty. His visit to Derville seemed to have changed the expression of his features, on which the attorney found the traces of a pleasant thought, a peculiar light which had been thrown upon them by hope.

"Does pipe smoke incommode you?" said he, offering to his attorney the chair of which half the straw was gone.

"But, colonel, you are horribly situated here!"

This phrase was drawn from Derville by the

mistrust natural to attorneys and by the deplorable experience which they early receive from the frightful and unknown dramas in which they take part. "Well," said he to himself, "here is a man who has certainly taken my money to satisfy the three theological virtues of the trooper,—gambling, wine and women!"

"That is true, monsieur, we do not shine here by luxury. It is a bivouac tempered by friendship, but—" here the soldier threw a profound look upon the man of law,—"but I have done no wrong to anyone, I have never turned anyone away, and I sleep in peace."

The attorney reflected that it would not be very delicate to ask an account of his client of the money which had been advanced him, and he contented himself by saying:

"Why have you not been willing to come into Paris, where you would have lived a little more expensively than here, but where you would have been better off?"

"But," replied the colonel, "the honest people with whom I am, took me in, took care of me gratis for a year! how then could I leave them the moment I had a little money? Then, the father of these three boys is an old *Egyptian*—"

"How, an Egyptian?"

"We give this name to the troopers who came back from the expedition to Egypt, of which I was a part. Not only are all those who came back a little like brothers, but Vergniaud was then in my regiment, we have shared our water in the desert; moreover, I have not yet finished teaching his little brats to read."

"He might have lodged you much better for your money, he might."

"Bah!" said the colonel, "his children sleep, as I do, on straw! His wife and himself have no better bed; they are very poor, do you see! they have taken an establishment beyond their resources. But, if I recover my fortune—In short, that is all!"

"Colonel, I should receive to-morrow, or the day after, your papers from Heilsberg. Your deliveress is still living."

"Curse the money! To think that I have none!" he cried, dashing his pipe to the ground.

A pipe *culottée* is a piece precious to a smoker; but this was by a gesture so natural, by a movement so generous, that all smokers and even the excise commissioners would have pardoned him this crime of *lèse-tabac*. The angels perhaps would have picked up the pieces.

"Colonel, your affair is excessively complicated," said Derville to him, leaving the chamber to go and walk in the sun along the front of the house.

"It appears to me," said the soldier, "perfectly simple. I was thought to be dead, here I am! Return to me my wife and my fortune; give me the rank of general to which I am entitled, for I was made colonel in the Imperial Guard the day before the battle of Eylau."

"Things do not go that way in the judicial world,"

replied Derville. "Listen to me. You are the
Comte Chabert, I am agreed; but it is a question
of proving it judicially to those who are going to
have an interest in denying your existence. Therefore, your certificates will be disputed. This discussion will bring up ten or twelve preliminary
inquiries. Everything will be carried, after the
hearing of both sides, up to the supreme court, and
will necessitate costly proceedings, which will be
long delayed, no matter what activity I put into
them. Your adversaries will demand an inquest,
which we cannot refuse, and will necessitate perhaps a commission of inquiry in Prussia. But supposing that everything goes smoothly; we will
admit that you are recognized promptly by the
courts as Colonel Chabert. Do we know how will
be decided the question raised by the very innocent
bigamy of the Comtesse Ferraud? In your case,
the legal point raised is outside the Code, and can
only be decided by the judges according to the laws
of conscience, as do the juries in the delicate questions presented by the social anomalies of some
criminal processes. Then, you had no children by
your marriage, and Monsieur le Comte Ferraud has
two by his; the judges may declare void that marriage in which the ties are the weaker, in favor of
that one which includes the stronger ones, from the
moment in which it was contracted in good faith by
both parties. Will you be in a very admirable
moral position, in stubbornly insisting upon having
at your age and in the circumstances in which you

find yourself, a wife who no longer loves you? You will have against you your wife and her husband, two powerful personages who may influence the courts. The suit has then in it elements of duration. You will have time to grow old in it, in the keenest chagrins."

"And my fortune?"

"You believe then that there is a large fortune?"

"Did I not have thirty thousand francs income?"

"My dear colonel, you executed, in 1799, before your marriage, a testament which left a quarter of your property to the hospitals."

"That is true."

"Well, when you were declared deceased, was it not necessary to proceed to an inventory, to a liquidation, in order to give this quarter to the hospitals? Your wife did not scruple to deceive the poor. The inventory, in which doubtless she was very careful not to mention the cash on hand, and the jewels, in which she produced very little silver, and in which the movable property was estimated at two-thirds of the real value, whether to favor her, whether to pay less duty to the exchequer, or because the appraisers are responsible for their estimation, the inventory, thus made, established a valuation of six hundred thousand francs. For her part, your widow was entitled to one-half. Everything was sold, bought in by her, she got the benefit of it all, and the hospitals received their seventy-five thousand francs. Then, as the public exchequer was one of your heirs, seeing that you had made no

12

mention of your wife in your will, the Emperor returned to her by a decree, the portion due the public
treasury.   Now then, to what are you entitled?
To three hundred thousand francs only, less the
costs."

"And you call that justice?" said the stupefied
colonel.

"Why certainly—"

"It is fine!"

"It is so, my poor colonel.   You see that what
you have thought easy, is not so.   Madame Ferraud
can keep even the portion which was given to her
by the Emperor."

"But, as she is not a widow, the decree is
void—"

"Agreed.   But everything can be argued before
the courts.   Listen to me.   Under these circumstances, I think that an agreement would be, for
you and for her, the best outcome of the suit.   You
will gain by it a fortune more considerable than
that to which you are entitled."

"That would be to sell my wife?"

"With twenty-four thousand francs of income,
you would have, in the position in which you
would be, women who would suit you better than
your wife, and who would render you more happy.
I intend to go to-day even to see Madame la Comtesse Ferraud in order to explore the ground; but I
did not wish to take this step without notifying
you."

"Let us go together to see her—"

"As you are now?" said the attorney. "No, no, colonel, no. You might lose your suit by it completely."

"Can my suit be won?"

"Under every head," replied Derville. "But, my dear Colonel Chabert, you neglect one thing. I am not rich, I have not yet entirely paid for my office. If the courts award you a provision, that is to say, a sum to receive in advance upon your fortune, they will not give it to you until after they have recognized you as Comte Chabert, grand officer of the Legion of Honor."

"That's a fact, I am grand officer of the Legion of Honor, I had forgotten it," he said naïvely.

"Well, until then," Derville went on, "will it not be necessary to plead the case in the courts, to pay the advocates, to raise and satisfy judgments, to set the bailiffs on foot, and to live? The costs of the preliminary actions will mount up, roughly speaking, to more than twelve or fifteen thousand francs. I have not got them, I who am crushed under the enormous interest which I pay to those who lent me the money to purchase my office. And you, where will you find them?"

The big tears fell from the faded eyes of the poor soldier and rolled down his withered cheeks. At the aspect of these difficulties, he was discouraged. The social world and the judicial world weighed upon his chest like a nightmare.

"I will go," he cried, "to the foot of the column in the Place Vendôme, I will cry there,—'I am the

Colonel Chabert who broke the great square of the Russians at Eylau.'   The bronze statue, he! he will recognize me.''

"And they will doubtless send you to Charenton.''

At this formidable name, the soldier's exaltation fell.

"Should I not have some favorable chances at the Ministry of War?''

"The Bureaus!'' said Derville.   "Go there, but only with a formal judgment which declares void your certificate of death.   The Bureaus would like to abolish all the servants of the Empire.''

The colonel rested for a moment overwhelmed, motionless, looking without seeing, sunk in a boundless despair.   Military justice is frank, rapid, it decides Turkish fashion, and nearly always judges justly; this justice was the only one that Chabert knew.   On perceiving the labyrinth of difficulties in which he would have to engage himself, on seeing how much money would be required to penetrate it, the poor soldier received a mortal blow in that power peculiar to man and which is named the *will*.   It seemed to him impossible to live as a suitor, it would be a thousand times more simple for him to remain poor; a beggar, to enlist as a trooper if some regiment would take him.   His sufferings, physical and moral, had already affected his body in some of the most important vital organs.   He was on the verge of one of those maladies for which the science of medicine has no name, the seat

of which is in some sort capable of motion, like the
nervous apparatus which seems to be the most often
attacked among all those of our bodily machine, an
affection which it would be necessary to designate
as the *spleen* of unhappiness. However grave this
affection, invisible but real, might be already it was
yet capable of being cured by a happy conclusion.
To shake completely this vigorous organization, it
would suffice that a new obstacle, that some unforeseen fact, should come to break the weakened
springs of action and produce those hesitations,
those uncomprehended, incomplete acts, which the
physicians observe in those ruined by distress.

In thus recognizing the symptoms of a profound
prostration in his client, Derville said to him:

"Take courage, the solution of this affair cannot
but be favorable to you. Only, consider if you can
give me your entire confidence, and accept blindly
whatever I judge best for you."

"Do whatever you like," said Chabert.

"Yes, but you give up to me like a man who is
going to his death?"

"Am I not going to remain without any position,
without a name? Is that tolerable?"

"I do not understand it so," said the attorney.
"We will secure, in friendly proceedings, a decision
which will annul your certificate of death and your
marriage, so that you can come into your rights
again. You will even be, through the influence of
Comte Ferraud, placed upon the army lists as general, and you will doubtless obtain a pension."

"Go ahead then!" replied Chabert, "I trust entirely in you."

"I will send you a power of attorney to sign,"
said Derville. "Adieu, have courage! If you are
in want of money, count on me."

Chabert shook Derville's hand warmly, and remained with his back leaning against the wall,
without the strength to follow him other than
with his eyes. Like all those who are inexpe-
rienced in judicial affairs he was terrified at this unforeseen contest. During this conference, there
had appeared several times beyond one of the
pilasters of the porte-cochère the head of a man
stationed in the street to watch for the coming
out of Derville, and who accosted him when he
appeared. It was an old man wearing a blue
vest, a sort of pleated white sack like those of the
brewers, and on his head an otter-skin cap. His
face was dark, hollowed and wrinkled, but reddened on the cheeks by excess of labor and tanned
by the open air.

"Excuse me, monsieur," said he to Derville,
stopping him by taking hold of his arm, "if I take
the liberty of speaking to you, but I thought to myself when I saw you that you were the friend of our
general."

"Well," said Derville, "how are you interested
in him? But who are you?" added the suspicious
attorney.

"I am Louis Vergniaud," he replied promptly.
"And I should like to say two words to you."

"And it is you who have lodged the Comte Chabert in the way he is?"

"Pardon, excuse me, monsieur, he has the best chamber. I would have given him mine if I had but one. I would have slept in the stable. A man who has suffered as he has, who is teaching my brats to read, a general, an Egyptian, the first lieutenant under whom I served,—you should see! He is the best lodged of anybody. I have shared with him what I had. Unluckily it was not very much, some bread, some milk, eggs; in short, you must suit yourselves to the times. It is all done willingly. But he has hurt us."

"He?"

"Yes, monsieur, hurt, there, to speak plainly— I have taken an establishment beyond my means, he sees it very clearly. That worries him, and he grooms the horse! I said to him,—'But, *mon général!*' 'Bah!' he said, 'I do not want to be like an idler, and I learned to do this long ago.' I have, then, given some notes in payment for my milk business to a man named Grados—Do you know him, monsieur?"

"But, my dear fellow, I have not the time to listen to you. Only tell me how the colonel has hurt you."

"He has hurt us, monsieur, as true as my name is Louis Vergniaud, and my wife has cried about it. He learned, through the neighbors, that we had not the first sou toward paying our note. The old growler, without saying a word, has kept together all that you have given him, has watched for the note, and paid it. It was wicked! When my wife and I, we knew that he had no tobacco, this poor old man, and that he did without it! Oh! now, every morning, he has his cigars, I would sell myself rather—No, we are hurt! Then, I wished to propose to you to lend us, seeing that he said to us that you were a fine man, a hundred écus on our establishment, so that we can make him have some clothes, that we can furnish his chamber. He has thought that he would square us up, did he not? Well, on the contrary, don't you see, the old man has put us in debt,—and hurt us! He ought not to have offered us this affront. He has hurt us, and among friends, too! On the word of an honest man, as true as that I am called Louis Vergniaud, I will promise rather than not to return you that money there—"

Derville looked at the milk-dealer, and took several steps backward for another look at the house, the court, the manure heaps, the stable, the rabbits, the children.

"Upon my word! I believe that one of the qualifications of virtue is not to be a proprietor," he said to himself. "Well, you shall have your hundred écus! and more even. But it is not I who will give them to you, the colonel will be amply rich enough to help you, and I do not wish to take that pleasure from him."

"Will it be soon?"

"Why, yes."

"Ah! *Mon Dieu!* how pleased my wife will be!"

And the sun-burned countenance of the milk-dealer seemed to expand.

"Now then," thought Derville, getting into his cabriolet again, "we will go to see our adversary. Do not let your own play be seen, endeavor to find out hers, and win the game by one stroke. It will be necessary to frighten her. She is a woman. At what are women the most frightened? But the women are only terrified at—"

He set himself to studying the countess's position, and fell into one of those meditations which absorb the great men of politics in arranging their own plans, in endeavoring to divine the secret of the enemy's cabinet. Are not attorneys in some measure statesmen charged with private affairs? A glance at the situation of Monsieur le Comte Ferraud and his wife is necessary here in order to understand the genius of the attorney.

Monsieur le Comte Ferraud was the son of a former counselor of the Parliament at Paris, who had emigrated during the Terror, and who, if he had saved his head, had lost his fortune. He returned during the Consulate, and remained constantly faithful to the interests of Louis XVIII., one of whose advisers his father had been before the Revolution. He therefore belonged to that party in the Faubourg Saint-Germain which nobly resisted all Napoléon's seductions. The reputation for ability which the young count, then known simply as Monsieur Ferraud, enjoyed, rendered him the object of the coquetries of the Emperor, who was

frequently as happy over his conquests among the
aristocracy as over the winning of a battle. The
count was promised the restoration of his title, that
of his property which had not been sold, he was
shown in the distance the post of minister, that of
senator. The Emperor failed. Monsieur Ferraud
was, at the period of Comte Chabert's death, a
young man of twenty-six, without fortune, with an
agreeable exterior, who had had some successes,
and whom the Faubourg Saint-Germain had
adopted as one of its glories; but Madame la Comtesse Chabert had known so well how to make the
most of her husband's inheritance that after eighteen months of widowhood she was still in the enjoyment of some forty thousand francs of income.
Her marriage with the young count was not altogether a piece of news to the coteries of the Faubourg
Saint-Germain. Happy at this marriage, which
carried out his ideas of fusion, Napoléon returned to
Madame Chabert the portion of her late husband's
estate which had fallen into the exchequer; but his
hopes were again disappointed. Madame Ferraud
not only loved her lover in the young man, she had
been seduced also by the idea of entering that dis-
dainful society which, notwithstanding its abase-
ment, dominated the Imperial court. All her vani-
ties as well as her passions were flattered by this
marriage. She was about to become a *femme comme
il faut*. When the Faubourg Saint-Germain learned
that the young count's marriage was not a deser-
tion, the salons opened to his wife. The Restoration

arrived.   The political advancement of Comte Ferraud was not rapid.   He understood the exigen-
cies of the situation in which Louis XVIII. found
himself, he was of the number of the initiated who
waited until *the abyss of the revolutions was closed,*
for this royal phrase, so derided by the Liber-
als, concealed a political meaning.   Nevertheless,
the ordinance cited in the long clerical phrase in
the commencement of this history had restored to
him two forests and an estate the value of which had
been considerably augmented during the seques-
tration.   At this moment, though the Comte Ferraud was councillor of State and director-general, he
considered his position as the beginning only of his
political fortune.   Absorbed by the cares of a devouring ambition, he had taken as his secretary a
former attorney, now ruined, named Delbecq, a
man more than skilful, who was admirably informed
in all the ruses of chicanery, and to whom he left
the conduct of his private affairs.   This shrewd
practitioner had comprehended his position in the
count's household well enough to remain honest
through calculation.   He hoped to succeed to some
position through the influence of his patron, whose
fortune was the object of all his cares.   His conduct
so gave the lie to his former life that he passed for
a calumniated man.   With the tact and the shrewdness with which all women are more or less endowed, the countess, who had justly estimated her
intendant, watched him adroitly, and knew so well
how to manage him that she had already secured a

very good position for the augmentation of her private fortune. She had been able to persuade Delbecq that she ruled Monsieur Ferraud, and had promised to have him appointed president of an inferior court for civil causes in one of the most important cities of France if he devoted himself entirely to her interests. The promise of a permanent position which would permit him to make an advantageous marriage, and to conquer later a high position in the political world by becoming a deputy, made of Delbecq the devoted tool of the countess. He had not allowed to escape him one of those favorable chances which the movements on the Bourse and the rise in values presented in Paris to skilful manipulators during the first three years of the Restoration. He had increased threefold the capital of his protectress, with so much the more facility that all methods had seemed good to the countess which might help to promptly increase her fortune to an enormous size. She employed the emoluments received by the count from his various positions for the household expenses so as to be able to form a capital from her revenues, and Delbecq lent himself to the calculations of this avarice without endeavoring to explain the motives to himself. Individuals of this species concern themselves only about secrets the discovery of which would be advantageous to their own interests. Moreover, he found the reason so naturally in that thirst for gold with which the greater number of the Parisiennes are affected, and so great a fortune was required to support the pretensions of Comte Ferraud, that the intendant thought sometimes that he saw in the avidity of the countess only an effect of her devotion to the man with whom she was still in love. The countess had buried the secrets of her conduct in the bottom of her heart. There rested the secrets of life and death for her, there lay precisely the key to this history. At the commencement of the year 1818, the Restoration was seated on a base apparently unshakable, its doctrines of government, comprehended by the most intellectual, seemed to them about to bring to France an era of new prosperity, then the Parisian society changed face. Madame la Comtesse Ferraud found that she had through chance made a marriage at once of love, of fortune and of ambition. Still young and beautiful, Madame Ferraud played the part of a fashionable woman, and lived in the atmosphere of the Court. Rich in her own right, rich through her husband, who, extolled as one of the most capable men of the royalist party and the friend of the king, seemed destined to be minister, she belonged to the aristocracy and partook of its splendors. In the midst of this triumph she was attacked by a moral cancer. There are sentiments which women perceive instinctively notwithstanding all the care which men take to conceal them. At the time of the first return of the king, Comte Ferraud had conceived some regrets because of his marriage. The widow of Colonel Chabert had brought him no alliance, he was alone and without support in a career full of dangers and

full of enemies.   Then, perhaps, when he became
able to judge his wife dispassionately he had recognized in her certain vices of education which rendered her unable to second him in his projects.   A
word which he had dropped apropos of Talleyrand's
marriage enlightened the countess, to whom it
was demonstrated that, if her marriage were still
to be accomplished, she would never be Madame
Ferraud.   This regret, what woman can ever forgive
it?   Does it not contain the germ of all insults, of
all crimes, of all repudiations?   But what a wound
would this word not open in the countess's heart if
it came to be supposed that she feared to see her
first husband reappear!   She had known that he
was living, she had repulsed him.   Then, during
the time in which she had no longer heard from him
she pleased herself by believing him dead at
Waterloo with the Imperial eagles, in company with
Boutin.   Nevertheless, she resolved to attach the
count to her by the strongest of bonds, by a golden
chain, and resolved to be so rich that her fortune
would render her second marriage indissoluble if
by chance Comte Chabert should appear again.
And he had reappeared, without her being able to
.explain to herself why the contest which she feared
had not already commenced.   Sufferings, disease,
had perhaps delivered her from this man.   Perhaps
he was half demented, Charenton might yet bring
him to terms.   She had not been willing to take
Delbecq or the police into her confidence, through
fear of giving herself a master, or of precipitating

the catastrophe. There are in Paris a great many
wives who, like the Comtesse Ferraud, live in the
company of a concealed moral monster, or who skirt
an abyss; they become callous in regard to their
evil, and are still able to laugh and to amuse themselves.

"There is something very singular in the situation of Monsieur le Comte Ferraud," said Derville
to himself as he came out of his long reverie at the
moment when his cabriolet stopped in the Rue de
Varennes, at the doors of the Hôtel Ferraud. "How
is it that he, so wealthy, a favorite of the king, is
not yet a peer of France? It is true that it is perhaps
a part of the king's policy, as Madame de Grandlieu
said to me, to give a very high importance to the
peerage by not distributing it too freely. Moreover, the son of a counselor of Parliament is neither
a Crillon nor a Rohan. Comte Ferraud can only
enter surreptitiously into the Upper Chamber.
But, if his marriage were annulled, could he not
assume, to the great satisfaction of the king, the
peerage of one of those old senators who have only
daughters? That will certainly be a good story to
begin with to frighten our countess," he thought as
he ascended the perron.

Derville had, without knowing it, put his finger
on the secret wound, buried his hand in the cancer
which was devouring Madame Ferraud. He was
received by her in a pretty winter dining-room in
which she was breakfasting while playing with a
monkey fastened by a chain to a sort of little post

furnished with iron bars for steps. The countess was enveloped in an elegant peignoir; the curls of her hair, carelessly fastened up, escaped from under a cap which gave her a little saucy air. She was fresh and smiling. The silver, the enamel, the mother-of-pearl, sparkled on the table, and there were around her flowers curiously arranged in magnificent vases of porcelain. When he saw the wife of Comte Chabert, wealthy with what he had left her, in the midst of luxury, in the highest society, whilst the unfortunate man was living in the house of a poor milk-dealer, among the cattle, the attorney said to himself:

"The moral of all this is that a pretty woman will never be willing to recognize her husband, or even her lover, in a man in an old box-coat, in a grass wig and boots full of holes."

A malicious and biting smile gave expression to the ideas half philosophical, half mocking, which might naturally come to a man sufficiently well placed to be acquainted with the true state of things notwithstanding the falsehoods under which the majority of Parisian families conceal their existence.

"Good day, Monsieur Derville," she said, continuing to give the monkey his coffee.

"Madame," said he brusquely, for he was offended at the light tone in which the countess had said to him, "Good day, Monsieur Derville,"—"I come to see you about an affair of considerable gravity."

"I am *in despair* to hear it, Monsieur le Comte is absent."

"I am enchanted to hear it, madame. He would be *in despair* if he assisted at our conference. I know, moreover, through Delbecq, that you like to conduct your affairs yourself, without wearying Monsieur le Comte."

"Then I will call Delbecq," she said.

"He will be useless to you, notwithstanding his skill," replied Derville. "Listen, madame, a word will suffice to render you serious. The Comte Chabert is living."

"Is it by saying such buffooneries as that that you wish to make me serious?" she said with a peal of laughter.

But the countess was suddenly mastered by the strange clearness of the fixed look with which Derville interrogated her, while seeming to read the depths of her soul.

"Madame," he replied with a cold and piercing gravity, "you are ignorant of the extent of the dangers which menace you.   I will not speak to you of the incontestable authenticity of the documents, or of the certainty of the proofs which attest the existence of the Comte Chabert. I am not the man to take up a bad case, that you know. If you oppose our proof of falsity of the certificate of death, you will lose this first suit, and this question decided in our favor will gain for us all the others."

"Of what then do you propose to speak to me?"

"Neither of the colonel, nor of yourself. I will not speak to you, either, of the memoirs which

13

might be drawn up by clever attorneys, armed with the curious facts of this case, and of the conclusions which they would draw from the letters which you received from your first husband before the celebration of your marriage with the second."

"That is false!" she cried with all the violence of a *petite maîtresse*. "I have never received any letters from the Comte Chabert; and if some one claims to be the colonel, he is only an adventurer, some liberated convict, like Cogniard perhaps. It makes you shiver, just to think of it. Could the colonel come to life again, monsieur? Bonaparte sent me a complimentary message on his death by an aide-de-camp, and I still have three thousand francs of pension awarded to his widow by the Chambers. I have had a thousand reasons to repulse all the Chaberts that have come, as I would repulse all those who may come."

"Fortunately we are alone, madame. We can lie at our ease," he said coldly, amusing himself by stirring up the anger which agitated the countess in order to wrest from her some indiscretions, a manœuvre familiar to the lawyers, accustomed to remain calm while their adversaries or their clients fly into a passion. "Well, then, it is between us two," he said to himself, inventing on the spur of the moment a trap to demonstrate to her her weakness. "The proof of the sending of the first letter exists, madame," he went on, aloud, "it contained some funds—"

"Oh! funds, it did not contain any at all."

"You have then received this first letter," resumed Derville smiling. "You are already caught
in the first trap which an attorney sets for you, and
you think yourself able to contend with justice—"

The countess reddened, paled, hid her face in her
hands. Then she shook off her mortification, and
replied with the self-possession natural to this kind
of women:

"Since you are the attorney of the pretended
Chabert, do me the pleasure to—"

"Madame," said Derville, interrupting, "I am
still at this moment as much your attorney as the
colonel's. Do you think that I wish to lose a practice as valuable as is yours? But you are not listening to me—"

"Speak, monsieur," she said graciously.

"Your fortune came to you from Monsieur le
Comte Chabert, and you have repelled him. Your
fortune is colossal, and you allow him to beg. Madame, the lawyers are very eloquent when the cases
are themselves eloquent; there are to be met with
here circumstances capable of raising public opinion
against you."

"But, monsieur," said the countess, impatient at
the manner in which Derville turned her and returned her on the gridiron, "admitting that your
Monsieur Chabert exists, the courts would maintain my second marriage because of the children,
and I should be quit of him by returning two
hundred and twenty-five thousand francs to Monsieur Chabert."

"Madame, we do not know in what manner the courts would look at the sentimental question. If, on the one side, we have a mother and her children, we have on the other a man overwhelmed by misfortune, aged by you, by your refusals. Where would he find a wife? Then, could the judges infringe the law? Your marriage with the colonel has on its side, legality, priority. But, if you are represented under odious colors, you might have against you an adversary whom you do not expect. There, madame, lies this danger from which I would wish to preserve you."

"A new adversary," she said: "who?"

"Monsieur le Comte Ferraud, madame."

"Monsieur Ferraud has too great an attachment to me, and, for the mother of his children, a too great respect—"

"Do not speak of these sillinesses," said Derville, interrupting her, "to lawyers accustomed to reading the bottoms of hearts. At this moment, Monsieur Ferraud has not the least desire to break your marriage, and I am persuaded that he adores you; but, if some one should come to say to him that his marriage might be annulled, that his wife would be arraigned as a criminal at the bar of public opinion—"

"He would defend me, monsieur."

"No, madame."

"What reason would he have for abandoning me, monsieur?"

"Why, that of marrying the only daughter of a

peer of France, the peerage of which would be transmitted to him by an ordinance of the king—"

The countess grew pale.

"We have got it!" said Derville to himself. "Good, I have it, the affair of the poor colonel is gained.—Moreover, madame," he resumed aloud, "he would have all the less remorse because a man covered with glory, general, count, grand officer of the Legion of Honor, would not be a poor second choice; and, if this man demanded of him again his wife—"

"Enough! enough, monsieur!" she said. "I shall never have any attorney but you. What is to be done?"

"Come to an agreement!" said Derville.

"Does he love me still?" she said.

"Why, I do not believe that he could do otherwise."

At this word the countess raised her head. A gleam of hope shone in her eyes; she figured perhaps upon working upon the tenderness of her first husband to gain her cause by some feminine ruse.

"I shall await your orders, madame, to know whether it will be necessary to notify you of our certificates, or if you will be willing to come to my office to draw up the basis of an agreement," said Derville, taking his leave of the countess.

A week after the two visits which Derville had made, and on a beautiful morning in the month of June, the husband and wife, disunited by an almost supernatural fortune, set out from the two points of Paris the most distant from each other, to meet in the office of their common attorney. The advances which Derville had generously made to Colonel Chabert permitted him to appear in a costume suitable to his rank. The defunct accordingly arrived established in a very neat cabriolet. He had his head covered with a wig suitable to his physiognomy, wore a suit of blue cloth, white linen, and carried under his waistcoat the red cross of the grand officers of the Legion of Honor. In resuming the costume of a comfortable life, he had found again his former martial elegance. He held himself upright. His countenance, grave and mysterious, on which were depicted happiness and all his hopes, appeared to have renewed its youthfulness and to have become more *grasse*, to borrow from painting one of its most picturesque expressions. He no more resembled the Chabert of the old boxcoat than a big sou resembles a forty-franc piece newly coined. On seeing him, the passers-by could easily have recognized in him one of those fine remnants of our old army, one of those heroic men upon whom our national glory is reflected, and who represent it, as a fragment of ice illuminated by the sun, seems to reflect all its rays. These old soldiers are at once paintings and volumes. When the count descended from his carriage to ascend Derville's steps, he leaped out as lightly as a young man could have done. Hardly had his cabriolet turned away when a handsome coupé

covered with armorial bearings arrived. Madame la
Comtesse Ferraud stepped from it in a simple toilet
which was yet skilfully contrived to display the
youthfulness of her figure. She had a pretty capote
lined with pink silk which framed in perfectly her
face, dissimulating its outlines and reanimating
them. If the clients had renewed their youth, the
office had remained like itself, and still presented
the scene with the description of which this tale
commenced. Simonnin was eating his breakfast,
his shoulder leaning against the window, which now
was open, and he was contemplating the blue of the
sky through the opening of this court surrounded by
four black buildings.

"Ah!" cried the little clerk, "who wants to bet a
theatre that the Colonel Chabert is a general and a
cordon rouge?"

"Our patron is a famous magician," said Godeschal.

"There is no trick to be played upon him to-day,
then?" asked Desroches.

"It is his wife who will take charge of that, the
Comtesse Ferraud!" said Boucard.

"Come now," said Godeschal, "the Comtesse
Ferraud will then have to do with two?—"

"Here she is!" replied Simonnin.

At this moment the colonel entered and asked for
Derville.

"He is here, Monsieur le Comte," said Simonnin.

"You are not deaf then, little scamp," said
Chabert, taking the *saute-ruisseau* by the ear and

twisting it to the great satisfaction of the clerks, who laughed and looked at the colonel with the curious consideration due to that singular personage.

The Comte Chabert was in Derville's apartment at the moment when his wife entered by the office door.

"I say, Boucard, there will be a singular scene in the patron's cabinet! There is a wife who can go on the even days to the Comte Ferraud and on the odd days to the Comte Chabert."

"In the bissextile years the *count* will be even," said Godeschal.

"Will you be quiet, messieurs! you can be overheard," said Boucard severely; "I have never seen an office in which the clients are made sport of as they are here."

Derville had consigned the colonel to the bedchamber when the countess presented herself.

"Madame," he said to her, "not knowing whether it would be agreeable to you to see Monsieur le Comte Chabert, I have separated you. If, however, you should desire—"

"Monsieur, this is an attention for which I thank you."

"I have prepared the draft of an agreement the conditions of which can be discussed by you and by Monsieur Chabert at the present sitting. I will go alternately from you to him, to present to you, alternately, your respective reasons."

"Let us see, monsieur," said the countess, making an involuntary gesture of impatience.

Derville read:

"Between the undersigned,

"Monsieur Hyacinthe, called *Chabert*, count, field-marshal, and grand officer of the Legion of Honor, living in Paris, Rue du Petit-Banquier, on one side:

"And la dame Rose Chapotel, wife of Monsieur le Comte Chabert, named above, née—"

"Go on," she said, "never mind the preamble, let us get to the conditions."

"Madame," said the attorney, "the preamble explains succinctly the position in which each of you finds yourself. Then, by Article I, you recognize, in the presence of three witnesses, who are two notaries and the dairyman in whose house your husband has lived, to whom I have confided your affair under the seal of secrecy, and who will maintain the most profound silence, you recognize, I say, that the individual designated in the certificates joined to the private deed, but whose condition will be found otherwise established by an *acte de notoriété* prepared by Alexandre Crottat, your notary, is the Comte Chabert, your first husband. By Article II, the Comte Chabert, in the interests of your happiness, engages himself to make use of his rights only in the cases provided for by the agreement itself.— And these cases," said Derville, making a sort of parenthesis, "are none other than the non-execution of the clauses of this secret agreement.—"On his part," he resumed, "Monsieur Chabert consents to procure, by mutual consent with you, a judgment

which will annul his certificate of death and will
decree the dissolution of his marriage."

"That does not suit me at all," said the astonished countess.   "I do not wish any suit drawn up.
You know why."

"By Article III," said the attorney, continuing
with an imperturbable phlegm, "you engage to constitute in the name of Hyacinthe, Comte Chabert, an
annuity of twenty-four thousand francs, inscribed
on the register of the public debt, but the capital
of which will revert to you at his death.—"

"But that is much too dear!" said the countess.

"Can you make a better bargain?"

"Perhaps."

"What do you wish then, madame?"

"I wish—I do not wish any suit; I wish—"

"That he should remain dead?" said Derville
quickly, interrupting her.

"Monsieur," said the countess, "if it requires
twenty-four thousand francs of income, we will go
to law—"

"Yes, we will go to law," cried, in a muffled voice,
the colonel, opening the door and appearing suddenly before his wife, one hand in his vest and
the other extended towards the floor, a gesture to
which the remembrance of his adventure gave a
horrible energy.

"It is he!" said the countess to herself.

"Too dear!" the old soldier went on.   "I have
given you nearly a million, and you haggle with
my misfortune.   Well, I want you now, you and

your fortune.   We have a community of goods, our marriage has not been broken—"

"But monsieur is not Colonel Chabert," cried the countess, feigning surprise.

"Ah!" said the old man in a tone of profound irony, "do you wish some proofs?   I picked you up in the Palais-Royal—"

The countess turned white.   In seeing her pale under her rouge, the old soldier, touched by the keen suffering which he was inflicting upon a woman formerly ardently loved, paused suddenly; but he received from her a look so venomous that he went on suddenly:

"You were in the house of—"

"Pray, monsieur," said the countess to the attorney, "make it convenient that I leave this place.   I have not come here to listen to such horrors."

She rose and went out.   Derville precipitated himself into the office.   The countess had taken wings and had as it seemed flown away.   Returning to his cabinet, the attorney found the colonel in a violent state of rage and traversing the room with great strides.

"In those times, each one took his wife wherever he wanted," he said; "but I made the mistake of choosing badly, of trusting to appearances.   She has no heart."

"Well, colonel, was I not right in entreating you not to come?   I am now certain of your identity. When you showed yourself, the countess made a

movement the signification of which was not doubtful.   But you have lost your suit, your wife knows
that you are unrecognizable!''

"I will kill her—''

"Nonsense, you will be taken and guillotined like
a wretch.   Moreover, perhaps you might miss your
stroke! that would be unpardonable, you should
never miss your wife when you wish to kill her.
Let me repair your blunders, you great child!   Go
away.   Take care of yourself, she would be capable of making you tumble into some trap and of
shutting you up in Charenton.   I am going to notify
her of our certificates in order to guarantee you from
any surprise."

The poor colonel obeyed his young benefactor,
and went away stammering excuses.   He slowly
descended the steps of the black staircase, lost in
sombre thoughts, overwhelmed perhaps by the blow
which he had just received, for him the cruelest,
the most deeply buried in his heart, when he heard,
as he reached the last step, the rustling of a dress
and his wife appeared.

"Come, monsieur," she said to him, taking him
by the arm with a movement similar to those which
were once familiar to him.

The action of the countess, the accent of her
voice which had become gracious again, sufficed to
calm the colonel's anger, and he allowed himself to
be led to the carriage.

"Well, get in!" said the countess to him when
the footman had let down the steps.

And he found himself, as if by enchantment, seated by the side of his wife in the coupé.

"Where will madame go?" asked the footman.

"To Groslay," she said.

The horses set off and traversed the whole of Paris.

"Monsieur—" said the countess to the colonel in a voice which revealed one of those emotions rare in life, and by which everything that we have within us is moved.

In these moments, heart, fibres, nerves, physiognomy, soul and body, everything, each pore even, shivers. Life seems to be no longer within us; it issues and springs out, it communicates itself like a contagion, transmits itself by the look, by the accent of the voice, by the gesture, in imposing our will on others. The old soldier shuddered on hearing this one word, this first, this terrible "Monsieur." But also it was at once a reproach, a prayer, a pardon, a hope, a despair, an interrogation, a response. This word comprehended everything. It would be necessary to be a comédienne to have been able to throw so much eloquence, so much feeling, into one word. The truth is not so complete in its expression, it does not set everything outside, it allows to be seen all that is within. The colonel experienced a thousand remorses for his suspicions, his demands, his anger, and lowered his eyes so that his trouble might not be perceived.

"Monsieur," resumed the countess after an imperceptible pause, "I recognized you indeed!"

"Rosine," said the old soldier, "that word contains the only balm that can make me forget my misfortunes."

Two great tears fell all warm on his wife's hands, which he pressed to express a paternal tenderness.

"Monsieur," she went on, "how was it that you did not perceive that it cost me a fearful price to appear before a stranger in a position as false as is mine? If I have to blush at my situation, let it at least be only in the midst of the family. Should not this secret rest buried in our hearts? You will absolve me, I hope, for my apparent indifference to the misfortunes of a Chabert in whose existence I should not believe. I received your letters," she said quickly, reading her husband's objections on his features, "but they reached me thirteen months after the battle of Eylau; they were opened, soiled, the writing was unrecognizable, and I could not but think, after having obtained the signature of Napoléon upon my new contract of marriage, that some adroit adventurer was trying to exploit me. In order not to trouble the peace of mind of Monsieur le Comte Ferraud, and not to disturb the family ties, I was obliged then to take precautions against a pretended Chabert. Was I not right? tell me."

"Yes, you were right; it is I who was a fool, an animal, a beast, not to have known how better to consider the consequences of such a situation. But where are we going?" said the colonel, seeing himself at the Barrière de la Chapelle.

"To my country house, near Groslay, in the valley of Montmorency.   There, monsieur, we will
reflect together on the position which we should
take.   I know my duties.   If I am yours by law, I
no longer belong to you in fact.   Can you wish that
we should furnish a story for all Paris?   Let us not
inform the public of this situation which for me has
a ridiculous side, and let us know how to preserve
our dignity.   You love me still," she went on,
throwing a gentle and sad look upon the colonel;
"but I, was I not authorized to form other ties?   In
this singular situation, a secret voice tells me to
hope in your goodness, which is so well known to
me.   Have I been in the wrong in taking you for
the sole and unique arbiter of my destiny?   Be both
judge and client.   I confide in the nobility of your
character.   You will have the generosity to pardon
me the results of innocent faults.   I will avow it to
you, then, I love Monsieur Ferraud.   I think myself
right in loving him.   I do not blush for this avowal
before you; if it offends you, it does not dishonor
us in the least.   I cannot conceal the facts from you.
When chance left me a widow, I was not a mother."

The colonel made a sign with his hand to impose
silence upon his wife, and they remained without
uttering a single word for the space of half a league.
Chabert thought he saw the two children before
him.

"Rosine!"

"Monsieur?"

"The dead are then very wrong to return?"

"Oh! monsieur, no, no! Do not think me un-
grateful. Only, you find a loving woman, a mother,
here where you left a wife. If it is no longer in
my power to love you, I know all that I owe to you
and can still offer you all a daughter's affection."

"Rosine," replied the old man in a gentle voice,
"I no longer bear any resentment against you. We
will forget everything," he added, with one of those
smiles the grace of which is always the reflection of
a fine soul. "I am not sufficiently wanting in delicacy to exact the semblance of love from a woman
who no longer loves me."

The countess threw upon him a look filled with
such gratitude, that the poor Chabert would have
been willing to have entered again his grave at
Eylau. Some men have souls sufficiently strong for
such devotions, the recompense for which is found
for them in the certainty of having given happiness
to a beloved person.

"My dear friend, we will talk of all this later,
and with quiet hearts," said the countess.

The conversation took another turn, for it was
impossible to continue long on this subject. Although
the husband and wife often returned to their grotesque situation, either by allusions or seriously,
they had a charming drive, recalling the events of
their former union and the things of the Empire.
The countess knew how to give a gentle charm to
these souvenirs, and diffused over the conversation
a tinge of melancholy that was necessary to maintain its gravity. She succeeded in reviving love

without exciting any desire, and allowed her first
husband to perceive all the mental accomplishments
that she had acquired, while endeavoring to accustom him to the idea of restricting his happiness to
those enjoyments only which a father tastes in the
presence of a cherished daughter.   The colonel had
known the countess of the Empire, he now saw a
countess of the Restoration.   Finally, the married
pair arrived by a cross-road at a great park situated
in the little valley which separates the heights of
Margency from the pretty village of Groslay.   The
countess there owned a charming house, in which
the colonel saw, on arriving, all the conveniences
necessary for his sojourn and that of his wife.   Misfortune is a species of talisman, the virtue of which
consists in strengthening our early constitution,—it
augments the suspicions and the wickedness of certain men, as it increases the goodness of those who
have an excellent heart.

Misfortune had rendered the colonel still better
and more helpful than he had been, he was then
able to appreciate the secret of those feminine sufferings which are unknown to the majority of men.
Nevertheless, notwithstanding his want of suspicion,
he could not prevent himself from saying to his
wife:

"You were then very sure of bringing me here?"

"Yes," she replied, "if I found Colonel Chabert
in the client."

The air of truthfulness which she was able to put
into this reply dissipated the slight suspicions which

14

the colonel was ashamed of having conceived.   For three days, the countess was admirable in the company of her first husband.   By tender cares and by her constant sweetness she seemed to wish to efface the memory of the sufferings which he had endured, and to procure her own forgiveness for the misfortunes which, as she admitted, she had innocently caused; she pleased herself by displaying before him—all the time causing him to perceive a sort of melancholy—the charms to which she knew he was susceptible; for we are more peculiarly susceptible to certain fashions, to those graces of the heart or of the mind which we do not resist; she wished to interest him in her situation, to revive his tenderness sufficiently to take possession of his mind and dispose of him absolutely.

Resolved to stop at nothing to attain her ends, she did not yet know what she should do with this man, but certainly she desired to annihilate him socially.   On the evening of the third day, she felt that, notwithstanding all her efforts, she could not keep concealed the mistrustfulness awakened in him as the result of her manœuvres.   To give herself a moment of relaxation, she ascended to her own apartment, seated herself at her secretary, removed the mask of tranquillity which she kept on before Comte Chabert, like an actress who, returning fatigued to her dressing-room after a painful fifth act, falls weary and half dead in the room, leaving to the house an image of herself, which she no longer resembles.   She set herself to finish a letter

already commenced, addressed to Delbecq, to whom
she wrote to go in her name and demand of Derville copies of the documents concerning Colonel
Chabert, to copy them and to come immediately to
her at Groslay.   She had scarcely finished when
she heard in the corridor the sound of the footsteps of the colonel who, anxious, had come in search
of her.

"Alas!" she said aloud, "I would I were dead!
My situation is intolerable—"

"Well, what is it that troubles you?" said the
worthy man.

"Nothing, nothing," she said.

She rose, left the colonel, and went down stairs
to speak without any witnesses to her femme de
chambre, whom she sent off to Paris, directing her
to give with her own hand to Delbecq the letter
which she had just written, and to bring it back to
her as soon as he had read it.   Then the countess
went to seat herself on a bench where she could
readily be seen so that the colonel could rejoin her as
soon as he wished.   The colonel, who was already
looking for his wife, hastened to her and seated
himself beside her.

"Rosine," he said to her, "what is it that troubles
you?"

She did not reply.   The evening was one of those
magnificent and calm ones, the hidden harmonies of
which in the month of June impart so much mild-
ness to the sunsets.   The air was pure and the
silence profound, so much so that there could be

heard in the distance in the park the voices of some children which added a kind of melody to the sublimities of the landscape.

"You do not answer me," said the colonel to his wife.

"My husband—" said the countess, who stopped, made a movement and interrupted herself to ask him, blushing as she did so,—"What shall I say in speaking of Monsieur le Comte Ferraud?"

"Call him your husband, my poor child," replied the colonel with a kindly tone; "is he not the father of your children?"

"Well," she resumed, "if monsieur asks me why I come here, if he learns that I have shut myself up here with an unknown man, what shall I say to him? Listen, monsieur," she went on, taking an attitude full of dignity, "decide my fate, I am resigned to anything—"

"My dear," said the colonel, taking his wife's hands in his own, "I have resolved to sacrifice myself entirely to your happiness—"

"That is impossible," she cried, with an involuntary convulsive movement. "Think of it, you would then have to renounce yourself, and in a formal manner—"

"How," said the colonel, "would not my word be sufficient for you?"

The word *formal* fell on the old man's heart and awakened in it involuntary mistrusts. He threw upon his wife a look which made her redden, she lowered her eyes, and he experienced a fear of being obliged to despise her. The countess was frightened at the possibility of having offended the untamed modesty, the severe probity of a man whose generous character, whose primitive virtues, were known to her. Although these thoughts darkened their brows for a moment, a good understanding was soon re-established between them. In this manner. The cry of a child re-echoed at a distance.

"Jules, let your sister alone!" cried the countess.

"What! your children are here?" said the colonel.

"Yes, but I have forbidden them to trouble you."

The old soldier comprehended the delicacy, the feminine tact, betrayed by so graceful a procedure, and took the hand of the countess to kiss it.

"Let them come," he said.

The little girl ran up to complain of her brother.

"Mamma!"

"Mamma!"

"It is he who—"

"It is she—"

The little hands were extended toward the mother, and the two infantile voices mingled. It was a picture, sudden and delightful.

"Poor children!" cried the countess, no longer restraining her tears, "I shall have to leave them; to whom will the courts award them? The heart of a mother cannot be divided, I want them myself!"

"Is it you who makes mamma cry?" said Jules, throwing an angry look on the colonel.

"Be still, Jules!" said the mother, imperiously.

The two children remained standing and silent,
examining their mother and the stranger with a
curiosity which it would be impossible to express in
words.

"Oh! yes," she went on, "if I am separated from
the count, may my children be left to me, and I will
be resigned to everything—"

This was a decisive word, which was as completely successful as she had hoped.

"Yes," cried the colonel as if he were com-
pleting a phrase commenced inwardly, "I should
go under ground again. I have already told myself so."

"Can I accept such a sacrifice?" replied the
countess. "If some men have died to save their mistresses' honor, they have given their life but once.
But, here, you would give your life every day!
No, no, that is impossible. If it were only a question of your existence, that would be nothing; but
to sign a declaration that you were not Colonel
Chabert, to admit that you were an impostor, to
give away your honor, to perpetrate a falsehood at
every hour of the day, human devotion would not
go so far as that. Think of it then! No. Were it
not for my poor children, I would already have flown
with you to the end of the world."

"But," replied Chabert, "can I not live here, in
your little pavilion, as one of your relatives? I am
as worn out as a condemned cannon, all I require is
a little tobacco and the *Constitutionnel*."

The countess melted into tears.   There ensued

between the Comtesse Ferraud and the Colonel Chabert a contest of generosity from which the soldier issued victorious. One evening, seeing this mother with her children, the soldier was seduced by the touching graces of a family picture, in the country, in the shade and the silence; he took a resolution to remain dead, and no longer terrified at the formality of a declaration, he asked what measures he should take to irrevocably assure the happiness of this family.

"Do as you like!" replied the countess, "I declare to you that I will not take any part in this affair. I should not do so."

Delbecq had arrived a few days before, and, following the verbal instructions of the countess, the intendant had been able to gain the old soldier's confidence. On the following morning then, Colonel Chabert set off with the former attorney for Saint-Leu-Taverny, where Delbecq had caused to be drawn up by a notary, a declaration conceived in such blunt terms that the colonel burst fiercely out of the office after having heard it read.

"*Mille tonnerres!* I should be a pretty fellow! Why, I should pass for a forger!" he cried.

"Monsieur," said Delbecq to him, "I do not counsel you to sign too quickly. In your place, I would claim at least thirty thousand francs income for this declaration, for madame would give them."

After having overwhelmed this knave *emeritus* with the flaming look of an honest man indignant,

the colonel fled, carried away by a thousand con-
tradictory sentiments.   He again became mistrustful, indignant and pacified alternately.

Finally he entered the park of Groslay by the
breach in the wall, and proceeded by slow steps to
rest himself and reflect at his ease in a cabinet arranged under a kiosk from which might be seen the
road to Saint-Leu.   The path being covered with
that sort of yellowish earth which is substituted for
the gravel of the river bed, the countess, who was
seated in the little salon of this kind of pavilion,
did not hear the colonel, for she was too much preoccupied with the success of her affair to pay the
slightest attention to the slight noise made by her
husband.   Neither did the old soldier perceive his
wife in the little pavilion above him.

"Well, Monsieur Delbecq, did he sign?" asked
the countess of her intendant whom she saw alone
on the road, beyond the hedge of a ditch.

"No, madame.   I do not even know what has
become of our man.   The old horse reared up."

"We shall have to end then by putting him in
Charenton," she said, "since we hold him."

The colonel, who found again the elasticity of
youth to leap the ditch, was before the intendant
in a twinkling, and applied to him the most beautiful pair of cuffs that were ever received on the two
cheeks of a *procureur*.

"Add that the old horses know how to kick!" he
said to him.

This anger dissipated, the colonel no longer felt in

him the strength to leap the ditch. Truth had shown herself in all her nakedness. The countess' speech and Delbecq's reply had unveiled the plot of which he was to have been the victim. The cares which had been lavished upon him were only a bait to lure him into a trap. This word was like a drop of some subtle poison which brought about in the old soldier the return of all his maladies physical and moral. He returned toward the kiosk by the gate of the park, walking slowly like a man over-burdened. Then, neither peace nor truce for him! From this moment, it would be necessary to begin with this woman that odious warfare of which Derville had spoken to him, to enter upon a life of litigation, to find nourishment in gall, to drink each morning a cup of bitterness. Then, frightful thought, where was the money to be found to pay the expenses of the first suits? So great a disgust of life took possession of him that if there had been any water near him he would have thrown himself into it; if he had had any pistols he would have blown out his brains. Then he fell again into that uncertainty of ideas which, since his conversation with Derville at the house of the milk-dealer, had affected his mental faculties. Finally when he came to the kiosk he ascended into the little aërial cabinet through the rose windows of which could be seen each of the charming distant slopes of the valley, and where he found his wife seated in a chair. The countess was looking at the landscape and preserved a calm countenance, guarding that

impenetrable physiognomy which the women determined to dare all know how to assume.   She wiped
her eyes as if she had been weeping, and played
absently with the long pink ribbon of her girdle.
Nevertheless, despite her apparent assurance, she
could not repress a shudder when she saw before her
her venerable benefactor, upright, his arms crossed,
his face pale, his brow severe.

"Madame," he said, after having looked at her
fixedly for a moment and caused her to blush, "madame, I do not curse you, I despise you.   At present,
I thank the chance that has disunited us.   I do not
even feel a desire for vengeance, I no longer love
you.   I wish for nothing from you.   Live tranquilly
on the faith of my word, it is worth more than the
scrawlings of all the notaries in Paris.   I will never
claim again the name which I have perhaps made
illustrious.   I am no longer anything but a poor devil
named Hyacinthe, who asks for nothing but his
place in the sunshine.   Adieu—"

The countess threw herself at the colonel's feet
and endeavored to retain him by taking his hands,
but he repelled her with disgust, saying to her:

"Do not touch me."

The countess made an untranslatable gesture
when she heard the sound of her husband's footsteps die away.   Then, with the quick shrewdness
which is given by deep villainy or the ferocious
egotism of the world, she thought that she might
live in peace under the promise and the contempt
of this loyal soldier.

Chabert in fact disappeared. The milk-dealer failed and became a driver of a cabriolet. Perhaps the colonel took up at first with some vocation of the same kind. Perhaps, like a stone thrown into an abyss, he fell from cascade to cascade till he sank into that mud of rags which multiplies itself in the streets of Paris.

Six months after this event Derville, who had heard nothing more either of Colonel Chabert or of the Comtesse Ferraud, came to the conclusion that they had doubtless made some arrangement between themselves which in revenge the countess had had drawn up in some other office. Therefore, one morning he computed the sums advanced to the aforesaid Chabert, added the costs, and requested the Comtesse Ferraud to procure from Monsieur le Comte Chabert this amount, presuming that she was aware of the whereabouts of her first husband.

The very next day the intendant of the Comte Ferraud, recently appointed president of an inferior court of civil causes in an important city, wrote to Derville this heart-breaking message:

"MONSIEUR,

"Madame la Comtesse Ferraud requests me to notify you that your client completely abused your confidence, and that the individual who called himself the Comte Chabert has admitted having unlawfully assumed a false character,

"Accept, etc.,

"DELBECQ."

"There are to be met with people like this, upon
my word of honor! really too stupid.   They have
stolen the very baptism," cried Derville.   "Be then
humane, generous, philanthropic and an attorney,
and you will be taken in!   There is an affair which
has cost me more than two notes of a thousand
francs each."

Some time after the receipt of this letter, Derville
was looking in the Palais for an advocate to whom
he wished to speak and who practised in the court
of the correctional police.   Chance directed it so
that Derville entered the sixth court at the moment
when the president condemned as a vagabond a
prisoner named Hyacinthe to two months of prison,
and ordered that he should afterward be conducted
to the almshouse of Saint-Denis, a sentence which,
in the jurisprudence of the prefects of police, is
equivalent to a perpetual detention.   On hearing
the name of Hyacinthe, Derville looked at the cul-
prit seated on the prisoners' bench between two
gendarmes, and recognized in the condemned man
his false Colonel Chabert.

The old soldier was calm, motionless, almost absent-minded.   Notwithstanding his rags, notwithstanding the misery depicted upon his countenance,
it seemed to have assumed a noble pride.   His look
had an expression of stoicism which a magistrate
should not have misapprehended; but, as soon as a
man falls into the hands of justice, he is no longer
anything but a moral being, a question of law or of
fact, as in the eyes of the statisticians, he becomes

a figure. When the soldier was conducted back to
the register office to be later carried away with the
batch of vagabonds who were then being tried,
Derville, making use of the privilege of the attorneys to enter anywhere in the Palais, accompanied him to the register and looked at him for
several moments, as well as at the curious assembly
of beggars among whom he was placed. The antechamber of the register offered at this moment one
of those spectacles which unfortunately neither the
legislators, nor the philanthropists, nor the painters,
nor the writers, come to study.

Like all the laboratories of fraud, this antechamber
is a dark and evil-smelling apartment, the walls of
which are adorned by a wooden bench blackened by
the perpetual occupancy of the unfortunate who
come to this rendezvous of all the social miseries,
and at which not one of them is missing. A poet
would have said that the light was ashamed to
illuminate this terrible sewer through which pass so
many misfortunes! There is not a single place in
which is not seated some crime in the germ, or con-
summated; not a single spot in which might not be
met some man who, driven to despair by the slight
brand which justice had imprinted upon him for his
first fault, had entered upon an existence at the end
of which inevitably rose the guillotine, or exploded
the suicide's pistol. All those who fall on the
pavements of Paris are thrown against these yellow
walls, on which a philanthropist who was not a
speculator could decipher the justification of the

numberless suicides of which the hypocritical
writers complain, incapable of taking a step to prevent them, and which are written in this antechamber, a sort of prelude to the dramas of the
morgue or to those of the Place de Grève.

At this moment, Colonel Chabert was seated in
the midst of these men whose faces were marked by
strong expressions, clothed in the horrible livery of
misery, silent at intervals and when they did
speak, doing so in low voices, for three gendarmes
on duty walked up and down the room, making their
sabres clank on the floor.

"Do you recognize me?" said Derville to the old
soldier, placing himself before him.

"Yes, monsieur," replied Chabert, rising.

"If you are an honest man," Derville went on in
a low voice, "how have you been able to remain
my debtor?"

The old soldier reddened as might have done a
young girl accused by her mother of some clandes-
tine love.

"What! Madame Ferraud has not paid you?" he
cried aloud.

"Paid me?—" said Derville. "She wrote me
that you were an adventurer."

The colonel lifted his eyes by a sublime movement of horror and of imprecation, as if to appeal to
Heaven against this new deceit.

"Monsieur," he said in a voice grown calm
again, "procure from the gendarmes the favor of
allowing me to enter the register room, I will

sign for you a draft which will certainly be honored."

With a word from Derville to the brigadier, he was permitted to take his client into the registry, where Hyacinthe wrote a few lines addressed to the Comtesse Ferraud.

"Send that to her," said the soldier, "and you will be reimbursed for your expenses and your advances. Believe me, monsieur, if I have not testified to you the gratitude which I owe you for your good offices, it is none the less there," he said, laying his hand on his heart. "Yes, it is there, full and complete. But what can the unhappy do? They can love, that is all."

"How is it," said Derville to him, "that you did not stipulate for some income?"

"Do not speak to me of that!" replied the old soldier. "You cannot know to what depth descends my contempt for that outward life to which most men attach so much importance. I was suddenly seized with a malady, the disgust of humanity. When I think that Napoléon is at Saint Helena, everything here below is indifferent to me. I can no longer be a soldier, that is all my unhappiness. In short," he added, making a gesture like a child's, "it is better to have luxury in your sentiments than on your clothes. For myself I fear nobody's contempt."

And the colonel returned to his place on his bench.

Derville went out. When he returned to his office, he sent Godeschal, then his second clerk, to the house of the Comtesse Ferraud, who, on reading the note, caused to be paid immediately to the attorney the sum due him from the Comte Chabert.

In 1840, toward the end of the month of June, Godeschal, then an attorney, went with Derville, his predecessor, to Ris. When they arrived at the avenue which leads from the high road to Bicêtre, they perceived under one of the elms of the road, one of those old hoary and broken men who have obtained the baton of marshal of the mendicants, living at Bicêtre as the indigent females live at the Salpêtrière. This man, one of the two thousand unfortunates lodged in the hospital of the *Vieillesse*, was seated on a curbstone and appeared to be concentrating all his intelligence on an operation very familiar to these pensioners, and which consists in drying in the sun the tobacco of their snuffy handkerchiefs, perhaps to avoid bleaching them. This old man had an interesting countenance. He was clothed in that gown of reddish cloth which the hospital accords to its inmates, a sort of hideous livery.

"See, Derville," said Godeschal to his traveling companion, "look at that old man. Does he not resemble those queer grotesques that we get from Germany? And that is living, and that is perhaps happy!"

Derville took his eyeglass, looked at the pauper, made an involuntary gesture of surprise and said:

"That old man, my dear fellow, is a complete poem, or, as the romanticists say, a drama. Have you not occasionally met the Comtesse Ferraud—?"

"Yes, she is a clever woman and very agreeable; but a little too pious," said Godeschal.

"This old inmate of the Bicêtre is her legitimate husband, the Comte Chabert, the former colonel; she has doubtless placed him there. If he is in this asylum, instead of inhabiting a hôtel, it is solely because he recalled to the pretty Comtesse Ferraud that he had taken her, like a hackney coach, on the public street. I remember still the look of a tigress which she threw upon him at that moment."

This prelude having excited Godeschal's curiosity, Derville related to him the preceding history. Two days later, on the Monday morning, on returning to Paris, the two friends looked over at Bicêtre, and Derville proposed to go and see Colonel Chabert.

Halfway up the avenue they found the old man seated on the stump of a fallen tree, holding a stick in his hand and amusing himself by drawing lines in the sand. On looking at him closely, they perceived that he had been breakfasting elsewhere than in the establishment.

"Good day, Colonel Chabert," said Derville to him.

"Not Chabert! not Chabert! my name is Hyacinthe," replied the old man. "I am no longer a man, I am number 164, seventh ward," he added, looking at Derville with a timorous anxiety, with the fear of an old man and of a child. "You have come to see the man condemned to death?" he said, after a moment of silence. "He is not married, he! He is very fortunate."

15

"Poor man," said Godeschal. "Would you like some money to buy tobacco?"

The colonel held out his hand eagerly to each of the strangers, with all the ingenuousness of a Paris street Arab. They each gave him a twenty-franc piece, and he thanked them with a stupid look, saying:

"Brave troopers!"

He "carried arms" with his stick, feigned to take aim at them, and cried, smiling:

"Salute of two guns! *vive Napoléon!*"

And he described with his cane in the air an imaginary arabesque.

"The nature of his wound has made him fall into second childishness," said Derville.

"He a child!" cried an old Bicêtrian who was looking at them. "Ah! there are days when it is not safe to tread on his toes. He is a shrewd old fellow, full of philosophy and of imagination. But to-day, what can you expect! this is his Monday. Monsieur, in 1820, he was already here. At that time, a Prussian officer, whose calèche was ascending the hill Villejuif, came along on foot. We were, we two, Hyacinthe and I, on the roadside. This officer was talking as he walked with another, with a Russian, or some animal of that kind, and when he saw this old fellow, the Prussian, a sort of a gabbler, said to him, 'There is an old voltigeur who must have been at Rosbach.' 'I was too young to be there,' he answered promptly, but I was old enough to find myself at Jena. Whereupon the Prussian slunk off, without asking any more questions."

"What a destiny!" cried Derville. "Come out of a foundling asylum, he returns to die in an old men's home, after having, in the interval, aided Napoléon to conquer Egypt and Europe.—Do you know, my dear fellow," resumed Derville after a pause, "that there exist in our society three men, the priest, the doctor and the man of law, who can form no just estimate of the world? They wear black robes, perhaps because they wear mourning for all the virtues, all the illusions. The most unfortunate of them all is the attorney. When a man comes in search of the priest, he comes to him urged on by repentance, by remorse, by those beliefs which render him interesting, which enlarge him, and which bring some consolation to the soul of the mediator, whose task is not without a sort of enjoyment; he purifies, he repairs and reconciles. But, we attorneys, we see the same evil sentiments repeating themselves, nothing corrects them, our offices are sewers that cannot be cleansed. How many things have I not learned while practising my profession! I have seen a father die in a garret, without a sou or a stitch, abandoned by two daughters to whom he had given forty thousand francs of income! I have seen wills burned; I have seen mothers despoiling their children, husbands robbing their wives, wives killing their husbands by making use of the love which they inspired in them to render them foolish or imbecile, so that

they might live in peace with a lover. I have seen
women giving to a child by a first marriage tastes
and habits which would bring about its death, so as
to enrich a love-child. I cannot tell you all that I
have seen, for I have seen crimes against which
justice is powerless. In short, all the horrors which
the romancers have been able to invent, are still
below the truth. You are going to encounter all
these pretty things, yourself; for my part, I am
going to live in the country with my wife. Paris
fills me with horror.''

"I have already seen some of these things in
Desroches' office,'' replied Godeschal.

Paris, February-March, 1832.

THE INTERDICTION

DEDICATED TO
MONSIEUR THE REAR-ADMIRAL BAZOCHE,
GOVERNOR OF THE ISLE OF BOURBON,

By the grateful author,
DE BALZAC.

IN THE RUE DU FOUARRE.

"*You should dress yourself more warmly when you go down to that parlor.*"

"*I do not like to keep them waiting, those poor people! Well, what is it that you wish of me?*"

"*Why, I come to invite you to dinner to-morrow at the house of the Marquise d'Espard.*"

*   *   *   *   *   *   *

"*And you want me to go and dine with her! Are you crazy?*" *said the judge.*

THE INTERDICTION

*

In the year 1828, about one o'clock in the morning, two men came out of a hôtel in the Rue du Faubourg-Saint-Honoré, near the Elysée-Bourbon: one of them was a celebrated physician, Horace Bianchon, the other, one of the most elegant men in Paris, the Baron de Rastignac, and they were old friends. Each had dismissed his own carriage, and there were no others to be found in the Faubourg, but the night was fine and the pavement dry.

"Let us walk as far as the boulevard," said Eugène de Rastignac to Bianchon, "you can get a carriage at the Club; they are to be found there till morning. You will accompany me to my door."

"Willingly."

"Well, my dear fellow, what do you say about it?"

"About that woman?" replied the doctor, coldly.

"There I recognize my Bianchon," cried Rastignac.

"Well, what?"

"But, my dear fellow, you speak of the Marquise d'Espard as of a patient to be placed in your hospital."

"Do you wish to know what I think, Eugène? If you leave Madame de Nucingen for this marchioness, you will barter your one-eyed horse for a blind one."

"Madame de Nucingen is thirty-six years old, Bianchon."

"And this one is thirty-three," replied the doctor, quickly.

"Her most vindictive enemies would not make her more than twenty-six."

"My dear fellow, when you are interested in discovering a woman's age, look at her temples and the end of her nose. Whatever the women may accomplish with their cosmetics, they can do nothing against these incorruptible witnesses of their experiences. Each one of their years has left there its stigmata. When a woman's temples are softened, lined, withered in a certain manner; when at the end of her nose you may find those little points which resemble the imperceptible black particles which settle down in London from the chimneys in which soft coal is burned—by your leave! the lady is over thirty. She may be beautiful, she may be charming, she may be loving, she may be everything that you could wish; but she will have passed thirty, but she is reaching her maturity. I do not blame those who attach themselves to a woman of this kind; only, a man as distinguished as you are should not take a rennet of February for a little api apple which smiles upon its branch and asks to be bitten. Love never goes to consult the civil registers; no one loves a woman because she is of such or such an age, because she is beautiful or ugly, stupid or witty: one loves because one loves."

"Well now, I, I love her for very different reasons. She is Marquise d'Espard, she was born a Blamont-Chauvry, she is the fashion, she has a soul in her, she has a foot as pretty as that of the Duchesse de Berri, she has perhaps an income of a hundred thousand francs, and I shall perhaps marry her some day! finally, she will enable me to pay my debts."

"I thought you were rich," said Bianchon, interrupting Rastignac.

"Bah! I have an income of twenty thousand francs, just enough to keep a stable. I have been broken up, my dear fellow, in the affair of Monsieur de Nucingen, I will relate that history to you. I have married off my sisters, that is the greatest advantage I have gained since we have known each other, and I am better pleased to have established them than if I had a hundred thousand écus of income. Now then, what do you wish that I should become? I am ambitious. To what could Madame de Nucingen lead me? In a year from now, I should be labeled, pigeon-holed, like a married man. I have all the disadvantages of marriage and those of a bachelor, without having the advantages of either; a false situation, to which come all those who remain too long attached to the same petticoat."

"Ah! and you think that here you have a sure

thing?" said Bianchon. "Your marchioness, my
dear fellow, is not at all to my taste."

"Your liberal opinions cloud your judgment. If
Madame d'Espard were a Madame Rabourdin—."

"Listen to me, my dear fellow, noble or bour-
geoise, she would always be soulless, she would
always be the most complete type of egotism. Believe me, the doctors are accustomed to judge men
and things; the most skilful among us confess the
soul in confessing the body. Notwithstanding that
pretty boudoir in which we have passed the evening, notwithstanding the luxury of that hôtel, it is
possible that Madame la Marquise is in debt."

"What makes you think so?"

"I do not assert it, I make the supposition. She
speaks of her soul as the late Louis XVIII. spoke of
his heart. Listen to me! this woman, frail, white,
with her chestnut hair, and who complains that she
may hear herself pitied, enjoys a robust health,
has an appetite like a wolf, the strength and the
treachery of a tiger. Never was gauze, or silk, or
muslin, more skilfully wrapped around a lie! *Ecco.*"

"You terrify me, Bianchon! You have then
learned a great many things since our sojourn in
the Vauquer establishment?"

"Yes, since that time, my dear fellow, I have seen
puppets, dolls and dancing-jacks! I know a little
about the manners of these beautiful ladies, the
health of whose bodies you guard, and that which
they have still more precious, their children, when
they love them, and their faces, which they always

adore. You pass your nights at their bedsides, you wear yourself out to save them the slightest alteration of their beauty, no matter where; you have succeeded, you keep the secret as if you were dead, they send to you for their bill, and find it horribly dear. What is it that has saved them? Nature. Far from commending you, they slander you, fearing that you may become the physician of their dear friends. My dear fellow, these women, of whom you say, 'They are angels!' I, I have seen them stripped of the little appearances under which they cover their souls, as well as of the dress under which they disguise their imperfections, without their manners and without their corsets,—they are not beautiful. We began by seeing a great many shoals, a great many filthy things under the waves of the world when we were cast ashore on the rock of the Vauquer establishment; that which we saw there was nothing. Since I have been going into the higher society, I have encountered monstrosities clothed in satins, Michonneaus in white gloves, Poirets bespangled with orders, grand seigneurs practising usury better than Papa Gobseck! To the shame of mankind, when I have wished to clasp hands with Virtue, I have found her shivering in a garret, pursued by slander, living from hand to mouth on fifteen hundred francs of income or of wages, and considered either as crazy, or original, or stupid. In short, my dear fellow, the marchioness is a fashionable woman, and it is precisely that kind of woman that I hold in horror.

Do you wish to know why? A woman who has
a lofty mind, a pure taste, a gentle spirit, a heart
richly endowed, who leads a simple life, has not
the slightest chance of being in the fashion.   That
is why!   A fashionable woman and a man in
power have certain analogies; but with this difference nearly, that the qualities which enable a man
to elevate himself above the others enlarge him and
constitute his glory; whilst the qualities by which
a woman attains her empire of a day are frightful
vices: she perverts herself to conceal her character,
she must—to lead this contentious worldly life—
have an iron health under a frail appearance.   As
a physician, I know that the goodness of the stomach
excludes the goodness of the heart.   Your fashionable woman has no feeling, her fury for pleasure
has its origin in a desire to warm up her cold nature,
she wishes to have emotions and enjoyments, just
as an old man stations himself on the stairway at
the Opéra.   As she has more head than heart, she
sacrifices to her triumph true passions and her
friends, as a general sends into the enemy's fire his
most devoted lieutenants that he may gain the battle.   The fashionable woman is no longer a woman;
she is neither mother, nor wife, nor lover,—she has
a sex in her brain, speaking medically.   Thus your
marchioness has all the symptoms of her monstros-
ity, she has the beak of a bird of prey, the clear and
cold eye, the soft speech; she is polished like the
steel of a piece of machinery, she excites everything, excepting the heart."

"There is some truth in what you say, Bianchon."

"Some truth?" replied Bianchon. "It is all true. Do you think that I did not feel to the bottom of my heart the insulting politeness with which she caused me to measure the imaginary distance which rank puts between us? that I was not moved by a profound contempt for her cattish blandishments in knowing her aim? In a year from now, she would not write a word to do me the slightest service, and this evening she overwhelmed me with smiles, thinking that I can influence my uncle Popinot, on whom the gaining of her lawsuit depends—"

"My dear fellow, would you have preferred that she had shown you nothing but stupidities? I admit the facts of your Catiline oration against fashionable women; but you are quite beside the question. I should always prefer for a wife a Marquise d'Espard to the most chaste, the most refined, the most loving creature on earth. Marry an angel! you would have to go and bury yourself in your happiness in the depths of the country. The wife of a political man is a governmental machine, a mechanism for fine compliments, for curtsies; she is the first, the most faithful of the instruments of which an ambitious man can make use; in short, she is a friend who can compromise herself without danger, and whom you can repudiate without fear of consequences. Suppose Mohammed were in Paris in the nineteenth century! his wife would be a Rohan, fine and flattering as an ambassadress, shrewd as Figaro. Your loving wife would lead to nothing, a

fashionable woman would lead to everything, she
is the diamond with which a man cuts all window
panes, when he has not the golden key which opens
all doors.   For the bourgeois, the bourgeois virtues;
for the ambitious, the vices of ambition.   Moreover,
my dear fellow, do you not suppose that the love of
a Duchesse de Langeais or De Maufrigneuse, of a
Lady Dudley, does not bring with it immense
pleasures? If you knew how the cold and severe
reserve of these women gives a value to the least
proof of their affection! what joy to see a periwinkle
lying under the snow!   A smile glancing under the
fan gives the lie to the reserve of an assumed attitude, and it is worth all the unbridled tendernesses
of your bourgeoises with their hypothetical devotion,
—for, in love, devotion is very near to speculation.
Then, a fashionable woman, a Blamont-Chauvry
has her virtues also!   Her virtues are fortune,
power, state, a certain scorn for everything which
is below her—"

"Thanks," said Bianchon.

"You old simpleton!" answered Rastignac, laughing.   "Come now, do not be commonplace, do like
your friend Desplein,—be a baron, be a Chevalier
of the Order of Saint Michael, become peer of France,
and marry your daughters to dukes."

"I, I wish that the five hundred thousand
devils—"

"La, la! you have no superiority then excepting
in medicine; truly you give me great pain."

"I hate this sort of people, I could wish for a

revolution that would deliver us from them forever."

"Therefore, dear Robespierre of the lancet, you
will not go to-morrow to your uncle Popinot's?"

"Oh! yes," said Bianchon, "when you are concerned, I would go to seek water in hell—"

"Dear friend, you melt me; I have sworn that
the marquis should be interdicted! Wait a minute,
I shall find an old tear with which to thank you."

"But," said Horace, continuing, "I do not promise
you to succeed according to your desires with Jean-
Jules Popinot. You do not know him; but I will bring
him the day after to-morrow to your marchioness,
she may beguile him if she can. I doubt it. All the
truffles, all the duchesses, all the mistresses, all the
axes of the guillotine may be there in all the grace
of their seductions; the king may promise him the
peerage, the good God may grant him the investi-
ture of Paradise and the revenues of Purgatory,—
not one of these inducements would persuade him
to pass a straw from one scale to the other of his
balance. He is a judge, as Death is Death."

The two friends had by this time arrived at the
entrance of the Ministry of Foreign Affairs, at the
corner of the Boulevard des Capucines.

"Here you are at your door," said Bianchon,
laughing, indicating to him the hôtel of the minister.
"And here is my carriage," he added, pointing to a
hackney coach. "Thus is the future summed up
for both of us."

"You will be happy at the bottom of the sea,
16

while I shall be always struggling on the surface
with the tempests until, when I sink, I shall come
to ask a place too in your grotto, old friend!"

"Till Saturday," replied Bianchon.

"Agreed," said Rastignac. "You promise me
the Popinot?"

"Yes, I will do all that my conscience will permit
me to do. Perhaps this petition for an interdiction
conceals some little *dramorama*, to recall by a word
our bad good time."

"Poor Bianchon! he will never be more than an
honest man," said Rastignac to himself, as he saw
the hackney coach disappear.

"Rastignac has charged me with the most difficult
of all the negotiations," thought Bianchon when he
rose the next morning, remembering the delicate
commission which had been confided to him. "But
I have never asked of my uncle the least little service at the Palais, and I have made for him more
than a thousand visits *gratis*. Moreover, between
ourselves, we feel no restraint. He will answer me
yes or no, and that will be all."

After this little monologue, the celebrated doctor
took his way, after seven o'clock in the morning,
towards the Rue du Fouarre, in which lived Monsieur Jean-Jules Popinot, judge of the inferior court
for civil causes of the department of the Seine.
The Rue du Fouarre, a name which signified formerly
Rue de la Paille, was in the thirteenth century the
most illustrious street in Paris. In it were the
schools of the University at the period when the

voice of Abelard and that of Gerson resounded through the world of learning. It is to-day one of the dirtiest streets of the twelfth arrondissement, the poorest quarter of Paris, that in which two-thirds of the population lack for wood in winter, that which throws most brats into the turning-box of the Foundling Hospital, most patients into the Hôtel-Dieu, most beggars into the streets, which sends the greatest number of rag-pickers to the corners of the gutters, the greatest number of invalid old men to sun themselves along the walls, the greatest number of unemployed workmen into the public squares, the greatest number of accused to the correctional police. In the middle of this always damp street, the gutter of which rolls toward the Seine the blackish waters of some dyeing establishments, is situated an old house, doubtless restored under François I., and constructed of bricks retained by quoins of cut stone. Its solidity seems to be attested by an exterior configuration which is not uncommon in some houses in Paris. If it be permitted to make use of the word, it has something like a belly produced by the swelling out of its first story, sinking under the weight of the second and the third, but sustained by the strong wall of the ground floor. At the first glance it would seem that the spaces between the windows, although strengthened by their borders in cut stone, would burst out; but the spectator soon perceives that, in this house as in the tower of Bologna, the old bricks and the old stones worn away still preserve invincibly their centre of

gravity.   At all seasons of the year, the solid courses
of the ground floor present the yellowish tone and
the imperceptible oozing which dampness gives to
stone.   The pedestrian has a chill in passing along
this wall the sloping edges of which protect it but
indifferently against the wheels of the cabriolets.
As in all the houses built before the invention of
carriages, the opening of the door forms an extremely
low archway, similar enough to the portal of a
prison.   At the right of this doorway are three
windows protected on the exterior by an iron net-
ting so close that it is impossible for the curious to
see the interior arrangement of the damp and dark
apartments, all the more so that the window panes
are dirty and dusty; at the left are two other windows like these, one of which, sometimes open, reveals the porter, his wife and his children swarming
about, working, cooking, eating and crying in an
apartment floored with planks, wainscoted, in which
everything is falling off in shreds and into which you
descend by two steps,—a depth which seems to indicate the progressive raising of the Parisian pavement.   If, on some rainy day, some passer-by
takes shelter under the long vault with protecting
and whitewashed rafters, which leads from the door
to the stairway, it would be difficult for him not to
look in on the scene which the interior of this house
presents.   At the left will be seen a little square
garden which would not permit you to make more
than four strides in any direction, a garden of black
earth in which there are trellises without any vine

branches, in which, in default of vegetation, there are in the shade of the two trees scraps of paper, old cloths, potsherds, rubbish fallen from the roof; an unfertile land in which time has deposited upon the walls, upon the trunks of the trees and their boughs, a powdery substance not unlike cold soot. The two square main buildings which constitute the house are lighted from this little garden, surrounded by the two neighboring houses built with upright joists in the partitions, decrepit, menacing ruin, in which may be seen on each floor some curious indication of the profession or vocation of the lodger. Here, there are long sticks supporting immense skeins of dyed wool drying; there, on a cord, are white shirts hanging; higher, rows of books newly backed display upon a board their freshly marbled edges; the women sing, the husbands whistle, the children cry; the cabinet-maker saws his planks, a coppersmith makes his metal resound,—all these industries combine to produce a noise which the number of instruments renders outrageous. The general system of the interior decoration of this passage, which is neither a court, nor a garden, nor a vault, and which partakes of all these, consists of wooden pillars supported upon square pedestals of stone and which form ogive arches. Two arcades open on the little garden; two others, which face the porte-cochère, allow a wooden stairway to be seen, the rail of which was formerly a marvel of ironsmith's work, so grotesque are the forms given to the metal, and of which the worn steps now

shake under foot.   The doors of each apartment
have casings brown with dirt, with grease and with
dust, and are furnished with double doors covered
with Utrecht velvet fastened with nails disposed in
lozenges and which have lost their gilding.   These
remnants of splendor announce that under Louis
XIV., this house was inhabited by some councillor
of Parliament, by rich ecclesiastics, or by some State
treasurer.   But these vestiges of ancient luxury now
bring a smile to the lips by the ingenuous contrast
which they offer between the present and the past.
Monsieur Jean-Jules Popinot lived on the first floor
of this house, where the want of light natural to
the first floors of Parisian houses was doubled by
the narrowness of the street.   This ancient dwelling
was known to the whole of the twelfth arrondissement, to whom Providence had given this magistrate
as it gives a beneficent plant to cure or to moderate
every malady.   Here is a sketch of this personage
whom the brilliant Marquise d'Espard wished to
seduce:

In his character as magistrate, Monsieur Popinot
was always clothed in black, a costume which contributed toward rendering him ridiculous in the eyes
of those accustomed to judge everything by a superficial examination.   Men who are jealous to preserve the dignity which this vestment imposes
should be able to submit to the most minute and
continual carefulness; but the dear Monsieur Popinot
was incapable of maintaining upon himself the Puritanical cleanliness which black requires.   His

pantaloons, always well worn, resembled crape, a stuff of which the robes of advocates are made, and his habitual attitude caused such a multitude of creases in them that there might be seen in places lines whitish, reddish or shining which revealed either a sordid avarice or the most heedless poverty. His heavy woolen stockings puckered in his shapeless shoes. His linen had that rusty tone which is contracted by a long sojourn in the wardrobe, and which announced that the late Madame Popinot had a certain mania for linen; according to the Flemish method, she doubtless gave herself only twice a year the trouble of a washing with lye. The coat and the waistcoat of the magistrate were in harmony with the pantaloons, the shoes, the stockings and the linen. He found a constant success in his carelessness, for, the very day on which he put on a new coat he brought it into appropriateness with the rest of his toilet by getting spots upon it with an inexplicable promptness. The good man waited until his cook apprised him of the shabbiness of his hat before procuring a new one. His cravat was always twisted without any preparation whatever, and never did he repair the disorder which his judge's band had occasioned in his tumbled shirt collar. He took no care of his gray hair, and shaved only twice a week. He never wore gloves, and buried his hands habitually in his empty pockets, the soiled openings of which, nearly always torn, added one trait the more to the negligence of his person. Anyone who has frequented the Palais de

Justice at Paris, a locality in which may be observed all the varieties of black garments, may readily imagine the style of Monsieur Popinot. The habit of sitting for entire days produces material changes in the bodily conformation, just as the weariness caused by the interminable pleadings affects the physiognomy of the magistrates. Enclosed in the ridiculously narrow court rooms, with no majesty of architecture and in which the air is speedily vitiated, the Parisian judge assumes through compulsion a frowning visage, aged by close attention, saddened through weariness; his complexion bleaches, contracts greenish or earthy tints according to his individual temperament. In short, within a given time, the most flourishing young man becomes a pale machine of *whereases*, a mechanism applying the Code to every possible case with the imperturbability of the fly wheels of a clock. If then, Nature had not endowed Monsieur Popinot with a very agreeable exterior, the magistracy had not embellished it. The scaffolding of his bodily frame presented many angles. His big knees, his great feet, his large hands, contrasted with a sacerdotal countenance which vaguely resembled a calf's head, mild to insipidity, badly lighted by mismatched, bloodless eyes, divided by a nose straight and flat, surmounted by a forehead without any protuberance, decorated by two immense ears which waved without any grace. His thin and scanty locks allowed his skull to be seen through several irregular openings. A single feature recommended this countenance to the physiognomist. This man had a mouth the lips of which breathed a divine kindliness. They were good, thick lips, red, with a thousand wrinkles, sinuous, mobile, in which Nature had expressed beautiful sentiments; lips which spoke to the heart and revealed in this man intelligence, perspicacity, the gift of second sight, an angelic spirit;—so that you would have comprehended him very badly by judging him only by his depressed forehead, his eyes without warmth and his pitiful carriage. His life corresponding with his physiognomy, it was filled with secret labors and concealed the virtue of a saint. Exhaustive legal studies had so well recommended him that, when Napoléon reorganized the administration of justice in 1806 and 1811, in accordance with the advice of Cambacérès, he was selected as one of the first to preside in the imperial court at Paris. Popinot was nothing of a self-seeker. At each new emergency, at each new solicitation, the minister pushed Popinot back a step,—he never set foot either within the doors of the high-chancellor or those of the chief justice. From the court, he was transferred to the rolls of the tribunals, then pushed gradually down to the last round of the ladder by the intrigues of active and stirring competitors. He was finally named assistant judge! A general outcry rose in the Palais: "Popinot assistant judge!" This injustice roused the judicial world, the advocates, the bailiffs, everybody excepting Popinot, who made no complaint at all. The first

clamor over, everyone found that all was for the best
in the best of all possible worlds, which certainly
should be the judicial world. Popinot was assistant
judge up to the days on which the most celebrated
Keeper of the Seals of the Restoration avenged the
injustices done to this noblest and silent man by the
chief justices of the Empire. After having been
assistant judge for twelve years, Monsieur Popinot
was doubtless going to die as a simple judge of the
tribunal of the Seine.

In order to explain the obscure destiny of one of
the superior men in the judiciary order, it is necessary here to enter into some considerations which
will serve to unveil his life, his character, and
which will show, moreover, some of the wheels
within wheels of that great machine that is called
Justice. Monsieur Popinot was classified by the
three presidents who presided successively over the
tribunal of the Seine in a category of *jugerie*—jurisdiction of a judge, his province,—the only word
which can express the desired idea. He did not
obtain in this company the reputation for capacity
to which his works had entitled him in advance.
In the same way that a painter is invariably included in the category of landscapists, portraitists,
historical, marine, or genre painters, by the public of the artists, the connoisseurs or the idiots,
who through envy, through critical omnipotence,
through prejudice, confine him in his intelligence,
believing, all, that there exist calli in all brains,
—a narrowness of judgment which the world

applies to writers, to statesmen, to all those who commence by a specialty before being proclaimed universal; in this same manner, Popinot arrived at his destination and was enclosed in his class. The magistrates, the advocates, the attorneys, all those who pasture in the judicial field, distinguish two elements in a lawsuit,—law and equity. The equity results from the facts, the law is the application of principles to the facts. A man may be right in equity, wrong in justice, without the judge being accusable. Between the conscience and the action there is a world of determining reasons which are unknown to the judge, and which condemn or justify the action. A judge is not God, his duty is to adapt facts to principles, to judge cases infinitely varied by making use of a determinate standard. If the judge had the power of reading the conscience and distinguishing the motives so as to render equitable judgments, each judge would be a great man. France requires about six thousand judges; no one generation has six thousand great men at its service, for the best of reasons it cannot find them, then, for its magistracy. Popinot was in the midst of the Parisian civilization a very skilful cadi, who, by the nature of his mind and through having thoroughly rubbed the letter of the law into the spirit of facts, had recognized the defect of wilful and violent applications. Aided by his judicial second sight, he pierced the envelope of double falsehoods in which the lawyers conceal the inner facts of the cases. A judge, as the illustrious Desplein was a surgeon, he penetrated the consciences as that learned man penetrated the bodies. His life and his habits had led him to the exact appreciation of the most secret thoughts by the examination of the facts. He delved into a case as Cuvier turned over the mould of the earth. Like that great thinker, he proceeded from deduction to deduction before coming to a conclusion, and reproduced the past of the conscience as Cuvier reconstructed an anoplo-therium. When it was a case of a report, he often woke up suddenly in the night, surprised by a gleam of truth which suddenly revealed itself in his thoughts. Struck by the profound injustice which characterizes these contests in which everything disserves the honest man, in which everything is in favor of the rogue, he often decided against the law and in favor of equity in all causes in which there were questions the truth of which might in some manner be divined. He therefore passed among his colleagues as sufficiently unpractical, his reasons, doubly deduced, moreover prolonged the delibera-tions; when Popinot remarked their unwillingness to listen to him, he gave his opinion briefly. It was said that he was but an indifferent judge in these cases; but, as he had a striking genius of apprecia-tion, as his judgment was lucid and his penetration profound, he was regarded as possessing a special aptitude for the dreary functions of *juge d'instruc-tion.** He remained therefore juge d'instruction

*Juge d'instruction—magistrate charged with the preliminary examination of the accused.—NOTE BY TRANSLATOR.

during the greater part of his judicial life.   Although his qualifications rendered him eminently fitted for this difficult position, and although he had the rep-utation of being a profound criminalist who found pleasure in his functions, the kindness of his heart kept him constantly in torture, and he was held be-tween his conscience and his pity as in a vise. Although better recompensed than those of *juge civil,* the functions of juge d'instruction would tempt no one; they are too slavish and confining.   Popinot, a man of modesty and of honest erudition, without ambition, an indefatigable worker, did not complain of his condition; he sacrificed to the public good his tastes, his compassion, and allowed himself to be deported into the lagunes of criminal examination, where he was able to be at once severe and benev-olent.   Sometimes his clerk of the court conveyed to the accused money for the purchase of tobacco, or for a warm garment in winter, in conducting him back from the judge's rooms to the Souricière, a temporary prison in which the accused are held at the disposition of the juge d'instruction.   He knew how to be at once an inflexible judge and a chari-table man.   Thus no one could obtain more readily than he, full confessions without resorting to any of the judicial machinery.   He had, moreover, all the shrewdness of a keen observer.   This man of an apparently silly goodness, simple and absent-minded, detected the tricks of the Crispins of the galleys, outwitted the most cunning of jades, and made the scoundrels tremble.   Very unusual circumstances

had sharpened his perspicacity; but, to relate them,
it is necessary to penetrate into his inward life; for
the judge was with him the social side; another
man, greater and less known, was to be found in
him.

Twelve years before the day on which this history
commences, in 1816, at the time of that terrible
scarcity which coincided fatally with the sojourn of
the so-called allies in France, Popinot was appointed
president of the extraordinary commission instituted
to distribute supplies to the poor of his quarter, at
the moment when he was proposing to abandon
the Rue du Fouarre, residence in which was no less
displeasing to him than to his wife.   This grand
jurisconsult, this profound criminalist, in whom
superiority seemed to his colleagues an aberration,
had for the last five years perceived judicial results
without discovering their causes.   In ascending into
garrets, in observing distress, in studying the cruel
necessities which gradually conduct the poor to
reprehensible actions, in measuring, in short, their
long struggles, he was filled with compassion.   This
judge became then the Saint Vincent de Paul of
these grown-up children, of these suffering workers.
His transformation was not complete at once.   Benevolence may be led along gradually, like the vices.
Charity empties the purse of a saint, as roulette
devours the gambler's wealth, gradually.   Popinot
went from misfortune to misfortune, from one alms-
giving to another; then, when he had lifted all
the rags which serve for this public misery as a

dressing under which festers a feverish wound, he
became, at the end of a year, the Providence of his
quarter. He was a member of the committee of
benevolence and of the bureau of charity. Everywhere that his gratuitous functions were to be exercised, he accepted them and performed them without
ostentation, after the manner of the *man with the
little cloak,** who passes his life in carrying soups
into the markets and into localities where the
famished are to be found. Popinot had the happiness to act within a larger circumference and in
a more elevated sphere;—he surveyed everything,
he prevented crime, he gave employment to idle
workmen, he found situations for the helpless, he
distributed his assistance with discernment at all
the threatened points, constituted himself the ad-
viser of the widow, the protector of homeless
children, the silent partner in small commercial
affairs. No one at the Palais or in Paris knew
anything of this secret life of Popinot. There are
virtues so brilliant that they permit of concealment;
men hasten to put them under a bushel. As to
those aided by the magistrate, all of them, working
during the day and fatigued at night, were but little
likely to sound his praises; they had all the in-
gratitude of children, who can never repay because
they owe too much. There are unnatural ingrati-
tudes; but what heart can sow good in order to
harvest gratitude and believe itself great? In the

**Homme au petit manteau bleu*—popular name given a celebrated philanthro-
pist named Champion, born in 1764, died in 1852.—NOTE BY TRANSLATOR.

second year of his secret apostleship, Popinot had ended by converting the ground floor of his house into a charity bureau, lit by the three windows with iron gratings. The walls and the ceiling of this large apartment had been whitewashed, and the furniture consisted of wooden benches, like those of the schools, of a cheap wardrobe, a walnut desk and an armchair. In the wardrobe were his charity registers, his models for bread-tickets, his day-book. He kept his accounts in a business-like manner, so as not to be the dupe of his own virtue. All the distresses of the quarter were figured, set down in a book in which each misfortune had its own account, like a merchant's debtors on his books. When he had doubts about a family, concerning a man to be helped, the magistrate found at his command the information of the detective police. Lavienne, a domestic made for his master, was his aide-de-camp. He withdrew or renewed the pledges in the pawn shops, and explored the most threatening localities while his master was occupied at the Palais. From four to seven o'clock in the morning in summer, from six to nine o'clock in winter, this apartment was full of women, of children, of the poor, to whom Popinot gave hearings. There was no need of a stove in winter,—the crowd thronged so thickly that the atmosphere became warm; but Lavienne spread some straw on the too-damp pavement. In the end, the benches became as polished as mahogany varnished; also up to the height of a man, the wall received an indescribable dusky painting, applied by the rags and the dilapidated garments of the poor. These unfortunates loved Popinot so much that, when, before the opening of his door, they had gathered there in the winter mornings, the women warming themselves with foot warmers, the men slapping their arms for the same purpose, there was never a murmur to trouble his slumber. The rag-pickers, the night wanderers, knew this dwelling, and often saw the magistrate's cabinet lit up at unseasonable hours. Even the thieves said in passing it: "That is his house," and respected it. His mornings were devoted to the poor, the middle of his day to the criminals, the evenings to judicial labors.

The genius of observation that had taken possession of Popinot was then necessarily *Bifrons*,*—he felt instinctively the virtues of poverty, the good sentiments frustrated, the fine actions conceived, the unknown devotions, as he sought in the depths of consciences the slightest traces of crime, the most delicate threads of misdemeanors, so as to discern all. The Popinot patrimony was worth a thousand écus of income. His wife, the sister of Monsieur Bianchon the father, doctor at Sancerre, had brought him twice as much. She had been dead for five years, and had left her fortune to her husband. As the salary of an assistant judge is not considerable, and as Popinot had not been a judge on full pay for

---

Bifrons—a demon who, when he assumes the human form, instructs his disciple in astrology and in the influence of the planets; he excels in geometry and knows the virtues of herbs, plants and precious stones.—NOTE BY TRANSLATOR.

17

but four years, it is easy to guess the reason of his
parsimony in all that concerned his own person or
daily life, considering the mediocrity of his revenue
and the extent of his charity.   Moreover, the indifference as to garments, which in Popinot indicated
the preoccupied man, is it not the distinctive mark
of a lofty science, of art cultivated furiously, of a
mind perpetually active?   To complete this portrait, it will suffice to add that Popinot was of the
very small number of judges of the tribunal of the
Seine to whom the decoration of the Legion of Honor
had not been given.

Such was the man whom the president of the
second chamber of the tribunal—to which Popinot
belonged, he having re-entered within the last two
years among the *juges civils*—had commissioned to
proceed to the examination of the Marquis d'Espard,
upon the petition presented by his wife in order to
obtain an interdiction.

The Rue du Fouarre, where so many unfortunates
swarmed in the early morning, became deserted
at nine o'clock and resumed its sombre and poverty-
stricken aspect.   Bianchon therefore hastened his
horse's trot, so that he might catch his uncle in the
midst of his audience.   He did not think without a
smile of the strange contrast which the judge would
produce by the side of Madame d'Espard; but he
promised himself to persuade him to assume a costume that would not render him too absurd.

"If my uncle has only a new coat?" said Bianchon to himself as he entered the Rue du Fouarre,

in which the windows of the charity bureau emitted a pale light. "I should do better, I imagine, to consult Lavienne on that point."

At the sound of the cabriolet, some ten poor people issued from under the porch in surprise and uncovered when they recognized the doctor; for Bianchon, who gratuitously attended the sick recommended to him by the judge, was not less well known than he to the unfortunates there assembled. Bianchon perceived his uncle in the midst of his bureau, the benches of which were, in fact, filled by the indigent who presented such grotesque singularities of apparel that the least artistic of passersby would have stopped in the middle of the street to look. Certainly, a designer, a Rembrandt, if there existed such a one in our day, would have there found material for one of his most magnificent compositions in seeing these miseries, frankly presented and silent. Here, the wrinkled countenance of an austere old man with a white beard, an apostolic head, presented a Saint Peter already made. His chest, partially uncovered, allowed the swelling muscles to be seen, the indications of a temperament of bronze which had served him for a base of resistance to sustain an epic of misfortune. There, a young woman was nursing her youngest child, that he might not cry, while holding another, of about five years, between her knees. This breast, the whiteness of which made a brilliant spot in the midst of the rags, this infant with its transparent skin, and its brother, whose attitude revealed the

gamin of the future, affected the sympathies by a
sort of half gracious opposition to the long line of
figures reddened by the cold in the midst of which
this family appeared. Farther on, an old woman,
pale and cold, presented that repulsive face of
pauperism in revolt, ready to take vengeance on
some day of sedition for all its past pains. There
was to be found also the young workman, debili-
tated, indolent, in whom the intelligent eye revealed
superior faculties repressed by necessities vainly
struggled against, silent under suffering, and in
peril of death for want of an opportunity to gain
entrance into that immense enclosure in which
struggle all those self-devouring miseries. The
women were in the majority; their husbands, gone
off to their workshops, had doubtless left to them the
charge of pleading the household cause with that
lively intelligence that characterizes the wife of the
poor, nearly always the queen in her own hovel.
You might have seen on all the heads, torn handkerchiefs, on all the bodies, dresses bordered with mud,
fichus in rags, jackets dirty and full of holes, but
everywhere eyes which glittered like so many living
flames. A horrible gathering, of which the aspect at
first inspired disgust, but which soon caused a kind
of terror as you came to perceive that the resignation, purely fortuitous, of these souls grappling with
all the daily necessities of life, was merely specu-
lating upon charity. The two candles which lit the
apartment flickered in a kind of fog caused by the
ill-smelling atmosphere of this badly-aired space.

The magistrate was not the least picturesque personage in this assembly. He had on his head a reddish cotton cap. As he was without a cravat, his neck, red with cold and wrinkled, showed itself plainly over the threadbare collar of his old dressing-gown. His weary countenance presented the semi-stupid appearance caused by absorbed attention. His mouth, like that of all those who work, was tightened like a purse of which the drawing-string is pulled. His contracted forehead seemed to support the burden of all the confidences which were made to him,—he felt, analyzed, and judged. As attentive as a usurer over his petty loans, his eyes left his books and his notes to penetrate to the innermost conscience of the applicants, whom he examined with the quickness of glance by which the avaricious express their disquietude. Standing behind his master, ready to execute his orders, Lavienne doubtless represented the police, and welcomed the newcomers, encouraging them to overcome their own bashfulness. When the doctor appeared, there was a general movement on the benches. Lavienne turned his head and was strangely surprised to see Bianchon.

"Ah! you here, my boy," said Popinot, stretching his arms. "What brings you here at this hour?"

"I feared that you would not make to-day, unless you saw me, a certain judicial visit concerning which I wish to see you."

"Well," resumed the judge, addressing a stout

little woman who was standing near him, "if you
do not tell me what is the matter with you, my
girl, I cannot guess it."

"Hurry up," said Lavienne to her, "do not take
up the time of others."

"Monsieur," said the woman finally, reddening
and lowering her voice so as not to be heard but by
Popinot and Lavienne, "I am a huckster, and I have
my last little one for whom I owe the nurse her
monthly wages.   Then, I hid my poor little
money—"

"Well, your husband took it?" said Popinot,
divining the termination of the confession.

"Yes, monsieur."

"What is your name?"

"La Pomponne."

"Your husband's?"

"Toupinet."

"Rue du Petit-Banquier?" resumed Popinot,
turning over the leaves of his register.   "He is in
prison," he said, reading a note on the margin of
the leaf on which the case of this household was
inscribed.

"For debt, my dear monsieur."

Popinot shook his head.

"But, monsieur, I have nothing with which to fill
my hand-cart, the landlord came yesterday and made
me pay him; otherwise, I should have been put out
on the street."

Lavienne leaned toward his master and said some
words to him in his ear.

"Well, how much do you need to buy your fruit at the market?"

"Why, my dear monsieur, I should need, to go on with my business, about—yes, I should certainly need ten francs."

The judge made a sign to Lavienne, who drew from a large bag ten francs and gave them to the woman, while the judge set down the loan in his register.   By the involuntary movement of joy which agitated her, Bianchon divined the anxieties which had tormented this woman on her way from her own house to the judge's.

"Your turn," said Lavienne to the old man with the white beard.

Bianchon drew the valet to one side, and asked him how long this audience would require.

"Monsieur has had two hundred persons this morning, and here are still eighty *to do*," said Lavienne; "Monsieur le Docteur will have time to make his first calls."

"My boy," said the judge, turning and seizing Horace by the arm, "see here, here are two addresses not far away,—one, Rue de Seine, and the other, Rue de l'Arbalète.   Run around there.   In the Rue de Seine, a young girl has asphyxiated herself, and you will find in the Rue de l'Arbalète a man to send to your hospital.   I will expect you at déjeuner."

Bianchon returned at the expiration of an hour. The Rue du Fouarre was deserted, the day was beginning to break, his uncle had remounted to his apartments, the last poor wretch whose misery had been soothed by the magistrate had gone away, Lavienne's bag was empty.

"Well, how are they getting on?" said the judge to the doctor as he mounted the steps.

"The man is dead," replied Bianchon, "the young girl will recover."

Ever since it had lost the supervising eye and hand of a woman, the apartment in which Popinot lived had assumed an aspect that harmonized with its master's. The carelessness of a man constantly preoccupied by one over-mastering thought left its curious seal on everything. Everywhere an inveterate dust, everywhere in the objects those changes from their original purpose the ingenuity of which recalled those of bachelor apartments. There were papers thrust into the flower vases, empty ink bottles on the furniture, forgotten plates, phosphorus boxes converted into candlesticks at the moment when it was necessary to search for something, partial takings down and packings up, commenced and forgotten; in short, all the accumulations and the emptyings caused by the abandonment of all thought of arrangement. But the magistrate's cabinet, especially stirred up by this incessant disorder, revealed his ceaseless action, the constant preoccupation of a man overwhelmed by affairs, pursued by conflicting necessities. The library was as if pillaged, the books were scattered about, some of them with their backs thrust into the open pages of others, some fallen face downward on the floor; the legal documents arranged in a row, through the greater part of the library, encumbered the floor. This floor had not been waxed for two years. The tables and the furniture were laden with the *ex-votos* brought by grateful poverty. Upon the cornucopias in blue glass which ornamented the chimney-piece were two glass globes, filled with various colors mingled together which gave them the appearance of some curious product of nature. Bouquets of artificial flowers, drawings in which the Popinot monogram was surrounded by hearts and immortelles, decorated the walls. Here, were boxes in cabinet work, pretentiously made, and which served for nothing. There, were paper-weights, manufactured in the style of those articles executed by convicts in the galleys. These masterpieces of patience, these *rebuses* of gratitude, these dried-up bouquets, gave to the judge's cabinet and chamber the air of a shop of children's playthings. The good man made *mementos* of these works, he filled them with notes, with forgotten pens, and with pieces of paper. These sublime testimonials of a divine charity were filled with dust, without freshness. A few birds, perfectly stuffed but devoured by worms, figured among this wilderness of trifles over which presided an Angora, Madame Popinot's favorite cat, which a naturalist without a sou had restored with all the appearance of life, repaying thus a slight alms with an eternal treasure. Some artist of the quarter whose heart had led his brushes astray, had also executed the portraits of Monsieur

and of Madame Popinot.   Even into the alcove of
the bedchamber there penetrated the embroidered
pincushions, the landscape made in needlework
and the crosses in folded paper, the twisting of
which revealed a senseless amount of labor.   The
curtains of the windows were blackened by smoke,
and the draperies had lost all their color.   Between
the fireplace and the large square table at which the
magistrate sat, the cook had served two cups of
coffee with milk on a small table.   Two mahogany armchairs upholstered in horse-hair waited
for the uncle and his nephew.

As the daylight, intercepted by the window panes,
did not penetrate thus far, the cook had left two
candles burning, the immeasurably long wicks of
which had formed "thieves" and threw out that
reddish light which saves the candle by the slow-
ness of the combustion,—a discovery due to the
misers.

"Dear uncle, you should dress yourself more
warmly when you go down to that parlor."

"I do not like to keep them waiting, those poor
people!   Well, what is it that you wish of me?"

"Why, I come to invite you to dinner to-morrow
at the house of the Marquise d'Espard."

"One of our relatives?" asked the judge with an
air of such naïve preoccupation that Bianchon
laughed.

"No, uncle; the Marquise d'Espard is a high and
very influential lady who has presented to the tribunal a petition to have her husband interdicted from

first to feel the effects of the evil, and that his prostration has left Monsieur le Marquis d'Espard a prey
to all the dangers of an incapacity fully established
by the following facts:

"'For a long space of time, all the revenues accru-
ing from the property of the Marquis d'Espard have
passed, without any apparent cause and without
any advantages, even temporary, to an old woman
whose repulsive ugliness is matter of general report,
and who is named Madame Jeanrenaud, living sometimes in Paris, Rue de la Vrillière, number 8; sometimes at Villeparisis, near Claye, department of the
Seine-et-Marne, and to the benefit of her son, thirty-
six years of age, an officer of the ex-Imperial Guard,
whom, by his influence, Monsieur le Marquis
d'Espard has placed in the Garde Royale with the
rank of chief of squadron in the first regiment of
cuirassiers. These persons, who, in 1814, were reduced to the utmost misery, have successively
acquired real estate of a very considerable value,
lately, among others, a hôtel in the Grande Rue
Verte, in which the Sieur Jeanrenaud is at present
expending considerable sums in order to establish
himself there with the Dame Jeanrenaud his
mother, in view of the marriage which he is contemplating; which sums already amount to more
than a hundred thousand francs. This marriage is
being brought about by the negotiations of the Marquis d'Espard with his banker, the Sieur Mongenod,
of whom he has asked his niece in marriage for the
aforesaid Sieur Jeanrenaud, promising to use his

credit to obtain for him the dignity of baron. This appointment was, in fact, established by an ordinance of His Majesty, dated the twenty-ninth of December last, upon the solicitations of the Marquis d'Espard, as can be established by his Grace, Monseigneur the Keeper of the Seals, if the tribunal judge it proper to have recourse to his testimony.

" 'That no reason, *even drawn from those which are reproved equally by morality and the law*, can justify the empire which the Dame Jeanrenaud, widow, has established over the Marquis d'Espard, who, moreover, sees her very rarely; or explain his strange affection for the aforesaid Sieur Baron Jeanrenaud, with whom his communications are infrequent; nevertheless, their authority over him is so great that, every time that they are in need of money, even were it to satisfy their slightest wishes, this dame or her son—'

"Eh! eh! *reason which morality and the law reprove!* What does the clerk or the attorney wish to insinuate to us?" said Popinot.

Bianchon laughed.

" 'This dame *or her son* obtains without any discussion from the Marquis d'Espard that which they ask, and, in default of cash, Monsieur d'Espard signs bills of exchange negotiated by the Sieur Mongenod, who has offered to the petitioner to testify to this effect.

" 'That, moreover, in support of these facts, it has

happened recently at the period of the renewal of the leases of the D'Espard estate, the farmers having given a sufficiently important sum for the continuation of their contracts, the Sieur Jeanrenaud caused the immediate delivery of these sums to himself.

" 'That the will of the Marquis d'Espard had so little to do with the abandonment of these sums, that, when he was spoken to about it, he did not appear to remember anything concerning it; that every time that he has been questioned by grave personages concerning his devotion to these two individuals, his responses have indicated so complete an abnegation of his ideas, of his interests, that there exists necessarily in this affair some occult cause upon which the petitioner requests the eye of justice, seeing that it is impossible that this cause should not be criminal, improper and unlawful, or of a nature to be appreciated by the medical jurisprudence, if indeed, this obsession be not of those which partake of the abuse of the moral powers, and which can be qualified only by making use of the extraordinary term *possession*—'

"The devil!" exclaimed Popinot, "what do you say to that, doctor? These facts are very strange."

"They might be," replied Bianchon, "an effect of some magnetic power."

"You believe then in the nonsense of Mesmer, in his magnetizing tub, in seeing through walls?"

"Yes, uncle," said the doctor, gravely. "While

listening to you reading this petition, I have been thinking of it.   I declare to you that I have verified, in another field of action, several facts analogous to these, relative to the boundless empire which one man can acquire over another.   I am, contrary to the opinion of my colleagues, entirely convinced of the power of the will, considered as a motive power. I have seen, all connivance and charlatanism aside, the effects of this *possession*.   The actions promised the *magnetizer* by the *magnetized* during the sleep have been scrupulously accomplished in the waking state.   The will of the one had become the will of the other.''

"Every species of action?''

"Yes.''

"Even criminal?''

"Even criminal.''

"It is well that it is you who say so, or I would not listen.''

"I will make you a witness of it,'' said Bianchon.

"Hum! hum!'' said the judge.   "Supposing that the cause of this pretended *possession* belongs to this order of facts, it would be difficult to establish it and to cause it to be recognized by the law.''

"I do not see, if this Dame Jeanrenaud is frightfully old and ugly, what other means of seduction she could have employed,'' said Bianchon.

"But,'' replied the judge, "in 1814, the date at which the seduction was accomplished, this woman must have been fourteen years younger; if she had become acquainted with Monsieur d'Espard ten years before that, these calculations of dates carry us back twenty-four years, to a period in which the lady may very well have been young and pretty, and have acquired, by very natural methods, for herself as well as for her son, over Monsieur d'Espard, an empire from which certain men are unable to escape. If the cause of this empire seem reprehensible in the eyes of justice, it is very justifiable in the eyes of nature. Madame Jeanrenaud may very well have been chagrined at the marriage contracted probably about that time by the Marquis d'Espard with Mademoiselle de Blamont-Chauvry; and there might be, at the bottom of all this, nothing more than a woman's rivalry, since the marquis has not lived for a long time with Madame d'Espard."

"But this repulsive ugliness, uncle?"

"The power of seduction is in direct ratio to ugliness; that is an old question! Moreover, the small-pox, doctor? But let us continue.

" '—That, since the year 1815, in order to furnish the sums required by these two persons, Monsieur le Marquis d'Espard has gone to live with his two children in the Rue de la Montagne-Sainte-Geneviève, in an apartment the poverty of which is unworthy of his name and of his quality'—You can live just as you please!— 'that he detains there his two children, the Comte Clément d'Espard and the Vicomte Camille d'Espard, in a manner of living not in accord with their future, with their name and

18

their fortune; that the want of money is frequently
so great that, recently, the landlord, one Sieur
Mariast, seized the furniture of these apartments;
that, when this due course of law was effected in
his presence, the Marquis d'Espard assisted the
sheriff's officer, whom he treated as a person of
quality, in offering him all the marks of courtesy
and attention which he would have displayed for a
person raised above himself in dignity of position—'

The uncle and the nephew looked at each other,
laughing.

" '—That, moreover, all the actions of his daily
life, outside of the facts alleged as to the Dame
Jeanrenaud, widow, and as to the Sieur Baron
Jeanrenaud, her son, are characterized by madness;
that, for nearly the space of ten years, he has occupied himself so exclusively with China, with its
manners and customs, with its history, that he
compares everything to Chinese methods; that,
when questioned upon this point, he confounds the
affairs of the present time, the events of the day
before, with facts relative to China; that he cen-
sures the acts of the Government and the conduct
of the King although, moreover, he loves him per-
sonally, in comparing them to the political events
of China.

" 'That this monomania has urged the Marquis
d'Espard to actions void of all sense; that contrary

to the customs of his rank and the ideas which he professes concerning the duty of the nobility, he has undertaken a commercial enterprise for which he daily signs obligations falling due at certain dates which threaten to-day his honor and his fortune, seeing that they represent him in the quality of a merchant, and can, if they are not met at the expiration of their term, cause him to be declared a bankrupt; that these obligations, contracted with paper merchants, printers, lithographers and colorists, who have furnished the materials necessary for this publication entitled: *Picturesque History of China,* and appearing in parts, are of such magnitude, that these same furnishers have entreated the petitioner to request the interdiction of the Marquis d'Espard in order that they may save their credit—'

"This man is a fool," cried Bianchon.

"You think so, you do!" said the judge. "It is necessary to hear him. Who listens to only one bell, hears only one sound."

"But it seems to me—" said Bianchon.

"But it seems to me," said Popinot, "that if one of my relatives wished to get possession of the administration of my property, and that, if instead of being a simple judge whose moral and mental condition can be examined any day by his colleagues, I were a duke and a peer, some attorney a little sharp, as is Desroches, might draw up a petition similar to this against me."

" '—That the education of his children has suffered because of this monomania, and that he has caused them to be taught, contrary to all the usages of instruction, the facts of Chinese history which contradict the doctrines of the Catholic religion, and has caused them to be taught the Chinese dialects—'

"Here, Desroches seems to me absurd," said Bianchon.

"The petition was drawn up by his head clerk, Godeschal, whom you know, who is not very Chinese," said the judge.

" '—That he frequently leaves his children deprived of the most necessary articles; that the petitioner, notwithstanding her repeated request, is not permitted to see them; that the Sieur Marquis d'Espard brings them to her only once a year; that, knowing the privations to which they are exposed, she has made vain efforts to procure for them articles the most necessary for their existence, and of which they are in need—'

"Ah! Madame la Marquise, this is nonsense. Who proves too much, proves nothing. My dear fellow," said the judge, dropping the papers on his knees, "where is the mother who has ever been so lacking in heart, in wit, in compassion, as not to rise even to the level of the inspiration of her natural instincts? A mother is as shrewd to get at her

children as a young girl is to successfully conduct a
love intrigue. If your marchioness had really
wished to take care of or to clothe her children, the
devil himself could not have prevented her, *hein?*
It is a little too long, this fine story, to be swallowed
by an old judge! Let us continue."

" '—That the age at which the said children have
arrived, requires that from the present time, precautions should be taken to protect them from the
fatal influence of this education, that they should be
provided for according to their rank, and that they
should not have before their eyes the example given
them by their father's conduct.

" 'That in support of the facts alleged in these
presents there exist proofs of which the tribunal
may readily obtain the evidence: very many times
Monsieur d'Espard has designated the judge of the
peace of the twelfth arrondissement as a mandarin
of the third class; he has often called the professors
of the College of Henri IV., the *lettered.*'—And they
resent it!—'With relation to the most simple
things, he has said that they are not so managed in
China; he will make allusion, in the course of an
ordinary conversation, either to the Dame Jeanrenaud, or to events that took place under the reign of
Louis XIV., and then remain plunged in the deepest
melancholy,—sometimes he imagines himself in
China. Several of his neighbors, notably the
Sieurs Edme Becker, student in medicine, Jean-
Baptiste Frémiot, professor, domiciled in the same

house, believe, after having conversed with the
Marquis d'Espard, that his monomania, in all that
concerns China, is the result of a plan formed by the
Sieur Baron Jeanrenaud and the Dame his mother,
widow, to complete the overthrow of the moral
faculties of the Marquis d'Espard, seeing that the
sole service which the Dame Jeanrenaud can render
Monsieur d'Espard is to procure for him everything
that relates to the Empire of China.

"'That, finally, the petitioner offers to prove to
the tribunal that the sums absorbed by the Sieur
and the Dame Jeanrenaud, widow, from 1814 to 1828,
amount to not less than a million francs.

"In confirmation of the preceding facts, the petitioner offers to Monsieur le Président the testimony
of persons who are in the habit of seeing Monsieur
le Marquis d'Espard, and whose names and qualities
are set down here below, among whom many have
earnestly requested the procuring of the interdiction
of Monsieur le Marquis d'Espard, as the sole method
of protecting his fortune from his deplorable administration, and of removing his children from his fatal
influence.

"'In consideration of this, Monsieur le Président,
and in view of the documents hereto adjoined, the
petitioner requests that it should please you, seeing
that the preceding facts prove incontestably the
state of dementia and of imbecility of Monsieur le
Marquis d'Espard, named hereinbefore, his quality
and his domicile, to order that, for the purpose
of securing the interdiction of the same, the present

petition and the documents in corroboration thereof shall be communicated to Monsieur le Procureur du Roi, and to commission one of Messieurs the judges of the tribunal to the end that a report may be made on a day that you may be pleased to indicate, in order that judgment may finally be decreed by the tribunal as it shall see cause, and you will do justice, etc.' "

"And here is," said Popinot, "the ordinance of the president who commissions me! Well, what does she want with me, the Marquise d'Espard? I know what to do. I will go to-morrow with my clerk to see Monsieur le Marquis, for this does not seem to me clear at all."

"Listen to me, my dear uncle, I have never asked of you the least little service relating to your judicial functions; well, I entreat you to have for Madame d'Espard the consideration to which her station entitles her. If she comes here, you will listen to her?"

"Yes."

"Well, go to hear her in her own house: Madame d'Espard is a sickly, nervous, delicate woman who would be very uncomfortable here in your rat's nest. Go there in the evening, instead of accepting the invitation to dinner, since the law forbids your eating and drinking in the houses of those under your jurisdiction."

"Does not the law forbid your receiving legacies from your dead patients?" said Popinot, thinking that he perceived a shade of irony on his nephew's lips.

"Come, uncle, since it is only for the sake of arriving at the truth in this affair, grant me my request. You will go there as *juge d'instruction*, since things do not seem to you clear. The deuce! the interrogation of the marchioness is not less necessary than that of her husband."

"You are right," said the magistrate, "it may very well be that she is the lunatic. I will go."

"I will come to get you: write down in your memorandum book: *To-morrow evening at nine o'clock, at Madame d'Espard's.* Good," said Bianchon, seeing his uncle make a note of the rendezvous.

The next evening, at nine o'clock, Doctor Bianchon mounted the dusty stairway of his uncle's, and found him working at the rendering of some thorny judgment. The new coat ordered by Lavienne had not been brought by the tailor, so that Popinot took his old coat, covered with spots, and was still the Popinot *incomptus* whose aspect excited the risibility of those to whom his private life was unknown. Bianchon succeeded, however, in putting his uncle's cravat in order and in buttoning his coat, he concealed the spots on the latter by crossing the revers of the skirts from right to left and thus presenting the part of the cloth that was still new. But in a very few minutes the judge pushed his coat up on his chest by the manner in which he thrust his hand into his trousers pockets according to his usual custom. The coat, multitudinously wrinkled behind and before, formed something like a hump in the middle of the back, and produced between the waistcoat and the pantaloons a space in which the shirt showed itself. To his misfortune, Bianchon did not perceive this excessively ridiculous effect until the moment when his uncle presented himself in the marchioness' salon.

A slight sketch of the life of this lady in whose dwelling the doctor and the judge were at this moment entering is necessary to render intelligible the conference which Popinot was about to hold with her.

Madame d'Espard had been, for the last seven years, very much *à la mode* in Paris, where *la Mode* alternately elevates and pulls down personages who, sometimes great and sometimes little,—that is to say, alternately in sight and forgotten,—become later insupportable persons—as are all the disgraced ministers and all the dethroned monarchs. Inconvenient because of their faded pretensions, these fawners of the past know all, slander all, and, like the ruined spendthrift, are the friends of all the world. To have been forsaken by her husband about the year 1815, Madame d'Espard must have been married early in the year 1812. Her children were, therefore, one fifteen and the other thirteen years of age. How had it come to pass that the mother of a family, thirty-three years of age, was *à la mode*. Although fashionable society be capricious, and though no one can designate its favorites in advance, though it often exalts the wife of a banker or some woman

of a doubtful elegance or beauty, it would seem
supernatural that it should have assumed constitutional features and adopted the *presidency of age*.
In this, society had done like all the rest of the
world, it accepted Madame d'Espard as a young
woman.　The marchioness was thirty-three years
of age in the registers of the State, and twenty-two
in the evenings in a salon.　But how many cares
and artifices!　Artificial ringlets concealed her temples.　She condemned herself in her own apartments
to a half-light, posing as an invalid in order to remain in the protecting shades of a light passed
through muslin curtains.　Like Diane de Poitiers,
she used cold water for her baths; like her, also, the
marchioness slept upon horse-hair, with her head
upon pillows of morocco leather, in order to preserve
her hair, ate but little, drank nothing but water,
combined all her movements so as to avoid fatigue,
and brought a monastic exactitude to the slightest
actions of her life.　This rude system has been, it
is said, carried to the extent of even using ice instead of water and cold aliments exclusively by an
illustrious Polish lady who, in our day, combines a
life already secular with the occupations, the customs of a studied elegance, of a *petite-maîtresse*.
Destined to live as long as did Marion Delorme, to
whom the biographies give a hundred and thirty
years, the wife of the former viceroy of Poland displays, at the age of nearly a hundred, a youthful
spirit and heart, a gracious face, a charming figure;
she can in her conversation, in which the *bon mots*

sparkle like vine-twigs in the fire, compare the men and the books of the literature of the day with the men and the books of the eighteenth century. Living in Warsaw, she orders her bonnets from Herbault. A great lady, she has the devotion of a young girl, she swims, she runs like a student, and knows how to throw herself on a divan quite as gracefully as any young coquette; she insults death and laughs at life. After having formerly astonished the Emperor Alexander, she can to-day surprise the Emperor Nicholas with the magnificence of her festivals. She can still cause some amorous young man to shed tears, for she is of the age in which it pleases her to have all the ineffable devotions of a grisette. In short, she is a veritable fairy story, if indeed she be not the fairy of the story. Had Madame d'Espard known Madame Zayonscek? did she wish to be her imitator? However this may be, the marchioness proved the beneficence of this régime, her complexion was pure, her forehead had no wrinkles, her body preserved, like that of the well-beloved of Henri II., the suppleness, the freshness, hidden charms which bring back love to a woman and make it permanent. The so-simple precautions of this régime, indicated by art, by nature, perhaps also by experience, found moreover in her a general constitution which came to their aid. The marchioness was endowed with a profound indifference for everything which was outside herself; the men amused her, but not one of them had ever caused her those great excitements which move

profoundly the two natures and break one against
the other.   She knew neither hatred nor love.
When offended, she took her revenge coldly and
tranquilly, at her ease, while waiting the occasion
to satisfy the evil thought which she preserved
against anyone who remained unforgiven in her
memory.   She did not stir herself, did not agitate
herself in the least; she spoke, for she knew that
in saying two words a woman can kill three men.
With a singular pleasure, she saw herself abandoned by Monsieur d'Espard—did he not carry away
with him two children who, at present, wearied her,
and who, in the future, could seriously injure her
pretensions?   Her most intimate friends, as her
least persevering adorers, seeing nowhere with her
those jewels of Cornelia who go and come proclaim-
ing without knowing it, their mother's age, all took
her for a young woman.   The two children, concerning whom the marchioness appeared to be so
much concerned in her petition, were, as well as
their father, as unknown to the world as the North-
east passage is unknown to the mariner.   Monsieur d'Espard was considered to be an eccentric,
who had left his wife without having against her
the slightest cause of complaint.   Finding herself
her own mistress at the age of twenty-two, and
mistress of her fortune, which gave her twenty-six
thousand francs a year, the marchioness hesitated
a long time before taking a part and deciding upon
her future existence.   Although she profited by the
outlay which her husband had made in his hôtel, of

which she kept the furniture, the equipages, the horses, in short, a complete establishment, she led at first a retired life during the years sixteen, seventeen and eighteen, an epoch in which the great families repaired their disasters occasioned by the political troubles. A member, moreover, of one of the most considerable and most illustrious families of the Faubourg Saint-Germain, her relatives advised her to lead a domestic life, after the compulsory separation to which she was condemned by the inexplicable caprice of her husband. In 1820, the marchioness shook off her lethargy, appeared at the Court, at the fêtes, and received in her own house. From 1821 to 1827, she held great state in her dwelling, caused herself to be remarked for her taste and by her toilets; she had her day, her hours, for receiving; then she presently seated herself on the throne on which had formerly shone Madame la Vicomtesse de Beauséant, the Duchesse de Langeais, Madame Firmiani, who, after her marriage with Monsieur de Camps, had resigned the sceptre into the hands of the Duchesse de Maufrigneuse, from whom Madame d'Espard had wrested it. The world knew nothing more of the private life of the Marquise d'Espard. She seemed to remain a long time on the Parisian horizon, like a sun on the point of setting but which never sets. The marchioness had entered into a close alliance with a duchess not less celebrated for her beauty than for her devotion to the person of a prince then in disgrace, but accustomed to entering always as the ruling

spirit into coming governments.   Madame d'Espard
was also the friend of a fair stranger in whose
society an illustrious and experienced Russian
diplomat was in the habit of analyzing public affairs.
Finally, an old countess, accustomed to shuffling the
cards of the great game of politics, had adopted her
in a maternal manner.   In the eyes of any man
with lofty views, Madame d'Espard was thus preparing herself to follow, with a silent but real influence, the public and frivolous empire which she
owed to fashion.   Her salon took a political consis-
tency.   These words: "What do they say of that
at Madame d'Espard's?   The salon of Madame d'Espard is against such a measure," were beginning
to be repeated by a sufficiently great number of
dunces to give to her flock of the faithful the
authority of a coterie.   A few crippled politicians,
cared for, flattered by her, such as the favorite of
Louis XVIII., who could no longer get himself taken
into consideration, and some former ministers
ready to return to power, declared her to be as
great a power in diplomacy as was the wife of the
Russian Ambassador at London.   The marchioness
had, on several occasions, given, either to the
deputies or to the peers, certain words and ideas
which from the tribune had afterward resounded
through Europe.   She had often formed an excellent
judgment on events of the day covering which
her coterie did not dare to venture an opinion.
The principal personages of the Court came to play
whist in her house in the evening.   She had,

moreover, the virtues of her defects. She was considered to be discreet, and was so. Her friendship seemed to be proof against anything. She served her protégés with a persistence which testified that she was less concerned about securing creatures of her own than about increasing her credit. This conduct was inspired by her ruling passion, vanity. The conquests and the pleasures which hold so high a place in the estimation of so many women, seemed to her but means to an end; she wished to live on all the points of the very greatest circle that life can describe. Among the men still young and for whom the future held something, who frequented her salon on important occasions, were to be seen Messieurs de Marsay, de Ronquerolles, de Montriveau, de la Roche-Hugon, de Sérizy, Ferraud, Maxime de Trailles, de Listomère, the two Vandenesses, du Châtelet, etc. Frequently she admitted a man without being willing to receive his wife, and her power was already sufficiently well established to impose these hard conditions upon certain ambitious personages, such as two celebrated royalist bankers, Messieurs de Nucingen and Ferdinand du Tillet. She had so carefully studied the strength and the weakness of Parisian life that she had always conducted herself in such a manner as to permit no man to have the slightest advantage over her. A very large price might have been offered for any note or letter that might compromise her, without finding a single one. If the dryness of her soul permitted her to play her part with such naturalness, her person served her not less well. She had a youthful figure. Her voice was, at her command, fresh and flexible, clear, hard. She possessed in an eminent degree the secrets of that aristocratic attitude by which a woman effaces the past. The marchioness knew perfectly the art of placing an immense space between herself and the man who believed himself entitled to certain rights to familiarity after a chance happiness. Her imposing regard knew how to deny everything. In her conversation, great and beautiful sentiments, noble determinations, seemed to flow naturally from a pure heart and soul; but she was in reality all calculation, and perfectly capable of disgracing a man who might be awkward in his transactions at the very moment in which she was carrying out without shame transactions for her own profit. In endeavoring to attach himself to this woman, Rastignac had well selected her as one of the most excellent of instruments: but he had not yet been able to make use of it; far from being able to manage her, he was already brayed in a mortar by her hands. This young *condottiere* of the intellect, condemned, like Napoléon, to forever give battle knowing that one defeat would be the tomb of his fortune, had encountered in his protectress a dangerous adversary. For the first time in his turbulent life, he was playing a serious game with a partner worthy of him. In the conquest of Madame d'Espard he perceived a future ministry; therefore he served her before making use of her: a dangerous début.

AT THE HOTEL D'ESPARD.

———

" *Monsieur Popinot.*"—" *Monsieur Bianchon.*"

The Hôtel d'Espard required a numerous train of domestics and the marchioness's household was very considerable. The grand receptions took place on the ground floor, but the marchioness lived on the first floor of her house. The style of the grand staircase, magnificently decorated, the apartments adorned in the noble taste which formerly prevailed at Versailles, indicated an immense fortune. When the judge saw the porte-cochère opening before his nephew's cabriolet, he examined with a rapid glance the lodge, the porter, the court, the stables, the arrangements of this dwelling, the flowers which embellished the stairway, the exquisite delicacy of the balustrade, the walls, the carpets, and counted the valets in livery who, at the sound of the bell, appeared on the landing. His eyes, which, the day before, had explored in his charity office the depths of wretchedness under the muddy garments of the people, now studied with the same clearness of vision the furnishing and the decoration of the apartments through which he passed, in order to discover the wretchedness of greatness.

"Monsieur Popinot."—"Monsieur Bianchon."

These two announcements were made at the entrance to the boudoir in which the marchioness was, a pretty room, recently refurnished, and which looked out on the garden of the hôtel. At this moment Madame d'Espard was seated in one of those ancient *rococo* arm-chairs which MADAME had made the fashion. Rastignac occupied near her, at her left, a low chair before the fireplace in which

19

he had established himself like the *primo* of an
Italian lady. A third personage was standing at
the angle of the chimney-piece. As the knowing
doctor had shrewdly divined, the marchioness was
a woman of a dry and nervous temperament: had it
not been for her régime, her skin would have taken
on the reddish color which is occasioned by a constant heat; but she increased her factitious whiteness by the shades and the vigorous tones of the
draperies by which she surrounded herself or in
which she dressed. The reddish browns, the chestnut colors, the bistre with golden reflections suited
her marvelously. Her boudoir, copied from that of
a celebrated lady then the fashion in London, was
furnished in tan-colored velvet; but she had added
numerous embellishments the pretty designs of
which lightened the excessive pomp of this royal
color. Her hair was arranged like that of a young
woman, in bandeaux terminated by curls which
emphasized the somewhat long oval of her face;
but, just as the round form is ignoble, so is the
oval shape majestic. The double mirrors with
facets which lengthen or flatten out at will the
faces reflected in them, furnish an evident confirmation of this rule as applied to the physiognomy.
When she saw Popinot, who stopped in the doorway
like a frightened animal, stretching his neck, his
left hand in his pocket, the right armed with a hat,
the lining of which was soiled, the marchioness
threw upon Rastignac a glance in which there was
the suggestion of derision. The somewhat silly

aspect of the good man was so in accordance with
his grotesque apparel, with his terrified air, that,
on seeing Bianchon's unhappy face, he feeling himself humiliated in his uncle, Rastignac could not
keep from laughing, turning away his head. The
marchioness made her salutation with a movement
of her head, and with a painful effort to rise from
her armchair, into which she fell back, not without
grace, in seeming to apologize for her impoliteness
by an assumed weakness.

At this moment the personage who was standing
between the chimney-piece and the door bowed
slightly, pushed forward two chairs which he offered
by a gesture to the doctor and the judge; then,
when he saw them seated, he leaned back again
against the hangings and crossed his arms. One
word as to this man. There is a painter of our day,
Decamps, who possesses in the highest degree the
art of making interesting whatever he presents to
your regards, whether it be a stone or a man. In
this respect, his pencil is happier than his brush.
Let him design a bare room and leave a broom leaning against the wall; if he chooses he can make you
shudder: you will believe that that broom has just
served as the instrument of a crime and that it is
wet with blood; it is the broom which the widow
Bancal used to sweep the apartment in which
Fualdès had his throat cut. Yes, the painter will
put his broom in such a dishevelled state as if it
were a man in a fury, he will make the splints
stand upright like your horrified hair; he will make

of it, as it were, an interpreter between the secret
poetry of his own imagination and the poetry which
reveals itself in yours.   After having frightened
you by the sight of this broom, he will design
another to-morrow, near which a sleeping cat, but
mysterious in its slumber, will reveal to you that
this broom serves the wife of a German shoemaker
to fly with to the Brocken.   Or else it may be some
peaceful broom, on which he will hang the coat of
some Treasury clerk.   Decamps has in his brush
that which Paganini had in his bow, a power mag-
netically communicative.   Well, it would be necessary to transport into literary style this compelling
genius, this *chic* of the pencil, to describe the erect
man, thin and tall, dressed in black, with long
black hair, who remained standing without saying
a word.   This seigneur had a hatchet face, cold,
bitter, the color of which resembled the waters of
the Seine when they are disturbed and when they
carry in their currents the coal dust of some sunken
barge.   He looked at the floor, listened and judged.
His attitude was terrifying.   He was stationed
there like the celebrated broom to which Decamps
has given the accusing power of revealing a crime.
Several times the marchioness endeavored during
the conference to obtain a tacit opinion from this
personage by turning her eyes for a moment upon
him; but no matter how searching the mute interrogation, he remained as grave and stiff as the statue
of the Commander.

The good Popinot, seated on the edge of his chair,

facing the fire, his hat between his legs, looked at
the gilded candelabra in *ormolu*, the clock, the curiosities crowded on the mantelpiece, the material
and the embellishments of the hangings, in short,
at all those pretty nothings which are so costly
and with which a fashionable woman surrounds
herself. He was drawn from his bourgeois contemplation by Madame d'Espard, who said to him
in a flute-like voice:

"Monsieur, I owe you a million acknowledgments—"

"A million acknowledgments," said the good man
to himself, "that is too many, there is not one."

"—For the trouble which you condescend—"

"Condescend!" he thought, "she is making fun
of me."

"—Condescend to take in coming to see a poor
client, who is too unwell to go out—"

Here the judge interrupted the speech of the marchioness by turning upon her the look of an inquisitor with which he examined the sanatory condition
of the poor client.

"She is perfectly well," he said to himself.
"Madame," he replied, assuming a respectful air,
"you owe me nothing. Although my proceeding
may not be usual according to the customs of the
court, we should spare ourselves nothing in order
to arrive at the truth in these cases. Our judgments are then determined less by the letter of the
law than by the inspirations of our own consciences.
Whether I search for the truth in my cabinet or

here, provided that I find it, everything is for the best."

While Popinot was speaking, Rastignac grasped Bianchon's hand, and the marchioness made to the doctor a little inclination of the head, full of graceful favors.

"Who is that gentleman?" said Bianchon in Rastignac's ear, indicating the man in black.

"The Chevalier d'Espard, the brother of the marquis."

"Monsieur your nephew has informed me," the marchioness replied to Popinot, "how many occupations you have, and I know already that you are good enough to wish to conceal a benefit, in order to relieve from their gratitude those whom you have favored. It seems that the court fatigues you extremely. Why do they not double the number of the judges?"

"Ah! madame, that is not the trouble," said Popinot, "it would not be any worse because of that. But, when that happens, the chickens will have teeth."

When he heard this phrase, which was so in harmony with the judge's appearance, the Chevalier d'Espard looked at him from top to bottom and appeared to say to himself: "We shall easily get the better of him."

The marchioness glanced at Rastignac, who leaned toward her.

"See," said the young dandy to her, "to what kind of men is given the power of deciding upon the interests and the life of individuals."

Like the greater number of men who have grown old in a profession, Popinot allowed himself readily to fall into the habits which he had contracted, habits of thought, moreover. His conversation smacked of the juge d'instruction. He loved to question his interlocutors, to drive them into unforeseen consequences, to make them say more than they wished to have known. Pozzo di Borgo amused himself, it is said, by surprising the secrets of his interlocutors, by catching them in his diplomatic snares; he thus displayed, through the force of an invincible habit, his crafty spirit. As soon as Popinot had, as it were, reconnoitred the ground on which he found himself, he concluded that it would be necessary to have recourse to the most skilful devices, the most carefully disguised, and the most beguiling known in the Palais, in order to discover the truth. Bianchon remained cold and grave, like a man who decides to submit to a torture in silence; but inwardly he wished for his uncle the power to tread on this woman as on a viper: a comparison which was suggested to him by the long dress, the curve of the attitude, the lengthened neck, the little head and the undulating movements of the marchioness.

"Well, monsieur," resumed Madame d'Espard, "whatever may be my repugnance to playing the egotist, I have been suffering for too long a time not to desire that you should soon come to a conclusion. May I expect soon a happy result?"

"Madame, I will do all that I can as far as I am

concerned to bring it to a conclusion," said Popinot
with an air of good humor. "Are you ignorant of
the cause which brought about the separation now
existing between yourself and the Marquis
d'Espard?" asked the judge, looking at the marchioness.

"Yes, monsieur," she replied, settling herself to
relate a story prepared in advance. "At the beginning of the year 1816, Monsieur d'Espard, who, for
the last three months, had completely changed in
his manners, proposed to me to go to live near
Briançon, on one of his estates, without any regard
for my health which that climate would have ruined,
without taking any account of my habits; I refused
to follow him. My refusals furnished him occasion
for reproaches so unfounded that, from that moment,
I began to doubt the soundness of his mental faculties. The next day he left me, leaving to me his
hôtel, the free disposition of my income, and went
to live in the Rue de la Montagne-Sainte-Geneviève,
taking from me my two children—"

"Permit me, madame," said the judge, interrupting, "what was that income?"

"Twenty-six thousand francs a year," she replied in a parenthesis. "I immediately consulted
old Monsieur Bordin to know what I should do,"
she went on; "but it appeared that the difficulties
in the way of taking from a father the control of
his children are such that I was obliged to resign
myself to living alone at twenty-two years of age, an
age at which very many young women might have

committed many foolish actions.   You have doubtless read my petition, monsieur, you are acquainted
with the principal facts upon which I base my request for the interdiction of Monsieur d'Espard?"

"Have you made any attempts, madame," asked
the judge, "to obtain your children from him?"

"Yes, monsieur, but they have all been fruitless.
It is very cruel for a mother to be deprived of the
affection of her children, above all when they could
give her those enjoyments which all women prize
so highly."

"The eldest must be sixteen years old," said the
judge.

"Fifteen!" replied the marchioness, quickly.

Here Bianchon looked at Rastignac.   Madame
d'Espard bit her lips.

"Of what importance is the age of my children to
you?"

"Ah! madame," said the judge, without appearing to attach any weight to the meaning of his
words, "a young lad of fifteen and his brother,
doubtless aged thirteen, have legs and wits, they
could readily come to see you secretly; if they do
not come, it is because they obey their father, and,
to obey him on this point, they must love him
greatly."

"I do not understand you," said the marchioness.

"You are ignorant, perhaps," replied Popinot,
"that your attorney pretends in your petition that
your dear children are very unhappy with their
father—"

Madame d'Espard said with a charming innocence:

"I do not know what the attorney has made me
say."

"Forgive me these inferences, but justice weighs
everything," Popinot replied. "Whatever I ask
you, madame, is inspired by the desire to become
thoroughly acquainted with the affair. According
to you, Monsieur d'Espard left you on the most
frivolous pretext. Instead of going to Briançon,
where he wished to take you, he has remained in
Paris. This point is not clear. Was he acquainted
with this Dame Jeanrenaud before his marriage?"

"No, monsieur," replied the marchioness with a
species of displeasure visible only to Rastignac and
the Chevalier d'Espard.

She was vexed to find herself put in the witness-
box by this judge, when she had proposed to herself
to pervert his judgment; but, as Popinot apparently
remained completely simple-minded through his
preoccupation, she concluded by attributing his
questions to the *interrogating* genius of Voltaire's
bailiff.

"My parents," she continued, "married me at the
age of sixteen to Monsieur d'Espard, whose name,
whose fortune and whose habits all answered to that
which my family required of the man who should
become my husband. Monsieur d'Espard was then
twenty-six, he was a gentleman in the English sense
of the word; his manners pleased me, he appeared
to be very ambitious, and I like the ambitious," she

said, looking at Rastignac. "If Monsieur d'Espard had not met that Dame Jeanrenaud, his qualities, his knowledge, his general attainments, according to the judgment of his friends at that time, would have carried him into the management of affairs; the king Charles X., then MONSIEUR, held him in high esteem, and the peerage, a post at the Court, an elevated position, all awaited him. This woman turned his head, and has destroyed the future of an entire family."

"What were at that time the religious opinions of Monsieur d'Espard?"

"He was," she replied, "he is still, of an exalted piety."

"You do not think that Madame Jeanrenaud has acted upon him through mysterious powers?"

"No, monsieur."

"You have a beautiful hôtel, madame," said Popinot brusquely, taking his hands out of his pockets, and rising to separate the skirts of his coat and warm himself. "This boudoir is very fine, those are magnificent chairs, your apartments are very sumptuous; you may well sigh, in fact, situated as you are here, to know that your children are badly lodged, badly clothed and badly cared for. For a mother, I cannot imagine anything more frightful!"

"Yes, monsieur. I would wish so much to procure some pleasure for those poor little ones, whom their father compels to labor from morning to night on that deplorable work on China!"

"You give beautiful balls, they would amuse

themselves at them, but they would perhaps acquire a taste for dissipation; however, their father may very well send them to you once or twice a winter."

"He brings them to me on New Year's Day and on my birthday. On those occasions, Monsieur d'Espard does me the kindness to dine with them at my house."

"This conduct is very singular," said Popinot, assuming the air of a man convinced. "Have you seen this Dame Jeanrenaud?"

"One day, my brother-in-law, who, through interest in his brother—"

"Ah! monsieur then," said the judge, interrupting the marchioness, "is Monsieur d'Espard's brother?"

The chevalier bowed without saying a word.

"Monsieur d'Espard, who has followed this affair, conducted me to l'Oratoire, where this woman goes to the service, for she is a Protestant. I saw her, there is nothing attractive about her, she is like a butcher's wife; she is extremely fat, horribly pitted by the small-pox; she has hands and feet like a man's, she squints,—in short, she is a monster."

"It is inconceivable," said the judge, appearing to be the most guileless of all the judges in the kingdom. "And this creature lives near here, in the Rue Verte, in a hôtel! There are then no more bourgeois?"

"A hôtel on which her son has expended insane sums."

"Madame," said the judge, "I live in the Fau-bourg Saint-Marceau, I do not know that sort of ex-pense,—what do you call expending insane sums?"

"Why," replied the marchioness, "a stable, five horses, three carriages,—a calèche, a coupé, a cab-riolet."

"That costs then a great deal?" said Popinot sur-prised.

"Enormously!" said Rastignac, intervening. "An establishment such as that, requires, for the stables, for the keeping of the carriages and the clothing of the servants, between fifteen and sixteen thousand francs."

"Do you think so, madame?" asked the judge with a surprised air.

"Yes, at the least," replied the marchioness.

"And the furnishing of the hôtel must have cost also a great deal?"

"More than a hundred thousand francs," replied the marchioness, who could not repress a smile at the vulgarity of the judge.

"The judges, madame," the good man resumed, are sufficiently incredulous, they are even paid to be so, and I am so myself. Monsieur le Baron Jean-renaud and his mother, if this be true, must have strangely plundered Monsieur d'Espard. Here is a stable which according to you, costs sixteen thou-sand francs a year. The table, the domestics' wages, the gross expenses of the household, must be the double of that, which would require fifty or sixty thousand francs a year. Do you believe

that these people, formerly so poor, can possess so
great a fortune as that? A million yields scarcely
forty thousand francs of income."

"Monsieur, the son and the mother placed the
funds given them by Monsieur d'Espard in the
Funds when they were at sixty or eighty. I believe
that their income must amount to more than sixty
thousand francs. The son has, moreover, some
very good appointments."

"If they expend sixty thousand francs," said the
judge, "how much do you spend then?"

"Why," replied Madame d'Espard, "nearly as
much."

The chevalier made a movement, the marchioness
reddened, Bianchon looked at Rastignac, but the
judge maintained an air of simple good nature which
deceived Madame d'Espard. The chevalier took no
further interest in this conversation, he saw that
everything was lost.

"These people, madame," said Popinot, "can be
brought before the criminal courts."

"Such was my opinion," replied the marchioness,
enchanted. "If they had been threatened with the
correctional police, they would have come to terms."

"Madame," said Popinot, "when Monsieur
d'Espard left you, did he not give you a power-of-
attorney to manage and administer your property?"

"I do not understand the object of these questions," said the marchioness with some heat. "It
seems to me that, if you should take into consideration the condition in which I am left by my

husband's madness, you should occupy yourself with him and not with me."

"Madame," said the judge, "we are coming to it. Before confiding to you or to others the administration of the property of Monsieur d'Espard, if he should be interdicted from managing it himself, the court should be informed as to how you have taken care of your own. If Monsieur d'Espard had given you a power-of-attorney, he would have shown confidence in you, and the court would appreciate this fact. Have you had his power-of-attorney? You may have purchased and sold real estate, and made investments?"

"No, monsieur; the Blamont-Chauvrys are not in the habit of going into business," she replied quickly, touched in her pride of nobility and forgetting all about her case. "My property has remained intact, and Monsieur d'Espard did not give me his power-of-attorney."

The chevalier put his hand over his eyes to conceal the lively vexation caused him by the want of foresight of his sister-in-law, who was ruining herself by her replies. Popinot had gone straight to the important fact, notwithstanding all the detours of his interrogation.

"Madame," said the judge, pointing to the chevalier, "monsieur doubtless is connected with you by ties of relationship? we can speak openly before these gentlemen?"

"Certainly," said the marchioness, astonished at this precaution.

"Well, madame, I concede that you should expend
only sixty thousand francs a year, and this sum will
seem well employed to whoever sees your stables,
your hôtel, your numerous domestics, and the customs of a household the luxury of which seems to me
to be superior to that of the Jeanrenauds."

The marchioness made a gesture of assent.

"Now," replied the judge, "if you should possess
only an income of twenty-six thousand francs, between ourselves, you could well be in debt to the
extent of a hundred thousand francs. The court
would then be entitled to believe that there existed
in the motives which led you to request the interdiction of monsieur your husband some personal
interest, some need of meeting your debts, if—you
—have—any. The recommendations which have
been made to me have interested me in your situation, examine it carefully, make your statement.
There would still be time, in case my suppositions
should prove to be well founded, to avoid the scan-
dal of a reproach which it would be within the attri-
butes of the court to express in the *whereases* of its
decision, if you should not render your position clear
and well-defined. We are obliged to examine the
motives of the plaintiffs as well as to listen to the
defence of the man to be interdicted, to investigate
if the petitioners are not controlled by passions, led
astray by mercenary motives unfortunately only too
common—"

The marchioness was on Saint Lawrence's gridiron.

"—And it is necessary for me to have explanations on this subject," said the judge. "Madame, I do not ask to have an accounting from you, but only to know how you have managed to maintain an establishment of sixty thousand francs a year, and that for several years. There are a great many women who accomplish this feat in their households, but you are not one of those women. Speak, you may have very legitimate resources, some royal favors, some sources of income from the indemnities recently awarded; but, in that case, the authorization of your husband would have been necessary to have enabled you to receive them."

The marchioness was mute.

"Reflect," said Popinot, "that Monsieur d'Espard may wish to defend himself, and his advocate will have the right to investigate to ascertain if you have any creditors. This boudoir has been recently refurnished, your apartments have not the furniture which Monsieur le Marquis left you in 1816. If, as you did me the honor to inform me, furnishing is costly for the Jeanrenauds, it is still more so for you, who are *une grande dame*. Although I am a judge, I am still a man, I may be deceived, enlighten me. Reflect upon the duties which the law imposes upon me, upon the vigorous research which it requires, and then that it is a question of pronouncing the interdiction of the father of a family, in the flower of his age. Therefore, will you excuse, Madame la Marquise, the objections which I have the honor to submit to you, and concerning which it is

20

easy for you to give me some explanations. When a man is interdicted because of dementia, a trustee is required; who will be the trustee?"

"His brother," said the marchioness.

The chevalier bowed. There was a moment of silence which was embarrassing for these five persons in each other's company. Without appearing to take it seriously, the judge had uncovered this woman's wound. The good-natured bourgeois countenance of Popinot, at which the marchioness, the chevalier and Rastignac had been disposed to laugh, had acquired in their eyes its true physiognomy. In looking at him by stealth, all three of them perceived the thousand significations of that eloquent mouth. The absurd man had become a sagacious judge. His interest in examining the boudoir was now explained;—he had taken the gilded elephant which supported the mantel-clock for his point of departure in questioning all this luxury, and he had come to read the very depths of this woman's heart.

"If the Marquis d'Espard is crazy on China," said Popinot, indicating the articles on the chimney-piece, "I am charmed to see that its products please you equally. But perhaps it is to Monsieur le Marquis that you owe the charming Chinese things there," he said, pointing to the precious trifles.

This neat jest made Bianchon smile, petrified Rastignac, and the marchioness bit her thin lips.

"Monsieur," said Madame d'Espard, "instead of being the defender of a wife placed in the cruel alternative of seeing her fortune and her children lost, or of appearing to be the enemy of her husband, you accuse me! you are suspicious of my intentions! You must admit that your conduct is strange—"

"Madame," replied the judge quickly, "the discretion which the court brings to these cases would have given you, in any other judge, a critic perhaps less indulgent than I am. Moreover, do you believe that Monsieur d'Espard's advocate will be very considerate? Will he not be sure to represent in the worst light intentions that may be pure and disinterested? Your life will all be open to him, he will investigate it without bringing to his researches the respectful deference which I have for you."

"Monsieur, I thank you," replied the marchioness ironically. "We will admit for the moment that I owe thirty thousand, fifty thousand francs, that would be, in the first place, a bagatelle for the houses of D'Espard and of Blamont-Chauvry; but, if my husband is not in the possession of his intellectual faculties, would that be any obstacle to his interdiction?"

"No, madame," said Popinot.

"Although you have interrogated me with a crafty keenness which I should not have thought to find in a judge, under circumstances in which frankness would have sufficed to learn everything," she resumed, "and though I consider myself authorized to say nothing more, I will reply to you without circumlocution that my position in the world, that all these efforts made to preserve my relations with it, are not in harmony with my tastes. I began life by dwelling for a long time in solitude; but the interests of my children appealed to me, I felt that I should make an effort to take their father's place. By receiving my friends, by maintaining all these relations, by contracting these debts, I have secured their future, I have prepared for them brilliant careers in which they will find aid and support; and, in order to secure that which they will thus have acquired, many shrewd calculators, magistrates or bankers, would willingly have paid all that it has cost me."

"I appreciate your devotion, madame," replied the judge. "It does honor to you, and I in no wise blame your conduct. The magistrate belongs to all; he should be acquainted with everything, it is necessary for him to weigh everything."

The tact of the marchioness and her habit of judging men enabled her to perceive that Monsieur Popinot could not be influenced by any consideration. She had counted upon some ambitious magistrate, she had encountered a man with a conscience. She instantly began to reflect upon other methods of securing the success of her affair. The servants brought in the tea.

"Has madame any other explanations to give me?" said Popinot, seeing these preparations.

"Monsieur," she replied haughtily, "carry out your commission; examine Monsieur d'Espard, and you will commiserate me, of that I am certain—"

She lifted her head and looked at Popinot with

mingled pride and impertinence; the good man bowed to her respectfully.

"He is very fine, your uncle," said Rastignac to Bianchon. "He seems to understand nothing at all? he does not know then what the Marquise d'Espard is, he is ignorant then of her influence, of her occult power in the world? She will have in her house to-morrow the keeper of the seals—"

"My dear fellow, what would you have me do?" said Bianchon; "did I not forewarn you? This is not a man to be cajoled."

"No," said Rastignac, "he is a man to be sunk."

The doctor was obliged to bow to the marchioness and her mute chevalier to hasten after Popinot, who, not being a man to remain in an awkward situation, was trotting away through the salons.

"That woman owes a hundred thousand écus," said the judge as he got into his nephew's cabriolet.

"What do you think of the case?"

"I," said the judge, "I never have any opinion until I have examined both sides. To-morrow, early, I will summon Madame Jeanrenaud before me, in my cabinet, at four o'clock, to demand some explanations from her, on the facts which concern her, for she is compromised."

"I should like very much to know the end of this affair."

"Eh! Mon Dieu! don't you see that the marchioness is only the tool of that tall, dry man who did not utter a word? There is a little of Cain in him, but a Cain who searches his club in the courts, where, unfortunately, we have some of Samson's swords."

"Ah! Rastignac," exclaimed Bianchon, "what are you doing in that company?"

"We are accustomed to seeing these little plots in families; not a year elapses that requests for interdiction are not non-suited. According to our customs, no one is dishonored by these attempts; whilst we send to the galleys a poor devil who has broken the window frame which separates him from a wooden bowl full of gold coins. Our Code is not without its defects."

"But the facts of the petition?"

"My boy, you are evidently unacquainted with the judicial romances which the clients impose upon their attorneys? If the attorneys condemned themselves to present nothing but the truth, they would not gain the interest on their dues."

The next day, at four o'clock in the afternoon, a fat lady with a sufficient resemblance to a cask on which some one had put a dress and a sash, panted and perspired as she mounted Judge Popinot's staircase. She had with great difficulty issued from a green landau which suited. her marvelously,—it would be impossible to conceive of the woman without the landau, or of the landau without the woman.

"It is I, my dear monsieur," she said, presenting herself at the door of the judge's cabinet, "Madame Jeanrenaud, whom you have summoned neither more nor less than if she were a thief."

These inelegant words were announced in an inelegant voice, scanned, as it were, by the involuntary whistlings of an asthma, and terminated by an attack of coughing.

"When I go through damp places, you would not believe how I suffer, monsieur. I shall not make any old bones, by your leave. Well, here I am."

The judge was quite stupefied at the aspect of this pretended Maréchale d'Ancre. Madame Jeanrenaud had a face pitted with an infinite number of holes, with a great deal of color, a low forehead, a turned-up nose, a face as round as a ball, for, with this good woman, everything was round. She had the keen eyes of a country woman, a frank air, a jovial speech, chestnut hair retained by a false cap under a green hat ornamented with an old tuft of auriculas. Her voluminous breasts were provocative of mirth and inspired fears of a grotesque explosion at each fit of coughing. Her great legs were of that species that cause it to be said of a woman by the street urchins of Paris, that she is built on piles. The widow wore a green dress trimmed with chinchilla, which suited her like a spot of wagon-grease on a bride's veil. In short, everything about her was in accord with her last words: "Here I am!"

"Madame," said Popinot to her, "you are suspected of having employed means of seduction upon Monsieur le Marquis d'Espard in order to procure for yourself considerable sums of money."

"Of what! of what!" she said, "of seduction?

But, my dear monsieur, you are a respectable man, and, moreover, as a magistrate, you should have good sense, look at me! Tell me if I am a woman to seduce anyone. I cannot tie my shoestrings, or stoop down. Here it is now twenty years, God be praised, since I have been able to put on a corset under penalty of sudden death. I was as slender as an asparagus at sixteen, and pretty, I can say so to you to-day. Then I married Jeanrenaud, an honest man, the captain of a salt barge. I had my son, who is a fine fellow: he is my glory; and, without disparaging myself, he is the best thing I have done. My little Jeanrenaud was a soldier to make Napoléon proud, and served him in the Imperial Guard. Alas! the death of my husband, who was drowned, changed everything for me;—I had the small-pox, I remained two years in my chamber, without budging, and I came out of it as big as you see me, ugly for ever, and as unhappy as the stones.—There are my seductions!''

"But, madame, what motives then can have induced Monsieur d'Espard to give you sums that are—''

"*In*mense, monsieur, say the word, I am quite willing; but, as to the motives, I am not authorized to declare them.''

"You would be in the wrong. At this moment, his family, justly disquieted, are about to see—''

"*Dieu de Dieu!*'' said the good woman rising with a bound, "is he liable to be tormented then on my account? the king of men, a man who has

not his equal! Sooner than that he should have
the slightest vexation, and, I dare to say it, one
hair the less on his head, we will give up everything, Monsieur le Juge. Put that down on your
papers. *Dieu de Dieu!* I will run and tell Jeanrenaud what is the matter. Ah! this is a nice
business!"

And the little old woman rose, went out, rolled
down the stairway and disappeared.

"She does not lie, that woman," said the judge
to himself. "Well, to-morrow I shall know all, for
to-morrow I shall go to see the Marquis d'Espard."

Those who have passed the age at which a man
expends his energies at random are aware of the
influence exerted upon important events by actions
that are in appearance immaterial, and will not be
surprised at the consequences attending the slight
incident that follows. On the following day, Popinot had a coryza, a malady unattended by any
danger, known by the improper and ridiculous
name of a cold in the head. Unsuspicious of the
seriousness of a delay, the judge who had a
slight fever, kept his room and did not go to interrogate the Marquis d'Espard. This day lost was,
in this affair, what on "Dupes Day" was the
bouillon taken by Marie de Médicis which, delaying
her conference with Louis XIII., permitted Richelieu
to arrive first at Saint-Germain and resume possession of his royal captive. Before following the
magistrate and his clerk to the house of the Marquis
d'Espard, perhaps it will be necessary to glance at

this household, at its interior and at the affairs of this father of a family represented as demented in his wife's petition.

There are to be met with here and there in the old quarters of Paris several buildings in which the archæologist recognizes a certain desire to ornament the city, and that pride of ownership which leads to construction with a view to durability. The house in which Monsieur d'Espard then lived, in the Rue de la Montagne-Sainte-Geneviève, was one of these antique monuments built in cut stone, and did not lack for a certain richness in the architecture; but time had blackened the stone, and the city revolutions had greatly altered it, without and within. The high personages who had formerly inhabited the quarter of the Université having departed with the great ecclesiastical institutions, this dwelling had come to shelter industries and inhabitants for which it was never designed. During the last century, a printing office had ruined the floors, soiled the woodwork, blackened the walls and destroyed the principal interior arrangements. Formerly the hôtel of a cardinal, this noble house was at present delivered over to obscure lodgers. The character of its architecture indicated that it had been built during the reigns of Henri III. of Henri IV. and of Louis XIII. at the period in which were constructed in the neighborhood the hôtels Mignon and Serpente, the palace of the Princesse Palatine and the Sorbonne. One old man remembered having heard it called in the last century the

Hôtel Duperron.   It appeared to be probable that this
illustrious cardinal had built it, or at least had lived
in it.   There exists, in fact, at the angle of the court,
a perron consisting of several steps by which the
house is entered; and in the middle of the interior
façade there is another perron by which you descend
to the garden.   Notwithstanding the dilapidation,
the luxury displayed by the architect in the balustrades and in the platforms of these two perrons
reveals the ingenuous intention of recalling the
name of the proprietor, a species of sculptural pun
which our ancestors frequently permitted to themselves.   Finally, in support of this testimony, the
archæologists are able to perceive in the tympanums
which ornament the two principal façades, some
traces of the cords of the Roman hat.   Monsieur le
Marquis d'Espard occupied the ground floor, doubtless
in order to have the use of the garden, which might
pass as being spacious for this quarter and which
faced the south, two advantages required for the
health of his children.   The situation of the house,
in a street the name of which indicates its steep
slope, secured for this ground floor a sufficiently
great elevation to preserve it against any dampness.
Monsieur d'Espard should have been able to lease his
apartment for a very modest sum, rents being low at
the period at which he came into this quarter so as to
be in the vicinity of the colleges and to be able to
supervise the education of his children.   Moreover,
the condition in which the property was at the time,
with everything out of repair, had necessarily

obliged the landlord to show himself very accommo-
dating.   Monsieur d'Espard had thus, without laying himself open to any charge of lack of judgment,
been able to expend some money on his dwelling in
order to establish himself comfortably.   The height
of the rooms, their disposition, their wainscotings,
the framework of which alone remained, the construction of the ceilings, everything breathed something of that grandeur which the priesthood has
imprinted on all things undertaken or created by it,
and which the artists find to-day in the slightest
fragments remaining of it, be it only a book, a
garment, a library panel or some armchair.   The
painting which the marquis had had done offered
those brown tones loved by the Hollanders, by the
ancient Parisian bourgeoisie, and which furnish to-
day such excellent effects to the painters of genre.
The panels were covered with a plain paper which
harmonized with the painting.   The windows were
furnished with curtains of an inexpensive material,
which had been chosen with a view of complet-
ing the general unity of the effect.   The pieces
of furniture were rare, and well placed.   Whoever
entered this dwelling could not resist a gentle and
peaceful feeling, inspired by the profound calm, by
the silence which there reigned, by the modesty
and the unity of the color—using this expression in
the sense in which it is employed by the painters.
A certain nobility in the details, the exquisite cleanliness of the furniture, a perfect accord between the
things and the inhabitants, everything brought to

the lips the word *agreeable*.   But very few persons
were admitted into these apartments inhabited by
the marquis and his two sons, the existence of whom
might seem mysterious to all the neighborhood.   In
a part of the main building at right angles with the
street, on the third floor, there are three large rooms
which remained in the state of dilapidation and the
grotesque bareness in which the printing office had
left them.   These three rooms, set apart for the
preparation of the *Picturesque History of China*, were
arranged in such a manner as to contain an office,
a store-room, and a cabinet in which Monsieur
d'Espard remained during a part of the day; for,
after the déjeuner, until four o'clock in the afternoon, the marquis occupied his cabinet on the third
floor, to supervise the publication which he had
undertaken.   His visitors usually found him there.
His two children, on their return from their classes,
frequently ascended to this office.   The apartment
on the ground floor thus formed a sanctuary in
which the father and his sons remained from dinner-
time until the next day.   His family life was thus
carefully secluded.   Of servants, he had only a
cook, an old woman who had long been attached to
his family, and a valet de chambre of the age of
forty, who had served him before he had married
Mademoiselle de Blamont.   The children's governess had remained with them.   The minute care
shown by the aspect of the apartment revealed the
spirit of order, the maternal love which this woman
displayed in the interests of her master in the

management of his house and in the government of
his children. Grave and taciturn, these three honest servitors seemed to have comprehended the
ideas which directed the inward life of the marquis.
This contrast between their habits and those of the
greater number of valets constituted a singularity
which threw over this household an air of mystery,
and which contributed greatly to the calumny for
which Monsieur d'Espard himself furnished occasion. Praiseworthy motives had induced him to
form a resolution not to associate with any of the
other inmates of the house. In undertaking the
education of his children, he wished to preserve
them from all contact with strangers. Perhaps also
he wished to avoid being wearied by his neighbors.
With a man of his quality, at a time when the Latin
Quarter was particularly agitated by Liberalism,
this conduct naturally excited against him small
animosities, feelings, the silliness of which is comparable only with their baseness, and which are
begotten by the gossip of porters, venomous gabbling
from door to door, of which Monsieur d'Espard and
his household remained ignorant. His valet de chambre passed for a Jesuit, his cook was a sly plotter,
the governess had an understanding with Madame
Jeanrenaud to plunder the lunatic. The lunatic, that was the marquis. The other lodgers came
gradually to attribute to folly a number of things
observed in Monsieur d'Espard and sifted through
their appreciation without their being able to find
any reasonable motives for them. Having very

little faith in the success of his publication upon China, they had finally persuaded the landlord that Monsieur d'Espard was without means, at the very moment when, by an oversight committed by very many busy persons, he had allowed the receiver of taxes to send him a writ for the payment of his dues in arrears. The landlord had at the same time claimed his rent from the first of January by the despatch of a receipt which the porter's wife had amused herself by not delivering. On the fifteenth of the month, a summons to pay having been served, the portress had tardily communicated with Monsieur d'Espard, who thought this to be some misunderstanding, without believing in the uncivil behavior of a man in whose house he had been living for twelve years. The marquis had his property seized by a bailiff at the moment when his valet was carrying the money for the rent to the proprietor. This seizure, insidiously communicated to those with whom he was in business relations for his publication, had alarmed some of them who were already in doubt as to the solvency of Monsieur d'Espard, because of the enormous sums which, it was said, were drawn from him by the Baron Jeanrenaud and his mother. The suspicions of the lodgers, of the creditors and of the landlord were, moreover, almost justified by the great economy which the marquis displayed in his living expenses. He carried himself like a ruined man. His domestics paid cash in the quarter for the slightest objects purchased for daily consumption, and acted like

persons who wish no credit; if they had asked for
anything whatever upon promise to pay, they
would perhaps have been refused, so much had the
slanderous gossip obtained credit in the quarter.
There are tradesmen who like those of their cus-
tomers who pay slowly but who permit of a friendly
intercourse; whilst they hate those, otherwise excellent, who keep themselves at such a distance as
to avoid all familiarity.   Men are thus constituted.
In almost all classes of society, they offer facilities to
those connected by slight ties or to base souls that
flatter them, favors refused to the superiority that
wounds them, in whatever manner it reveals itself.
The shopkeeper who clamors against the Court has
his own courtiers.   In short, the daily habits of
the marquis and his children aroused naturally the
evil dispositions of their neighbors, and insensibly
urged them on to that degree of malice in which
persons recoil before no act of baseness that may
injure the enemy whom they have created for
themselves.   Monsieur d'Espard was a *gentil-
homme,* as his wife was a *grande dame,*—two magnificent types, already so rare in France that the
observer may readily enumerate all those that offer
a complete realization of it.   These two personages
are based upon primitive ideas, upon beliefs that
are, so to speak, innate, upon habits acquired in
company, and which no longer exist.   To believe in
blue blood, in a privileged race, to place one's self
in thought above other men, is it not necessary to
have measured from birth the space which separates

the patricians from the people? To command, is it
not necessary to have known no equals? Is it not
necessary, in short, that education should inculcate
the ideas with which nature inspires the great men
upon whose brows she had placed a crown before
their mothers could there press a kiss? These ideas
and this education are no longer possible in France,
where, for the last forty years, chance has arrogated
to itself the right of making nobles by dipping them
in the blood of battle-fields, by gilding them with
glory, by crowning them with the aureole of genius;
where the abolition of entail and of majorats, by
crumbling up the estates, obliges the noble to occupy
himself with his own affairs instead of with those
of the State, and where personal grandeur can no
longer be anything but a grandeur acquired by long
and patient labors,—an era completely new. Considered as a remnant of that great body called
Feudalism, Monsieur d'Espard was entitled to a
respectful admiration. If he believed himself
elevated by birth above other men, he believed
equally in all the obligations of nobility; he possessed the virtues and the strength which it requires. He had educated his children in his
principles, and had communicated to them from the
cradle the religion of his caste. A profound sentiment of their own dignity, the pride of their name,
the certainty of being great in themselves, engen-
dered in them a royal pride, the courage of the
paladins and the protecting bounty of the lords of
the manor; their manners, in accord with their

21

ideas, and which would have seemed admirable in
the company of princes, offended all the world of
the Rue de la Montagne-Sainte-Geneviève, a land of
equality if there were any, where, moreover, Monsieur d'Espard was believed to be ruined, where,
from the very meanest up to the greatest, everyone
refused the privileges of nobility to a noble without
money,—for the reason that each allowed them to be
assumed by burghers grown rich. Thus the want
of intercourse, spiritual and physical, between this
family and those around it, was complete.

With the father as well as with the children, the
outward aspect and the soul within were in harmony.
Monsieur d'Espard, then about fifty years of age,
might have served for a type to express the noble
aristocracy of the nineteenth century. He was
slender and blond; his countenance had, in the
outline and in the general expression, a native dis-
tinction which revealed elevated sentiments; but it
bore the imprint of an intended coldness which
commanded respect a little too austerely. His
aquiline nose, slightly twisted at the end from left to
right, a slight deviation which was not unattrac-
tive; his blue eyes, his high forehead, sufficiently
advanced at the eyebrows to form a heavy projec-
tion which caught the light, thereby shading the
eye, indicated an upright spirit, capable of perse-
verance, a grand loyalty, but gave at the same time
a strange aspect to his physiognomy. This flexure
in the forehead might well have been taken, in
fact, as an indication of a slight degree of mental

unsoundness, and his thick eyebrows which joined
added something more to this apparent oddness.
He had the white and carefully cared-for hand of a
gentleman, his feet were narrow and arched. His
speech was undecided, not only in the pronunciation,
which resembled that of a stammerer, but also in
the expression of his ideas, his thoughts and his
manner of speaking produced in the hearer's mind
the effect of a man who comes and goes, who, to
employ a familiar expression, meddles, tries at
everything, interrupts himself in his gestures, and
accomplishes nothing. This defect, purely exterior,
was in strong contrast with the decision expressed
by his firmly closed mouth, with the sharply cut
character of his physiognomy. His walk, which
was slightly jerky, suited his manner of speech.
These singularities served to corroborate his as-
serted dementia. Notwithstanding his elegance, he
was systematically economical concerning his own
person, and wore for three or four years the same
black frock coat, brushed with an extreme care by
his old valet de chambre. As to his children, they
were both handsome and endowed with a grace
which did not exclude the expression of an aristocratic disdain. They had that lively color, that
freshness in the regard, that transparency of the
flesh, which reveal pure habits, an exact regimen,
regular habits of work and of amusement. Both
had black hair and blue eyes, the nose twisted
like their father's; but it was their mother perhaps
who had transmitted to them that dignity of speech,

of look, and of bearing, which is hereditary in the Blamont-Chauvrys. Their voices, clear as crystal, had the power to move their hearers and that softness which exercises such powers of seduction; in short, they had the voice which a woman would have wished to hear after she had received the flame of their looks. They preserved, above all, the modesty of their pride, a chaste reserve, a *noli me tangere* which, later, might have seemed to be calculated, so much did their aspect inspire the desire to know them. The elder, the Comte Clément de Nègrepelisse, had just entered his sixteenth year. For the last two years he had abandoned the pretty little English vest which his brother, the Vicomte Camille d'Espard, still wore. The count, who, within the last six months, had ceased going to the College Henri IV., was dressed as a young man enjoying the first pleasures of a high position. His father had not wished to impose upon him a useless year of philosophy, he endeavored to give to his accomplishments a sort of bond by the study of the higher mathematics. At the same time the marquis instructed him in the Oriental languages, the diplomatic law of Europe, heraldry, and history from the great sources, history in the charters, in authentic documents, in the collections of ordinances. Camille had lately taken up the study of rhetoric.

The day on which Popinot proposed to himself to go and interrogate Monsieur d'Espard was a Thursday, a holiday. Before their father had arisen, about nine o'clock, the two brothers were amusing themselves in the garden. Clément was defending himself ineffectively against the urgency of his brother, who wished to go shooting for the first time, and who desired his support in the request he was going to make to his father. The viscount always made a little too much of his weakness, and often took pleasure in contesting with his brother. Both of them now fell to quarreling and to fighting in sport, like two schoolboys. As they ran about the garden, one after the other, they made noise enough to waken their father, who came to the window without being perceived by them, so warm was the combat. The marquis pleased himself by looking at his two children who were turning in and out like two serpents, and showed in their faces the animation caused by the exercise of their faculties; —their countenances were white and pink, their eyes shot light, their arms and legs twisted about like cords in the fire; they fell down, rose again, renewed their forces like two athletes in the arena, and gave to their father one of those happinesses which recompense for the keenest pains of an agitated life. Two persons, one on the second, the other on the first floor of the house, looked out in the garden, and said that the old lunatic was amusing himself by making his children fight. Immediately several heads appeared at the windows; the marquis perceived them, said a word to his children, who, quickly climbing up to his window, leaped into his chamber, and Clément obtained

the permission asked for by Camille.   In the house,
nothing was heard of but the new proof of the marquis's lunacy.

When Popinot, accompanied by his clerk, presented
himself about noon at the door, where he asked
for Monsieur d'Espard, the portress conducted him
up to the third floor, relating on the way how Monsieur d'Espard, no later than that very morning,
had caused his children to fight, and had laughed
like the monster that he was, on seeing the younger
bite the elder till he bled, and how, doubtless, he
wished to see them destroy each other.

"If you ask me why!" she added, "he does not
know, himself."

As she uttered this definite statement, she brought
the judge to the third landing of the stairway, in
front of a door placarded with posters which announced the issue of the successive parts of the
Picturesque History of China. This muddy landing,
this dirty hand-rail, this door on which the printing trade had left its black marks, this broken
window and these ceilings on which the appren-
tices had amused themselves by designing monstrosities with the smoky flame of their candles,
the collection of paper and rubbish piled up in the
corner, either purposely or through carelessness; in
short, all the details of this picture which presented
itself to the eye, were so in accord with the facts
alleged by the marchioness that, notwithstanding
his impartiality, the judge could not but believe
them.

"Here you are, messieurs," said the portress, "here is the *manifacture* where the Chinese eat up what would nourish the whole quarter."

The clerk looked at the judge and smiled, and Popinot had some trouble to maintain his own gravity. They both entered the first room, in which they found an old man who doubtless served at once as attendant in the office, as attendant in the storeroom and as cashier. This old man was the Maître Jacques de la Chine. The walls of this room were furnished with long planks on which were piled up the published sections of the work. At the back, a wooden partition and open-work screen furnished with a green curtain on the interior, shut off a cabinet. An opening through which the écus were intended to be received or passed out, indicated the cashier's seat.

"Monsieur d'Espard?" said Popinot, addressing this man, who wore a gray blouse.

The attendant opened the door of the second chamber, in which the magistrate and his clerk perceived a venerable old man with white hair, dressed simply, decorated with the cross of Saint-Louis, seated before a desk, who interrupted his occupation of comparing sheets of colored paper to look up at the two visitors. This room was a modest office, filled with books and proofs. There was in it a table of black wood at which doubtless worked some person now absent.

"Monsieur is Monsieur le Marquis d'Espard?" asked Popinot.

"No, monsieur," replied the old man, rising. "What do you wish with him?" he added, advancing toward them, and giving evidence by his manner of the refined habits and customs of a gentleman.

"We wish to speak with him concerning matters which are strictly personal," replied Popinot.

"D'Espard, here are some messieurs who wish to see you," said this old man, entering the last apartment in which the marquis was occupied in reading the newspapers at the corner of the fire.

This last cabinet had a worn carpet, the windows were furnished with curtains of gray linen; there were only some mahogany chairs, two armchairs, a cylinder secretary, a desk à la Tronchin, and on the mantel a shabby clock and two old candelabras. The old man preceded Popinot and his clerk, pushed forward two chairs for them as if he were the master of the house, and Monsieur d'Espard permitted him to do so. After the respective salutations, during which the judge narrowly observed the alleged lunatic, the marquis naturally inquired the object of their visit. At this, Popinot looked at the old man and at the marquis with a sufficiently significative air.

"I believe, Monsieur le Marquis, that the nature of my functions and the inquiry which brings me here require that we should be alone, although in the spirit of the law, in these cases, the interrogatory receives a sort of domestic publicity. I am judge of the Inferior Civil Court for the Department of the Seine, and am commissioned by Monsieur le Président to interrogate you concerning the facts set forth in a petition for interdiction presented by Madame la Marquise d'Espard."

The old man withdrew. When the judge and his witness were alone, the clerk closed the door, established himself without ceremony at the desk á la Tronchin, where he unrolled his papers and prepared his *procès-verbal*. Popinot had not ceased to observe Monsieur d'Espard,—he watched the effect upon him of this declaration, so wounding to a reasoning man. The Marquis d'Espard, whose face was ordinarily pale, as are those of blond persons, became suddenly red with anger, he shook slightly, sat down, placed his newspaper on the mantel, and lowered his eyes. He resumed immediately his dignity of the gentleman, and looked at the judge, as if to seek in his countenance the indication of his character.

"How is it, monsieur, that I have not been notified of such a petition?" he asked.

"Monsieur le Marquis, the persons whose interdiction is requested, not being considered to be in the possession of their reason, the notification of the petition is useless. The duty of the tribunal is to verify, before everything, the allegations of the petitioners."

"Nothing can be more just," replied the marquis. "Well, monsieur, will you indicate to me the manner in which I should proceed—"

"You have only to reply to my questions, omitting no details. However delicate may be the reasons which have led you to act in the manner

which has given Madame d'Espard the pretext for
her petition, speak without fear. It is unnecessary
to observe to you that the magistracy is aware of
its duties, and that under similar circumstances the
most profound secrecy—"

"Monsieur," said the marquis, whose features
expressed a keen pain, "if from my explanations
there should ensue some censure for the line of conduct pursued by Madame d'Espard, what would
happen?"

"The Court might express a censure in the
reasons given for its judgment."

"Is this censure optional? If I should stipulate
with you, before replying to you, that nothing in-
jurious to Madame d'Espard should be set forth in
case your report should be favorable to me, would
the Court take into consideration my request?"

The judge looked at the marquis, and these two
men exchanged sentiments of an equal nobility.

"Noël," said Popinot to his clerk, "retire to
the next room. If I have need of you, I will call
you.—If, as I am at this moment inclined to believe," he resumed, addressing the marquis when
the clerk had left them, "there should be encountered in this affair some misunderstandings, I can
promise you, monsieur, that, on your request, the
tribunal would act with courtesy. There is a first
fact, alleged by Madame d'Espard, the gravest of
all, and concerning which I entreat you to enlighten
me," said the judge, after a pause. "It is a question of the dissipation of your fortune for the benefit

of a Dame Jeanrenaud, the widow of a captain of
a barge, or rather, for the benefit of her son, the
colonel, whom you have placed, for whom you have
exhausted the favor in which you are held by the
king, in short, for whom you have extended your
protection so far as to procure him a fine marriage.
The request causes it to be thought that this friendship exceeds in devotion all natural sentiments,
even those reproved by morality—"

A sudden flush invaded the cheeks and the brow
of the marquis, there even came tears into his eyes,
his lashes were moist; then a just pride suppressed
this evidence of feeling which, in a man, is taken for
weakness.

"In truth, monsieur," he replied in an altered
voice, "you place me in a strange perplexity. The
motives of my conduct were condemned to die with
me.—To speak of them, I shall be obliged to discover
to you secret wounds, deliver up to you the honor
of my family, and—a delicate thing which you will
appreciate—speak of myself. I hope, monsieur, that
everything will remain secret between us. You will
know how to find in the judicial methods a form
which will permit you to draw up a decision without
there being in it any question of my revelations—"

"In this connection, everything is possible, Monsieur le Marquis."

"Monsieur," said Monsieur d'Espard, "some time
after my marriage, my wife had expended such
sums that I was obliged to have recourse to a loan.
You are acquainted with the condition of the noble

families during the Revolution? I was not permitted to have either an intendant or a man of business. To-day, noblemen are, nearly all of them, obliged to look after their own business affairs. The greater number of my titles to property had been brought from Languedoc, from Provence or from Comtat to Paris by my father, who feared, with sufficient reason, the investigations which the family titles, and what were then called the parchments of the privileged, would draw down on their proprietors. We were Nègrepelisses in our own name. D'Espard is a title acquired under Henri IV. by an alliance which gave us the property and the titles of the house D'Espard, on condition of placing in the middle of the shield in our arms the coat-of-arms of the D'Espards, an old family of Béarn, allied to the house D'Albret through the wives,—*gold, three pales sable, quartered with azure with two griffins' claws argent armed gules posed saltier* with the famous DES PARTEM LEONIS for device. In the days of this alliance we lost Nègrepelisse, a little city as celebrated during the religious wars as was my ancestor who then bore the name. The Capitaine de Nègrepelisse was ruined by the conflagration of his property, for the Protestants did not spare a friend of Montluc. The Crown was unjust to Monsieur de Nègrepelisse, he received neither the baton of marshal, nor command, nor indemnity; the king Charles IX., who loved him, died without having been able to recompense him; Henri IV. indeed brought about his marriage with Mademoiselle d'Espard, and secured for him the domains of that house; but all the property of the Nègrepelisse had already passed into the hands of the creditors. My great-grandfather, the Marquis d'Espard, was, like myself, placed at an early age at the head of his family by the death of his father, who, after having dissipated his wife's fortune, left her only the entailed lands of the house D'Espard, which, moreover, were burdened with a jointure. The young Marquis d'Espard found himself all the more crippled that he had a position at Court. Particularly esteemed by Louis XIV., the king's favor was to him a brevet of fortune. Here, monsieur, there was thrown upon our coat-of-arms a horrible, unheard-of spot, a spot of blood and of mud which I am trying to remove. I discovered this secret in the titles relating to the lands of Nègrepelisse, and in the files of correspondence."

At this solemn moment the marquis spoke without stammering, without any of those repetitions which were habitual with him; but everyone has been able to observe for himself that those persons who in the ordinary affairs of life are affected by these two defects, lose them at the moment when some lively passion animates their discourse.

"The Revocation of the Edict of Nantes took place," he resumed. "Perhaps you are ignorant, monsieur, that this brought an accession of fortune to very many of the royal favorites. Louis XIV. gave to the grandees of his court, lands confiscated from the Protestant families which had not arranged

for the sale of their property. Some persons high
in favor, as was then said, went hunting for Protestants. I have acquired the certainty that the present fortune of two ducal families is composed of
lands confiscated from the unhappy merchants. I
will not explain to you, a man of the law, the
manœuvres employed to entrap those refugees who
had large fortunes to carry away: it will suffice for
you to know that the estate of Nègrepelisse, consisting of twenty-two parishes and right of taxation in
the city, that that of Gravenges, which formerly
belonged to us, were originally in the possession of
a Protestant family. My grandfather came into
possession of them through the grant made to him
by Louis XIV. This grant was based upon facts
stamped by frightful iniquity. The proprietor of
these two estates, believing that it would be possible
to return to France, had made an apparent sale and
then had gone to Switzerland to rejoin his family,
which he had sent there at the first alarm. He
wished, doubtless, to take advantage of all the delays
accorded by the ordinance, in order to regulate his
business affairs. This man was arrested by an
order of the governor, the feoffee admitted the facts,
the poor merchant was hanged, my father received
the two estates. I would willingly suppress the
part which my ancestor took in this intrigue; but
the governor was his maternal uncle, and I have
read, unhappily, a letter in which he requests him
to apply to Déodatus, a name for the king which
had been agreed upon among the courtiers. There

prevails throughout this letter a jesting tone at the expense of the victim which fills me with horror. In fact, monsieur, the sums of money sent by the refugee family to purchase the life of the poor man, were retained by the governor, who none the less dispatched the merchant."

The Marquis d'Espard stopped, as though these souvenirs were still too painful for him.

"This unfortunate was named Jeanrenaud," he resumed. "This name will explain to you my conduct. I have not been able to reflect, without keen pain, on the secret shame which weighed on my family. This fortune permitted my grandfather to espouse a Navarreins-Lansac, an heiress of the property of that younger branch, at that time much richer than was the elder branch of the Navarreins. My father found himself from that time one of the most considerable landed proprietors in the kingdom. He was able to marry my mother, who was a Grandlieu of the younger branch. Though ill-acquired, this property has strangely profited with us! Resolved to repair the wrong promptly, I wrote to Switzerland, and received no reply until the moment when I was on the traces of the heirs of the Protestant. I finally discovered that the Jeanrenauds, reduced to the utmost poverty, had left Fribourg, and that they had come back to live in France. At last I discovered in Monsieur Jeanrenaud, a simple lieutenant of cavalry under Bonaparte, the heir of this unfortunate family. In my eyes, monsieur, the right of the Jeanrenauds was clear. In order to establish it, would it not be necessary for them to attack the present holders? To what authority would the refugees address themselves? their tribunal was above, or, rather, monsieur, the tribunal was here," said the marquis, striking his heart. "I have not wished that my children should have the same opinion of me that I have of my father and of my ancestors; I have wished indeed to leave them a heritage and an escutcheon without stain, I have not been willing that nobility should be a lie in my person. In short, speaking politically, should the noble émigrés, who protest against the confiscations of the Revolution, keep for themselves property which is the fruit of confiscations obtained by crime? In Monsieur Jeanrenaud and in his mother I have met with a rough honesty,—if you listened to them, you would think that they were robbing me. In spite of my insistence they have accepted only the value which the property had when my family received it from the king. This value was agreed between us to be eleven hundred thousand francs, which they gave me the privilege of paying at my own convenience, without interest. In order to do this, I have been obliged to forego my revenues for a long time. It was here, monsieur, that there first commenced the destruction of certain illusions which I had cherished concerning the character of Madame d'Espard. When I proposed to her to leave Paris and to go to live in the provinces where, with the half of our income we could live honorably, and thus be enabled to make more promptly a restitution of which I spoke to her without revealing to her the gravity of the facts, Madame d'Espard considered me a lunatic. I then discovered the true character of my wife, she would have approved unscrupulously of my grandfather's conduct, and would have derided the Huguenots. Terrified at her coldness, at the slightness of her attachment to her children, whom she abandoned to me without regret, I resolved to leave her in the possession of her own fortune, after having liquidated our common debts. It was not for her, moreover, she told me, to pay for my stupidities. Having no longer sufficient revenues to keep up my mode of life and provide for the education of my children, I decided to bring them up myself, to make of them men with honorable feelings, gentlemen. By investing my money in the public funds, I have been enabled to pay much more promptly than I hoped, for I profited by the opportunities presented by the rise in Rentes. By reserving four thousand francs for my sons and myself, I should have been able to pay only twenty thousand écus a year, which would have required nearly eighteen years to accomplish my liberation, whereas I have lately paid the last of my eleven hundred thousand francs due. Thus I have the happiness of having accomplished this restitution without having wronged my children in the slightest. These are, monsieur, the reasons for the payments made to Madame Jeanrenaud and her son."

"Thus," said the judge, suppressing the emotion

22

which this recital caused him, "Madame la Marquise is acquainted with the motives of your retreat?"

"Yes, monsieur."

Popinot made a sufficiently expressive gesture, rose suddenly and opened the door of the cabinet.

"Noël, you may go," he said to his clerk. "Monsieur," he resumed, "although what you have said to me is sufficient to enlighten me, I desire to hear you concerning other facts alleged in the petition. Thus, you have undertaken here a commercial enterprise which is not in accord with the habits of a man of quality."

"We cannot well speak of that here," said the marquis, making a sign to the judge to pass out. "Nouvion," he continued, addressing the old man, "I am going down stairs to my apartment, my sons will soon be in, you will dine with us."

"Monsieur le Marquis," said Popinot on the stairway, "this is, then, not your apartment?"

"No, monsieur, I have rented these rooms for the offices of this enterprise. You see," he said, pointing to a poster, "this history is published under the name of one of the most honorable publishing houses in Paris, and not by me."

The marquis caused the judge to enter into the ground floor rooms, and said to him:

"This is my apartment, monsieur."

Popinot was moved, very naturally, by the poetry rather found than sought for, which prevailed in this dwelling. The weather was magnificent, the windows were open, the air from the garden diffused through the salon the fresh vegetable odors; the rays of the sun lightened and animated the somewhat darkened tones of the wainscoting. Popinot came to the conclusion, as he saw this pleasant aspect, that a lunatic would scarcely be capable of inventing the agreeable harmony which appealed to him at this moment.

"I should have a similar apartment myself," he thought. Then he asked aloud: "You will leave this quarter soon?"

"I hope so," replied the marquis; "but I shall wait until my younger son shall have finished his studies, and until the character of my children shall have been formed, before introducing them into the world by their mother's side; moreover, after having imparted to them the solid instruction which they now possess, I wish to complete it by making them travel through the capitals of Europe, in order that they may become acquainted with men and things, and acquire facility in speaking the languages which they have been studying. Monsieur," he said, causing the judge to be seated in the salon, "I could not speak to you concerning the publication upon China before an old friend of my family, the Comte de Nouvion, returned from the emigration after the Revolution without any fortune whatever, and in connection with whom I have undertaken this affair, less for myself than for him. Without confiding to him the reasons for my retreat, I said to him that I was ruined, like himself, but that I had enough money to undertake a speculation

in which he might make himself of service. My
preceptor was the Abbé Grozier, whom, at my
recommendation, Charles X. appointed his libra-
rian at the library of the Arsenal, which was given
him when the prince was still MONSIEUR. The
Abbé Grozier was profoundly informed concerning
China, its manners and customs; he had made me
his heir at an age in which it is difficult not to de-
velop an enthusiasm for that knowledge which is
acquired. At the age of twenty-five I was acquainted with Chinese, and I admit that I have
never been able to preserve myself from an exclu-
sive admiration for this people, which has conquered its conquerors, whose annals incontestably
ascend to an epoch much more remote than are the
mythological or biblical times; which, by its im-
movable institutions, has preserved the integrity of
its territory, whose monuments are gigantic, whose
administration is perfect, with whom revolutions
are impossible, who have considered the ideal of the
beautiful in art as unfruitful, who have carried
luxury and industry to so high a degree, whom we
cannot surpass in any point, whilst they equal us
in those things in which we think ourselves superior. But, monsieur, if I frequently permit myself to jest in comparing with China the actual
condition of the European states, I am not a Chinese,
I am a French gentleman. If you should have any
doubts concerning the financial success of this enterprise, I can prove to you that we count at this
moment two thousand five hundred subscribers to

this monument, literary, iconographic, statistical
and religious, the importance of which is generally
appreciated; our subscribers are scattered through
all the nations of Europe, we have only twelve hundred in France. Our work will cost about three
hundred francs, and it furnishes the Comte de
Nouvion, for his part, with six or seven thousand
francs income, for his comfort was the secret
motive for undertaking this enterprise. As far as
I am concerned, I have seen in it only the possibility of giving some pleasures to my children. The
hundred thousand francs which I have made, very
much in spite of myself, will pay for their fencing
lessons, their horses, their clothes, their theatres,
their lessons in deportment, the canvases which
they try to paint, the books which they wish to
buy, in short, all those little whims which it gives
the fathers so much pleasure to satisfy. If it had
been necessary for me to refuse these enjoyments to
my poor children, so deserving, so constant in their
studies, the sacrifice which I am making to the
honor of our name would have been doubly burden-
some. In fact, monsieur, the twelve years during
which I have retired from the world in order to edu-
cate my children have procured for me the most
complete oblivion at Court. I have forsaken the
career of politics, I have lost all my historic fortune,
all the new distinctions which I might have left to
my children; but our house will have lost nothing,
my sons will be distinguished men. If I do not attain to the peerage, they will conquer it nobly in

consecrating themselves to the conduct of their
country's affairs, and in rendering to her those services which are not forgotten. At the same time
that I have purified the past of our house I have assured it a glorious future,—is not that to have accomplished a fine task, although secretly and without glory? Have you now, monsieur, any other
subjects on which you wish to be informed?"

At this moment the noise of several horses was
heard in the court.

"There they are," said the marquis.

The two young men presently entered the salon,
simple yet elegant in their appearance, booted,
spurred, gloved, flourishing their riding whips gaily.
Their animated countenances brought in the freshness of the open air, they were sparkling with
health. Both came to grasp their father's hand,
exchanging with him, as between friends, a look
full of silent tenderness, and they saluted the judge
coldly. Popinot considered it entirely useless to
interrogate the marquis on his relations with his
sons.

"Did you enjoy yourselves?" their father asked
them.

"Yes, father. For the first time, I cut down six
puppets in twelve strokes!" said Camille.

"Where did you ride?"

"In the Bois, where we saw mother."

"Did she stop?"

"We were going so fast at that moment that she
doubtless did not see us," replied the young count.

"But why then did you not go and present yourselves to her?"

"I have thought that I have noticed, father, that she is not very well pleased when we speak to her in public," said Clément in a low voice. "We are somewhat too old."

The judge's ear was fine enough to catch this phrase, which clouded the brow of the marquis. Popinot pleased himself by the contemplation of the spectacle which was presented to him by the father and the sons. His eyes, filled with a sort of tenderness, returned to the face of Monsieur d'Espard, whose features, whose look and whose manners represented to him probity under its finest form, probity spiritual and chivalrous, nobility in all its beauty.

"You—you see, monsieur," said the marquis to him, resuming his stammering, "you see that justice—that justice can enter here—here, at any hour; yes, at any hour here. If there are any crazy people—if there are any crazy people, they can only be the children, who are a little crazy over their father, and the father who is very crazy over his children; but that is a lunacy of good sterling quality."

. At this moment the voice of Madame Jeanrenaud was heard in the antechamber, and the good woman came into the salon notwithstanding the remonstrance of the valet de chambre.

"I am not going in a roundabout way, I am not!" she cried. "Yes, Monsieur le Marquis," she said, making a general salute to the company, "I must speak to you at this very minute. *Parbleu!* I have come too late, after all, for there is Monsieur the criminal judge."

"Criminal!" said the two youths.

"There were very good reasons why I did not find you at your house, since you were here. Oh, bah! justice is always about when it is a question of making mischief. I come, Monsieur le Marquis, to say to you that I am of the same mind as my son to return everything to you, since it concerns our honor, which is attacked. My son and I, we would rather refund all to you than to cause you the slightest vexation. In truth, one would have to be as stupid as the pots without handles to be willing to see you interdicted—"

"Interdict our father!" cried the marquis's two sons, pressing up against him. "What is the matter?"

"Chut, madame!" said Popinot.

"Leave us, children," said the marquis.

The two young men withdrew to the garden without making any observation, but full of anxiety.

"Madame," said the judge, "the sums of money which Monsieur le Marquis has paid over to you were legitimately due you, though they have been given you in virtue of a principle of probity which is carried to an extreme length. If all those who are in possession of property that has been confiscated, in any manner whatever, even through perfidious methods, were obliged to make restitution after a hundred and fifty years, there would be found in France very little legitimate ownership. The wealth of Jacques Cœur has enriched twenty noble families; the unjust confiscations of the English in favor of their adherents, when the English were in possession of a part of France, have made the fortunes of several princely houses. Our laws permit Monsieur le Marquis to dispose of his revenues by free gift without exposing himself to the charge of dissipation. The interdiction of a man is based upon the absence of all reason in his actions; but here, the cause of the restitutions which have been made to you is found in the most sacred, the most honorable motives. Therefore you may keep everything without remorse, and allow the world to put its own evil interpretation on this fine action. In Paris, it is the purest virtue that is made the object of the vilest calumnies. It is unfortunate that the present state of our society makes the conduct of Monsieur le Marquis seem sublime. I could wish, for the honor of our country, that such acts should seem quite simple; but our manners are such that I am forced, by comparison, to regard Monsieur d'Espard as a man to whom a crown should be awarded instead of being threatened with a judgment of interdiction. During the course of a long judicial life, I have never seen or heard anything that has moved me more than that which I have just seen and heard. But there is nothing extraordinary in finding virtue in its most beautiful form, there where it is practised by men who belong

to the most elevated class.—After having thus explained myself, I hope, Monsieur le Marquis, that
you will be sure of my silence, and that you will
have no inquietude concerning the judgment to be
pronounced, if judgment there be."

"Well, good enough!" said Madame Jeanrenaud,
"here is a judge of the right kind! Really, my
dear monsieur, I would embrace you if I were not
so ugly; you talk like a book."

The marquis offered his hand to Popinot, and
Popinot placed his own into it softly, turning a look
full of penetrating accord upon this man, so great in
private life, to which the marquis replied by a
gracious smile.   These two natures, so full, so rich,
the one bourgeois and divine, the other noble and
sublime, had come into unison with each other
gently, without shock, without outbreak of passion,
as if two pure flames had commingled.   The father of
his whole quarter felt himself worthy to press the
hand of this man twice noble, and the marquis knew
by a movement in the depths of his heart that the
hand of the judge was one of those from which incessantly flow the treasures of an inexhaustible
benevolence.

"Monsieur le Marquis," added Popinot as he
bowed, "I am happy to have to tell you that, from
the first words of this interrogation, I considered my
clerk superfluous."

Then he approached the marquis, drew him into
the embrasure of the window and said to him:

"It is time that you should return to your own

house, monsieur; I believe that in this affair Madame la Marquise has been subject to influences which you should begin to combat from to-day."

Popinot went out, and, as he walked, turned it over more than once in his mind in the court and in the street, moved to tenderness by the memory of this scene. It was one of those effects which implant themselves in the mind, to flower again in remembrance at certain hours in which the soul seeks consolation.

"That apartment would suit me very well," he said to himself on his arrival at his own house. "If Monsieur d'Espard should leave it, I would take up his lease—"

The next day, about ten o'clock in the morning, Popinot, who, the evening before, had drawn up his report, took his way to the Palais with the intention of doing prompt and sound justice. As he entered the vestry to assume his robe and put on his band, the attendant of the chambers said to him that the president of the tribunal requested him to pass into his cabinet, where he was waiting for him. Popinot immediately went there.

"Good day, my dear Popinot," said the magistrate to him. "I was waiting for you."

"Monsieur the president, is it a question of anything serious?"

"A piece of nonsense," said the president. "The keeper of the seals, with whom I had the honor to dine yesterday, drew me aside into a corner. He had learned that you had been to take tea with

Madame d'Espard, with whose affair you were commissioned. He has caused me to understand that
it is advisable that you do not sit in this cause—"

"Ah! Monsieur the president, I can affirm that I
left Madame d'Espard's at the moment when the tea
was served; moreover, my conscience—"

"Yes, yes," said the president, "the whole tribunal, the two courts, the Palais, know you. I
will not repeat to you what I said of you to His
Grace; but you knew that *Cæsar's wife should be
above suspicion.* Therefore we will not make of
this nonsense a matter of discipline, but a question
of the proprieties. Between ourselves, it is less a
case of you than of the tribunal."

"But, Monsieur the president, if you were acquainted with the case," said the judge, endeavoring to draw his report from his pocket.

"I am convinced in advance that you have
brought to this affair the strictest independence. I,
myself, when I was in the provinces, a simple
judge, I have often taken much more than a cup of
tea with persons whose cases I had to judge; but it
is sufficient that the keeper of the seals has spoken
of it, that you may be gossiped about, to cause the
tribunal to avoid any discussion on the subject. All
conflict with public opinion is always dangerous for
a constitutional body, even when it has right on its
side, for the weapons are not equal. The newspapers may say everything, suppose everything;
and our own dignity forbids us to do anything, even
to reply. Moreover, I have conferred concerning it

with your president, and Monsieur Camusot has just been commissioned, on the recusation which you will give. It is a matter all arranged in the family. In short, I ask of you your recusation as a personal service; in return, you shall have the cross of the Legion of Honor, which has been so long due you, I will make it my own affair."

As he saw Monsieur Camusot, a judge recently called from a court of appeals to that of Paris, and who now came forward, bowing to the judge and the president, Popinot could not repress an ironical smile. This young man, blond and pale, filled with hidden ambition, seemed equally willing to hang or to unhang, at the good pleasure of the kings of the earth, the innocent as well as the guilty, and to follow the example of the Laubardemonts rather than those of the Molés. Popinot retired, bowing to the president and the judge; he disdained to notice the lying accusation brought against him.

Paris, February, 1836.

LIST OF ETCHINGS

———

VOLUME XX